Being Al

By

Charlie Laidlaw

ISBN: 9798796957783

This is a work of fiction. Names and characters are the product of the author's imagination and any resemblance to actual persons, living or dead, is entirely coincidental.

PUBLISHNATION
www.publishnation.co.uk

By the same author:

The Things We Learn When We're Dead
The Space Between Time
Love Potions and Other Calamities
Everyday Magic

Dedicated to all those whose lives have been touched by Covid-19, and to all those who are working, in whatever capacity, to get us through it.

"A politician needs the ability to foretell what is going to happen tomorrow, next week, next month, and next year. And to have the ability afterwards to explain why it didn't happen."
Winston Churchill

The beginning

In late January, two Chinese nationals were the first to test positive for coronavirus in the UK. The first officially recorded fatality took place in China on January 11th.

It was a morning like any other when the Prime Minister, Winston Spragg, received a phone call. He was in the middle of breakfast – croissants (plural), sausages (also plural), bacon, beans, mushrooms, eggs (fried and poached), fried potato and tomato – and didn't much like to be disturbed that early in the day. He had not long been Prime Minister and was rather enjoying the luxury of having very little to do, having delegated virtually everything to other people who, he rather hoped, were more competent than he was. Not that he was entirely *in*competent; after all, he could speak Latin although, he had to concede, there weren't many people alive he could have a conversation with. An early morning phone call was therefore something to be wary of.

On the line was the British Ambassador to China informing him of a new disease in China and that it had the potential to spread internationally. "It's centred on a place called Wuhan," he added helpfully.

"Never heard of it," said the PM.

"China or Wuhan?"

The PM let this attempt at juvenile humour pass. He had known Sir Humphrey Maddox, Her Majesty's Ambassador to the People's Republic, since they were schoolboys chasing each other naked down corridors with wet towels. The PM knew that the ambassador hadn't forgotten and, with retirement imminent, was planning to write his memoirs. The PM had already considered speaking to the SAS on the matter.

"Wuhan," said the PM.

"It's a city rather larger than London. I just thought you should know."

"But, so what?" the Prime Minister demanded.

"Well, it could be something serious. At the moment we just don't know," said the official.

"You don't know?"

"Nobody knows, Prime Minister."

"Then why are you phoning me?"

"Because you're the prime minister, Prime Minister."

"Then phone me back when you *do* know something," replied the PM and replaced the receiver. As a former Foreign Secretary, he was used to useless briefings from under-employed diplomats and, now chewing the last of his sausages, felt rather pleased with his blunt handling of an irrelevant phone call, even if it had been from an old schoolfriend, who might soon merit an obituary in *The Times*.

He ran a hand through his neatly combed hair to make sure it was properly messy, having learned early on in his political career that voters rather liked someone who evidently didn't have time to brush their hair.

Breakfast over, he sent a TOP SECRET email to the Health Secretary asking him to find out everything he could about this new disease, and if Wuhan actually existed.

The Health Secretary, Kevin Kock, was also new to his job and still felt that he was just getting his feet under the desk. However, as his desk was extremely large, this shouldn't have been a difficult task. Tall and rather thin, he looked permanently like an underfed rabbit caught in the headlights. He still remembered his meeting with the PM, when the latter was elected as Party leader.

"I'd like you to be Health Secretary," the PM said, his jaw jutting out.

"But I don't know anything about health," he'd replied, rather alarmed.

"You must know something," the PM prompted.

"Well, I once had measles."

"There, that makes you eminently qualified," said the PM. "Of course, you have my full confidence until that is, I mean to say, when you don't have my full confidence."

Kevin Kock couldn't confide to the Prime Minister that he had a phobia about sickness, would faint at the sight of blood (even underdone beef made him queasy), and took an array of tablets every morning to ward off everything from the common cold to diphtheria. His daytime was therefore spent in a miasma of worry. His wife frequently chastised him about his hypochondria, although it had become part of him, part of who he was.

However, unlike the PM, the Health Secretary was already at his desk but, unlike the Prime Minister, was actually trying to think of something useful to do. But the problem of holding high office, he'd discovered, was that the real work was done much further down the chain of command, people who Kevin Kock knew must exist but had never encountered.

He phoned his Permanent Secretary, Sir Roger Smallwood. "I've just had a confidential email from the PM," he began.

"That's nice," said the Permanent Secretary.

"Actually, it isn't nice at all. Apparently, there's an illness that's somehow magically sprung up in China."

"Where?"

"China. It's in Asia I believe."

"No, I meant *where* in China?"

The Health Secretary consulted the PM's email. "Wuhan, or so I'm informed."

"Never heard of it," said the official, then cleared his throat. "What would you like me to do, Minister?"

This was the one question that the Health Secretary always dreaded, because he rarely knew what anybody should do. "Not sure, to be honest, but I'm sure you'll think of something. Maybe first find out if Wuhan is actually a real place."

The Secretary of State for Health was a pragmatic man, despite health phobias, having been an economist at the Bank of England. He was therefore well versed in plucking random facts out of thin air and cobbling them together as national fiscal policy. Although he wasn't much worried by this new illness in a place he had never heard of, emails from the PM were rare and therefore required rapid response. In the absence of anything else to do, he therefore started plucking.

His computer now switched on, he quickly discovered that "Wuhan is the capital city of Hubei Province in the People's Republic of China. It is the largest city in Hubei and the most populous city in Central China, with a population of over 11 million, the ninth most populous Chinese city…"

With admirable efficiency, Sir Roger was back on the phone within an hour. "I have the information you requested, Minister."

The Health Secretary marvelled, as ever, at the efficiency of the British civil service, that could always be counted on the get to the bottom of things.

"Wuhan" said the Permanent Secretary, "is the capital city of Hubei Province in the People's Republic of China. It is the largest city in Hubei and the most populous city in Central China, with a population of over 11 million…"

"Wait, wait, wait," interrupted the Health Secretary, "you're just quoting from Wikipedia."

"I know," said Sir Roger, "but it's the only link the Foreign Office could send me."

A tracking app developed by King's College London later suggested that Covid-19 was first present in the UK from January, and perhaps earlier.

Breakfast over, the Prime Minister sat back, buttons on his shirt strained to breaking point, while an efficient, if rather chubby, flunkey cleared his dirty plates away, and asked if he'd like more coffee or orange juice, which he would like, thank you very much. Both. All in all, what with a fine breakfast and batting away an irritating ambassador, his day was going rather well.

"You really shouldn't eat so much, Winston," said the flunkey and it took the PM some moments to realise that she was in fact his girlfriend, Caroline. "You'll get fat. Or more fat than you already are."

"Fiddlesticks!" he retorted. "Breakfast is, I should remind you, an important meal in anybody's day. No, perhaps *the* most important meal of the day. Imparts stamina for the day ahead. Stamina, by the way, is from the Latin *stamina*, meaning threads. Imparts is also from the Latin *impartire*. Also, I am not fat. Anyway, while I don't in any way want to seem rude, so forgive me for mentioning it, but I could say the same about you."

"I'm pregnant, Winston."

"Good God!"

Caroline sighed. "You are joking, aren't you? Please tell me you're joking."

"Of course, of course," said the PM, who now did remember that he was about to become a father for the fourth time. Fifth time? Eighth time? He had always been rather vague about the number of children he had, or what their names were, or their birthdays. There again, that's what his personal assistant was for. "Anyway, how has your day been so far?" he asked to change the subject.

"I have merely got out of bed and had a shower. Oh, and then I spent at least an hour cleaning red wine off the sofa."

"Don't we have cleaners to do that?"

"We do, but you'd also spilled wine on the walls, carpet, several arm chairs and the dog. I thought it best to keep our private life private and do the cleaning myself."

"Dilyn won't mind," said the PM, thinking fondly of their Jack Russell, and remembering vaguely that he and Caroline had had an argument the night before but unable to remember about what.

"He licked it all off," said Caroline. "He's now blind drunk and fast asleep."

Warning signs

In early February, a British businessman tested positive for coronavirus having been on a business trip to Singapore. Late in February, the first person in the UK to officially catch the virus without having been abroad was diagnosed.

"Covid-19 is a disease caused by a new strain of coronavirus. CO stands for corona, VI for virus, and D for disease. Formerly, this disease was referred to as '2019 novel coronavirus' or '2019-nCoV.' The Covid-19 virus is a new virus linked to the same family of viruses as Severe Acute Respiratory Syndrome and some types of common cold." The Health Secretary beamed around the Cabinet table, having used several large words and a dollop of credible science. Several of his colleagues were writing notes, others were looking vacantly out the windows or at the ceiling. Old Mick Gore, minister for something-or-other that Kevin Kock couldn't quite remember, seemed to be asleep.

"The common cold?" echoed the Chancellor, Vijay Patel.

"It's rather difficult to know what it is," interrupted the Foreign Secretary, Timothy Raambo, a rather commanding figure whose background usefully included having been abroad, and who therefore knew his stuff. "The Chinese aren't being very cooperative."

"In what way?" asked the Prime Minister.

"In an uncooperative way," he replied.

"Quite so," said the PM, as if this explained everything. "SARS was quite scary wasn't it? How many died in that outbreak, Health Secretary?"

"I don't believe that there were any UK fatalities, Prime Minister."

"But there were fatalities elsewhere," came a soft but menacing voice from the line of chairs behind the Cabinet table. Despite speaking in almost a whisper, the Prime Minister's chief advisor, Derek Goings, had the unholy knack of silencing everything. Papers ceased to rustle, pens stopped tapping, and

Mick Gore stopped snoring. "A total of 8,098 people caught the disease and, of these, 774 died, mostly in Asia."

The Health Secretary, sitting immediately in front of the advisor, could distinctly detect a whiff of sulphur from behind him. It smelled of decay and utter darkness. He also wondered, not for the first time, how Derek Goings seemed to know everything about everything, without having to consult files or notepads. He also wondered, not for the first time, whether Derek Goings simply made things up as he went along. The Health Secretary wrote 774 in large letters in the first file that came to hand, and made a mental note to quiz his Permanent Secretary on it later.

"It would seem," continued the advisor, "that Covid-19 is a mutated form of a virus more commonly found in an animal species as yet undetermined." The smell of sulphur was becoming stronger, and several Cabinet members were wrinkling their noses. "It's likely that SARS mutated from bats, bird flu from birds, HIV from monkeys, and swine flu from pigs."

"Health Secretary?" asked the Prime Minister.

"On the basis of intelligence coming from the Chinese authorities, the scientific evidence, and on what my officials know so far, I would concur," said Kevin Kock, looking at his stack of files, none of which contained much of interest.

"Both SARS and Covid-19 have a great deal in common," continued the PM's advisor in his throaty whisper, eyes invisible behind dark glasses. Kevin Kock had never seen him without dark glasses, even on dark evenings. "The best theory is that the virus mutated from a live animal market selling both wild and domestic animals."

"Wild animals? Tigers, elephants, that kind of thing?" asked the PM, now entirely ignoring his Health Secretary.

"Perhaps bats. Perhaps snakes or porcupines. I don't yet know," replied Derek Goings, with just the hint of an admission that he didn't yet possess the power of unlimited knowledge. "However, how the virus came about isn't right now of importance."

"Why not?" asked Raambo.

"Because," said the advisor with chilling precision, "I say so."

In early February, the government still believed that Covid-19 could be contained, merely advising against all but essential foreign travel and suggesting that UK nationals abroad should return home. It was also recognised, at least by the scientific community, that the response to Covid-19 had to be guided, not by its similarity to SARS or other coronaviruses, but by its differences – most importantly, by its rate of infection. As it soon became clear that Covid-19, compared to other coronaviruses, was very infectious, the prudent option would have been to lock down the country as soon as possible.

The Prime Minister believed otherwise. On 3rd February, speaking at a post-Brexit talk in Greenwich, he said that there is 'a risk that new diseases such as Coronavirus will trigger a panic and a desire for market segregation that go beyond what is medically rational to the point of doing real and unnecessary economic damage.' He went on to say that at this moment 'humanity needs some Government somewhere that is willing at least to make the case powerfully for freedom of exchange, some country ready to take off its Clark Kent spectacles and leap into the phone booth and emerge with its cloak flowing as the supercharged champion, of the right of the populations of the earth to buy and sell freely among each other… I can tell you in all humility that the UK is ready for that role.'

Lockdown was an option that was considered during the month, particularly since infections were quickly detected in Taiwan, Japan, Thailand, South Korea and the United States, and by the end of the month would be present in forty-nine countries. Instead, what was considered of greatest importance was to hold a meeting of the government's COBRA emergency committee, to demonstrate to the country that the government was taking everything very, very seriously – although the Prime Minister didn't hold the first one for some time, and then didn't attend several others that followed.

The Health Secretary was looking forward to his first COBRA meeting. Not only would be it a novel experience, but he was fully expecting the secret COBRA conference room to be an exciting place fashioned from brushed aluminium, with glass screens behind which shadowy operatives would be grouped in front of digital maps of Europe and the world, with little twinkly lights pinpointing places of interest. It would, he assumed, have a sterile atmosphere, with high-tech air-filtration to protect against biological or chemical attack and not, therefore, a room in which he need worry about sanitising gel or aerosol disinfectant.

First, he was disappointed to find out that COBRA stood for Cabinet Office Briefing Room A, a room within the Cabinet Office in Whitehall, just around the corner from Downing Street and a short, convenient stroll for the Prime Minister. For Kevin Kock, less conveniently situated in Victoria Street, it would require a slightly longer stroll. He chose instead to make the journey by ministerial car, because he didn't like to mingle with the public, who probably didn't share his high hygienic standards, and because there was a light drizzle and he didn't want to get his hair wet.

Second, he was alarmed to find that Cabinet Office Briefing Room A was simply just another room, the kind of soulless room with which he was intimately acquainted, having sat in hundreds of identical rooms across Whitehall and beyond. The walls, devoid of decoration, were painted bureaucratic grey, and the large plain mahogany table was dotted with bottles of water and glasses. While it was undoubtedly a sterile environment (the Health Secretary had made an immediate note of ambient dust levels, to determine the likely concentration of particulate matter in the atmosphere), there were no glass walls or banks of computer screens or twinkly lights. There was, however, a whiteboard behind the chair at the far end of the table, at which the Prime Minister sat. On it was written COVID-19, in the PM's bold and almost unintelligible scrawl, in case anybody was uncertain about the meeting's purpose, or had wandered in by mistake.

"Welcome, Health Secretary," said the Prime Minister, passing a note to the secretary on his left. "Now that we're all here, perhaps we should begin. I know how busy you all are," he added with a small laugh. The Health Secretary looked around the room, wondering if any of them were really busy or whether, like him, they had merely developed strategies to give the impression of being busy. "The purpose of this meeting is to decide what we should be thinking about in terms of this virus, and how we should all stand up to it, but not being in any way intimidated by it because, as I'm sure you all know, Britain is an island, which gives us a unique immunity from invasion, and which should make our response more nuanced to that of our former friends on the continent who don't have our geographical advantages or British spirit. Moreover, we are a country filled with a fit and healthy population, and therefore well able to ward off illness, should it come to our shores. I hope that's clear?" A few heads nodded although, as always, the PM had said nothing that made any sense, perhaps even to him. "Good. In which case, could I ask Professor Whittle for an update."

Most of the nodding heads belonged to people who were known by name to the Health Secretary, either as colleagues in Cabinet or in more junior office, or simply recognisable faces from the various health briefings he was obliged to attend from time to time. Brian Whittle, he knew particularly well. Not only was he the Chief Medical Officer of England, he was also the Chief Medical Advisor to government and Chief Scientific Advisor to the Department of Health. Kevin Kock marvelled how he could wear so many hats all at once, which was perhaps the reason why Brian Whittle was bald.

"We are all, of course, more than aware of the spread of the virus and the different ways in which jurisdictions elsewhere are responding to it or planning for it. We are therefore in the position of being able to assess best practice from countries which are more affected than us. Also, as an island nation, and as the Prime Minister has so sensibly pointed out, we can stop this virus in its tracks at Dover." Kevin Kock wondered whether anybody had considered Heathrow or Gatwick but, perhaps wisely, let this pass. "Quite apart from our own highly-expert teams who are already working around the clock to understand the virus and how we can defeat it, we have some other allies on our side. For example, the Global Outbreak Alert and Response Network, the Coalition for Epidemic Preparedness Innovations, and the Global Research Collaboration for Infectious Disease Preparedness, all supported by the World Health Organisation's Research Blueprint and Global Coordinating Mechanism. Together, they are accelerating our joint response to the outbreak and rapidly initiating technical platforms for the development of vaccines and therapeutics."

"*Per aspera ad astra,*" breathed the Prime Minister. Although the RAF's motto was lost on virtually everyone in the room, it seemed clear that the PM, jaw jutting out, was perhaps thinking fondly of Spitfires criss-crossing the skies. In place of a cigar, he was chewing on a red pen which, rather spoiling the effect, had leaked down his chin, making the Prime Minister resemble a rather dishevelled but well-fed vampire.

"Quite so," said Mick Gore from behind thick glasses, the one person in the room who the Health Secretary thought might actually understand Latin, wondering also whether the two of them stayed up late in the PM's apartments above Downing Street to discuss the lives of the Caesars and drinking Italian red. Kevin knew that the PM had a fondness for red wine.

"At present," continued Professor Whittle whose grandfather, Kevin Kock remembered, had invented the jet engine or the pencil-sharpener or something else entirely, "cases in China remain in the Hubei region. At present, we only have one confirmed UK case, that of a businessman who had been to Singapore."

"Weren't there two cases last month?" asked the Chancellor, who had thoughtfully placed a calculator on top of his stack of files as a useful prop to demonstrate who he was.

"Two Chinese nationals," said Whittle. "On holiday in York."

"York?" echoed the Chancellor.

"It's a city in the north of England," replied Whittle simply importing a fact, without apparent humour. He was, as far as the Health Secretary was concerned, a man devoid of any human emotions, being entirely devoted to disease and death.

"I went there once," said an elderly woman at the far end of the table whom Kevin Kock didn't recognise. "It was filled with little shops."

"The Shambles," said someone else, an elderly man on the other side of the table. "It's a jolly nice place, by the way. Well worth a visit."

"I had an ice cream," said the old lady, smiling broadly at the memory.

"Why, so did I!" said the old man, smiling broadly at the old woman, and no doubt wondering if she was free that evening.

"Thank you both so much," said Whittle, writing in his notebook. It would be the last time, no doubt, that COBRA would ever hear of those two again. "It would, however, be wise to consider the links we have with China. For example, Wuhan University has partnerships with Aberdeen, Glasgow, Birmingham and Leeds universities."

"Not Oxford or Cambridge?" asked the PM.

"Apparently not, Prime Minister. I should also add that approaching two million Chinese nationals were granted UK visas last year, and that student applications, in just one quarter last year, rose by 30,000."

There was a short silence around the table, while everyone privately pondered on the interconnected nature of the modern world, and how even Chinese people could come here in such large numbers.

It was left to the Prime Minister to sum up. "This has been a most useful meeting of minds, and I thank you all for coming. We are, as I have said, an island nation, with a spirit of purpose and perseverance that has seen us through many crises in the past. However, while I see this virus as something we should keep our eye on, I don't feel it's something that need take up a great deal of our attention. Perhaps, Foreign Secretary, you should consider limiting travel to the UK from China?" The Prime Minister looked happily around the room, having made a decision that Derek Goings could spin as fast and robust government action. Unfortunately, he had again been sucking on his red pen, and wiping a hand across his face, so that the PM now resembled, not so much a cherubic vampire, but a badly made-up clown. "Does anybody disagree?"

There were various grunts from around the table, which might have been *yes* or *no*, or *don't know*.

"In which case," said the PM, "*vale et tibi gratias ago*."

Only Mick Gore stood up. "It means thank you and goodbye," he told everyone.

Six people were later found to have died during February in the UK from Covid-19, although the first death was not officially announced until March.

Back at HQ, the Health Secretary was in conference with his Permanent Secretary, Sir Roger Smallwood. Sir Roger, Kevin noted approvingly, had brought with him a small notebook and pen.

"And how was the COBRA meeting, Minister?"

"Rather tedious."

"That is, alas, the case with most COBRA meetings. Don't forget that COBRA's primary purpose is to reassure the public that there is an emergency committee being busy with an emergency."

"I thought it was to decide things?"

"No, Minister, that's what Cabinet does. COBRA is there to determine if a national emergency exists, the nature of that emergency and whether existing legislation and regulations are sufficient to deal with the emergency, if it is deemed to be an emergency, and, if it is, to then provide Cabinet with broad policy options for further consideration."

Kevin Kock was well used to this kind of waffle. "Well, it didn't really do any of those things. It merely and rather vaguely discussed things."

"A meeting long on rhetoric but short on policy?"

"That would sum it up," the Health Secretary replied. He could hear traffic on Victoria Street; a car blowing its horn, a lorry grinding gears.

"Did you expect otherwise, Minister?"

Kevin hadn't known what to expect, and so couldn't answer this question directly. "I'm not sure that the PM has a firm plan in mind."

"And did you expect the PM to have something in mind?" asked Sir Roger, knowing full well that the PM's go-to strategy on everything was prevarication, on the political principle that if a problem was ignored for long enough it would generally sort itself out. "After all, our options are somewhat limited until we know more precisely how the virus intends to spread itself."

Kevin glanced sharply at his civil servant who was smiling benignly. Sir Roger seemed to be giving the virus an intelligence beyond what it could possibly possess. "How it intends to spread itself?" he echoed.

"To survive, any living thing must replicate, Minister," said Sir Roger.

"Yes, but we're not exactly talking about procreation and babies."

"Quite so, but we are talking about Covid-19's ability to reproduce itself. That requires a continuous cycle of new infection."

"Yes, quite so," said the Health Secretary, "I understand the biology that's involved."

"Then you'll also understand that all living things have to have successful reproduction strategies."

Kevin was momentarily distracted by the thought of his wife getting out of bed that morning and walking to the toilet in her see-through nightie – not, of course, that any reproductive strategies or activities had subsequently taken place. "You seem to be suggesting that the virus is a living thing, Sir Roger."

"As I assume you're aware, Health Secretary, so forgive me if I appear patronising, a virus consists of nucleic acids enclosed in a protein coat and therefore, of itself, does not appear to be an organism. However, once it enters a host cell, it induces that cell to reproduce the intruder's own DNA or RNA and make more viral protein. Hey presto, Minister! More virus. It therefore has a life cycle involving birth and death and suggests, as some scientists do, that a virus is indeed a living thing."

The Health Secretary chose only to nod wisely at his Permanent Secretary, in a way that suggested that, of course, he knew everything about viruses, although inside he was horrified. His obsession with germs and microbes was based on a fear of very small and very inanimate things. He had no idea that these things could be *living* things.

Taking a deep breath, he replied: "That may be so, but my concern is that we don't seem to know the full range of possible outcomes and, therefore, what strategies we could adopt along different timelines."

Sir Roger looked visibly impressed that the Health Secretary should have articulated a viable approach to dealing with the impending crisis – if, indeed, there was to be a crisis – not knowing that his minister was simply quoting from an article in *The Guardian*, a newspaper which Kevin knew Sir Roger detested and never read.

"In which case, Minister, what would you like me to do? he asked, opening his notebook.

Again, the question that Kevin always dreaded. "What we need is the best scientific advice," he suggested rather lamely.

"Wasn't Brian Whittle at the meeting?"

"Yes, but he didn't really say anything. Merely that we have lots and lots of people working on it."

"Doing what, Minister?"

Kevin sighed, unable to quite remember what Brian Whittle had actually said. "He didn't say, although he did sound rather confident."

"Minister, could I remind you that I am your Permanent Secretary?"

"I hardly need reminding, Sir Roger."

"I do therefore know what *this* department is doing in some detail. Of most importance, what we're doing is trying, in partnership with research laboratories and statisticians, to generate useful data on transmission, infection and, therefore, likely fatalities."

"*Fatalities*?"

"It's when someone dies, Minister."

"Yes, yes, I do rather understand the meaning of death, Sir Roger. So, what you're suggesting is that we do absolutely nothing until we know what might happen?"

"If it indeed it does happen, Minister."

"And if nothing much does happen, we can then say that we had, of course, prepared for the worst."

"Quite so, Minister."

"But if the worst does happen, are we absolutely prepared?"

"That depends on how you define *worst*, Minister."

"I don't need to define it, Sir Roger. I'm merely asking if this ministry is prepared for what might, or might not, happen."

"We are, of course, as prepared as we can be, against a threat that neither of us can define and which, I should remind you, may transpire not to be a threat."

"So, until we know what might, or might not, happen we can't make any real plans."

"In a nutshell, Minister."

"Or preparations?"

"Correct, Minister. As yet, we don't have the definitive scientific advice on which we can rigorously and properly base any contingency preparations."

"Leaving aside COBRA, Brian Whittle must have said something to you," said the Health Secretary, wondering why he had a scientific advisor and if, what with wearing so many hats, his health ministry hat kept falling off.

"What I do know is that he's co-ordinating a most vigorous and urgent research programme. That work is being coordinated through the government's Special Advisory Group for Emergencies."

Kevin Kock thought for a few moments. "Did you know that if you take the first letters of that group, it spells SAGE." He looked rather triumphantly at his Permanent Secretary.

"That's why this group is actually called SAGE, Minister."

His Permanent Secretary seemed to be mistaking scientific ignorance with stupidity. "But you don't know when this vigorous and urgent research might turn up some results?" he asked, trying to sound as he rather imagined a Secretary of State should sound.

"Research takes time, Minister."

"In other words, we can't follow scientific advice, because there isn't any."

"Also, in a nutshell, Minister. But once we have that advice, we *must* follow it to the letter."

"Of course, of course." Then, after some thought, "Why?"

"Because, if it all goes horribly wrong, you can point the finger of blame at the scientists."

Kevin didn't much like the word *you*. "Don't you mean, *we*, Sir Roger?"

"No, Minister. You're the Secretary of State, and I am merely your civil servant. Or, as the Prime Minister would say, *culpa cadit in eos, qui ducunt.*" Sir Roger closed his notebook without having written anything in it.

"Thank you, Sir Roger."

"Thank you, Minister."

Kevin waited until his Permanent Secretary had closed the door before interrogating a language translation site.

Blame falls on those who lead, he read. Why was it, he thought, that everyone these days seemed to speak Latin?

On 21st February 2020, a key government committee, the new and emerging respiratory virus threats advisory group (NERVTAG), concluded, three weeks after the World Health Organisation had declared a public health emergency of international concern, that they had no objection to Public Health England's 'moderate' risk assessment of the disease to the UK population. The editor-in-chief of the Lancet *medical journal, said in* The Guardian *newspaper 'that was a genuinely fatal error of judgement.'*

While Kevin Kock pondered the strategic logic of doing very little, while also spraying an industrial strength aerosol around his office, an aerosol that he hoped capable of suppressing all germs, microbes and alien life-forms, the PM had his feet up on a coffee table and was playing Candy Crush on his mobile phone. "Hard day, dear?" asked Caroline, who was flat out on a cream sofa, one hand on her distended belly.

"As always, as always," he replied, alternately tapping on his phone and slurping from a glass of Merlot. "It's a hard job, you know."

"Of course, Prime Minister. It's also a hard job being pregnant."

"You don't have to call me prime minister," said the Prime Minister.

"I was using it ironically, sarcastically or sardonically or, perhaps, as a term of endearment. Maybe all of them," said Caroline, patting her tummy. "God, I hate this place!"

The PM checked his phone's email icon and saw that he had 103 emails requiring his attention. After a moment's thought, he deleted them all. Why, when he kept dogs, should he be expected to bark all the time? "What's wrong with this place? It's comfortable enough, if somewhat functional."

"Functional doesn't get close! It's your office, Winston. Downstairs are other offices. Down more stairs, more offices. Offices, offices, offices, with us perched on top of them."

"It's also our home," he reminded her. "Well, maybe not our proper home which is, quite obviously, and I quite agree, somewhere else but, while I'm prime minister, it's also our *temporary* home, although I am, of course, also hoping that it won't be too temporary."

Caroline sighed, while the Prime Minister finished his glass of red wine and went off to the kitchen for a refill.

His red phone started to ring the moment he had sat back down and about to resume his game of Candy Crush. It was one of his downstairs aides, a chirpy matriarch who had served many prime ministers without seeming to like any of them.

"I've just had a message from the Foreign Office, Prime Minister," said the matriarch in a lilting Irish accent, which was infinitely more attractive than the person it belonged to. "They've had word that a British citizen has died from Covid-19."

"Good God! Why wasn't I informed immediately?"

"They say that they sent you an email."

"Well, maybe they did," said the PM in voice that suggested, as the recipient of so many emails, messages and phone calls, that he couldn't be immediately expected to deal with everything.

"The deceased was a passenger on the cruise liner *Diamond Princess*, Prime Minister."

"Where?"

"Japan."

"How absolutely marvellous!" replied the Prime Minister, pleased that his strategy – if it was one – of stopping the virus (from the Latin meaning *poison*) in its tracks at Dover was bearing rich fruit.

Comings and Goings

In late February, according to a Sunday Times *report, at a private event, the Prime Minister's chief advisor outlined the government's strategy at the time and which was summarised by someone present as 'herd immunity, protect the economy, and if that means some pensioners die, too bad.'*

In early March, the Prime Minister told the nation that, while the virus was likely to become a more significant problem, 'this country is very, very well prepared. However, the final sentence of his message didn't appear on his official Twitter page: "I wish to stress that, at the moment, it is very important that people consider that they should, as far as possible, go about business as usual.'

By and large, Derek Goings was both universally loathed and feared. It was assumed that he either had access to supernatural forces or was, in fact, one of the Undead. Even the Archbishop of Westminster would cross himself when the two met, which was rarely – at the archbishop's request. Partly, he was loathed because of his role as the PM's chief advisor, with almost permanent access to the Prime Minister's ear. Partly, it was also because the PM usually did what his advisor told him to do, and that this was somehow undemocratic. Partly, too, it was because he smelled of sulphur. Nobody could therefore understand how he was married, shared a marital bed and had fathered a child. However, the sceptics pointed out, only his marriage was a matter of record. Whether he slept with his wife, and who the father of his child was, were grey areas best not explored.

Derek, his critics often complained, although never to his face or to his few friends, had somehow appeared from nowhere. One minute, nobody had ever heard of him; the next minute, his name, and the smell of the underworld, was everywhere. Derek's great achievement, agreed on by friends and foes, was to have leaped successfully onto the political stage without ever having done anything useful. Okay, he had once helped a relative run a nightclub in the north of England, and never mind that it had been voted the second worst in Europe. (The worst subsequently burned down, accidentally or on purpose, handing the crown to Derek's relative). Okay, he had also tried to start an airline in either Prague or Moscow (nobody was entirely sure which) but that hadn't got off the ground, either literally or metaphorically.

Having therefore done nothing of note, he then appeared as if in a puff of black and menacing smoke on the Westminster stage, immediately making enemies of virtually everyone. However, having enemies only seemed to increase his powers because, say what you might about him, he did get things done. In a Whitehall dominated by men in grey suits, and all either from Oxbridge or interbred, the proper way to get things done had always been the old-fashioned way. After all, the British way was the traditional way; decisions were made over Pimm's at Wimbledon; gin and tonics at Twickenham, and whatever was available at Henley. Decisions were rarely made in Whitehall, where they were supposed to be made. Derek, of course, thought otherwise, facing up to the grey suits in either jeans or tracksuit, with a mission to bring the British Civil Service at least into the 20th century. Perhaps, even for him, the 21st century was too big a task, at least for now. This wrecking-ball of a man, with his glittering career in night-time entertainment and air travel, therefore found himself in endless conflict with the mandarins who were supposed to be running the country.

Derek's meteoric rise through the government's advisory ranks was extraordinary; so too the growth of his reputation as someone who could end a political career with the merest nod of his head. He was, it was agreed, either Machiavellian or Svengalian – generally the former, because few civil servants or politicians had ever read a 19th century novel, and therefore didn't quite know who Svengali was.

Kevin Kock was, of course, all too aware of the PM's advisor, having been in numerous meetings with him and having seen how even the most confident minister could be brought to his or, sometimes, her knees with a cursory glance. It was therefore with alarm bordering on panic that he received the news from his Permanent Secretary that Derek Goings was on his way round for a 'bit of a chin-wag.'

"But I'm busy," he'd squeaked to Sir Roger.

"No, you're not. I manage your diary, Minister."

The Health Secretary could have said that he had a completely separate diary in which he, as Health Secretary, kept his Top Secret meetings; or that he was ill; or could have chosen from any one of the many excuses that he'd used over the years, mostly to cover up his blood and germ phobias. Now, of course, thanks to his Permanent Secretary, his alien life-form phobia because, in his mind, Covid-19 was now sentient and possibly intelligent – like a jellyfish, but with a more deadly sting. He then spent some minutes spraying his office with air freshener and disinfectant, and covering his desk with large piles of files. He even undid the top button of his shirt to demonstrate his dedication to the British people except, of course, Derek Goings.

His arrival was signalled, not by a deferential knock on his office door or a bleep from his internal phone, but by the smell of decay. The Health Secretary closed his eyes for just a moment and took several deep breaths only to find, when he opened his eyes again, that the PM's advisor was already standing on the other side of his desk.

"Derek, good gracious! How nice to see you!" The Health Secretary automatically stuck out a hand, before realising that Derek Goings still had both hands in the pockets of his jeans. Only the Prime Minister was still shaking everyone's hand, particularly on hospital visits.

The PM's advisor sat in the chair opposite and sniffed the air. "Very wise," he remarked. "As Health Secretary, it's good to see that you're setting an example."

"Am I?"

"You can't be too careful, Minister, because you never know who might be harbouring infection. Sterilising your office is possibly or probably a good thing." The advisor's eyes, hidden behind dark glasses, were black discs. His soft voice carried with it both menace and good hygienic advice.

"Am I to assume that you're here for a reason?" the Health Secretary asked, hoping to sound business-like and brusque, having rehearsed this opening line as he sprayed the room. "Because I am, as I'm sure you are, rather busy."

"No, you're not, Health Secretary. I looked at your diary."

"Sir Roger had no right…."

"I have every right, Minister."

Before Kevin could think of a suitably outraged reply, there was a soft knock on the door and Sir Roger himself appeared, carrying a notebook. Without asking, he took the other available seat next to Derek and neatly crossed his legs.

"I am here, Minister, to determine whether this country is prepared." The PM's advisor's voice was barely a whisper. "After all, we are now beginning to see the first Covid-19 fatalities on British soil."

"I did know that, Derek."

"We will certainly see more fatalities, Minister, which brings me neatly to the reason why I am here. I merely wish to determine if *you* have made adequate preparations. Particularly the provision of personal protective equipment."

This was a question that the Health Secretary, even panic-stricken, had foreseen. "Of course, Derek. We have, for example, a reserve of over one billion items of PPE. One *billion*, Derek." The Health Secretary smiled brightly at his nemesis on the other side of the desk, using the advisor's first name twice in the space of a few seconds, a useful trick that he'd learned on some management course he'd attended. Sir Roger picked imaginary spots of dust from his immaculate trousers and looked out the window.

"Yet, I am led to believe, Minister, that this figure includes things like cleaning products, waste bags, detergents and paper towels," said the advisor, still in his stage whisper.

"Does it?" replied Kevin. "I mean, yes it does. At least, possibly it does. But a billion is still rather a lot of stuff, I'm sure you would agree."

"Not necessarily," said the advisor. "For example, your inventory lists 547 million protective gloves."

"So?"

"So, a more accurate figure would be 273.5 million *pairs* of gloves, or am I missing something?"

"Pairs of gloves?"

"Your inventory lists each glove separately."

The Health Secretary looked wildly at his Permanent Secretary, who merely shrugged. "I did send you the inventory last year, Minister. Which you approved," he added with a smile.

"Well, you know what they say, Derek."

"No, I don't know what they say, Minister."

"That there are only three kinds of people in the world. Those who can count, and those who can't." The Health Secretary gave a small laugh, which wasn't echoed from across the table.

"I hardly think that this is a time for levity, Minister." The smell of sulphur had risen several notches, and a green vapour seemed to be filling the room. "I also just hope the media don't get hold of the story. I dread to think what *Panorama* would make of it."

"I'm sure they won't, Derek."

"However, if things deteriorate, PPE will get eaten up pretty quickly," said the advisor, whose eyes had never left Kevin's face, or maybe they had because, behind dark glasses, he could be looking anywhere.

"We are, of course, setting up new procurement channels to ensure against any and every contingency, aren't we, Sir Roger?"

His Permanent Secretary shifted uncomfortably in his seat. "Of course, Minister," and then actually wrote something in his notebook.

"Very well, then I will assume that you have the needs of the health service and its gallant staff fully covered. But what about the care sector?"

"What about the care sector?" asked the Health Secretary.

The advisor was quiet for a moment. "Well, you are the person responsible for it."

"What!" Kevin almost pushed himself upright.

"You are, as I assume you must realise, Secretary of State for Health *and* Social Care."

"What!"

Sir Roger cleared his throat. "I did send you a memo, Minister."

The Cabinet met in the first week of March to discuss what, if anything, to do next. In February, the government had already introduced the Health Protection (Coronavirus) Regulations 2020, a statutory instrument made under the Public Health (Control of Disease) Act 1984, intended merely to delay the spread of the virus, with powers to detain and isolate anyone believed to be carrying Covid-19. Hospitals also set up screening services, and the Chief Medical Officer for England outlined a strategy of contain, delay, research and mitigate – which sounded excellent, if only on paper.

However, two modelling teams from Imperial College London and the London School of Hygiene & Tropical Medicine had separately concluded that if the government's simple delay strategy was continued, about 250,000 deaths could result. These findings were relayed to the government's scientific advisory group for emergencies on 3rd March, which was also attended by government officials, but who might not have thought them important enough to pass on to government ministers.

For Kevin Kock, who had introduced the new health regulations as well as drive-through screening at hospitals, and had at the time been very pleased with himself, it now seemed as if the virus wasn't listening, no matter how much disinfectant he sprayed around his office. It was spreading, no doubt about that, with cases now reported across all the nations of the UK.

The Prime Minister was, as always, in an ebullient mood, while simultaneously trying to look sombre. This simply made him look like a menacing walrus. "Gentlemen," he began, misogynistically ignoring the women present, including the pretty Home Secretary, Lovely Rasool, who sighed loudly. The Prime Minister ignored her, as he usually did. "We are facing an existential crisis in the form of a virus we cannot see but over which we shall prevail. Make no mistake, colleagues, we will fight this virus with vigour and determination and it is up to us to determine what we should be vigorous about." The Prime Minister smiled broadly around the table, so that nobody knew whether he was being inarticulate or jovial. "Health Secretary, could you give us an update?"

Kevin Kock consulted his notes. "As of now, there are just over five thousand confirmed cases, Prime Minister."

"Which, quite frankly, and trying to look on the bright side, isn't as many as it could be," the Prime Minister observed.

"It's over one thousand more than yesterday, Prime Minister."

"Well, in the scheme of things, it still isn't that many."

"Maybe not, but cases are doubling every three days." Sir Roger had been quite forceful on this point, having been briefed by someone-or-another.

"Okay, so what does the World Health Authority say about it?"

"Organisation," the Health Secretary corrected.

"Excellent idea! That's precisely what we need! We absolutely require coordinated organisation."

There was a lengthy silence in which tea cups were rattled and Lovely Rasool helped herself to another Danish pastry, plates of which were dotted down the Cabinet table. The Prime Minister brushed ineffectually at crumbs down his shirtfront.

"What we need, Prime Minister, is a phased approach to curtailing large gatherings," suggested Lovely Patel who, as Home Secretary, probably had more responsibility for British large gatherings than anyone else round the table.

"Quite, quite," the PM agreed and several Cabinet members nodded. "But my view is that we must also look back to the war for our inspiration, because World War Two wasn't a conflict that we rushed into willy-nilly. No, on the contrary, there was a phoney bit at the start of the war in which there was little or no fighting. We used that period to prepare for the dark days we knew would inevitably lie ahead and that, colleagues, is what we should be doing now. Rather than fighting the virus, we should be preparing to fight the virus."

"That may be so, Prime Minister," said the Home Secretary loudly, "but other countries have already introduced lockdown and quarantine measures. Countries such as New Zealand, South Korea and Vietnam."

"Yes, but they're quite near China."

"The virus travels between people, Prime Minister, not by geography."

The Prime Minister was going to say something about fighting it on the beaches, or being prepared to fight it on the beaches, then wisely thought otherwise, wondering also why he had seen fit to promote this Lovely woman to be Home Secretary. "I am perfectly aware of that," he replied.

"Specifically," she continued, refusing to shut up, "there is a full programme of football still scheduled for this weekend, five horse racing meetings and a Six Nations match at Twickenham."

"England against Wales," said the PM. "I shall of course be attending that event. In my capacity, naturally, as president of the Rugby Football Union."

"No, you're not," replied the Home Secretary. "Peter Wheeler is the president."

"The ex-player? Good grief!" The PM helped himself to yet another Danish pastry and signalled for more tea. "Well, they did invite me," he grumbled. "I just assumed it was because I was president and had, what with everything I have to remember, forgotten that I was president."

"Not because you're the prime minister, Prime Minister?" the Home Secretary suggested.

"Scotland are also playing France at Murrayfield this weekend," the Scottish Secretary added, to demonstrate that the UK was more than England with a few inconvenient bits stuck on.

"Exactly!" replied the Home Secretary. (*On the same day that Scotland played France, 8th March, the French government banned all gatherings of more than 1,000 people*). "Next week, I should also add, some 250,000 people will be going to the Cheltenham Festival. It would surely be remiss of us to allow that event, and other large events *this* weekend" – looking pointedly at the PM – "to go ahead."

"I'd forgotten it was the gee-gees next week," said the Business Secretary, Dave Clegg, who had once briefly helped run a bookshop in Swindon, and whose demeanour suggested that he was already planning to attend.

"Not to mention Liverpool's Champions League match against Atletico Madrid," said the Environment Secretary rather too brightly who, it was rumoured, was a secret football fan but, to further his career, had always kept it secret. "For what it's worth, Prime Minister, my view is that we have to carefully calibrate our response to the virus. I just don't think that the British people will tolerate their freedoms being infringed at this stage. We have to take the people with us, not dictate measures that they will consider un-British."

"I agree," said Dave Clegg. "Our democracy is nothing if it doesn't have consensus. That is at the fundamental and unwritten heart of our unwritten constitution. Cancelling sporting events at this juncture in time would be to break that consensus, not to mention rewrite our unwritten constitution and, perhaps, also break the people's trust in their government."

"But do many football supporters vote Conservative?" asked the PM.

"They did at the last general election," replied the Business Secretary. "Voters from the north of England who had always been Labour supporters. They turned their backs on Socialism to put you in that chair, Prime Minister."

"Yes, I do vaguely remember," said the PM.

"Therefore, it would be unwise for us to turn our backs on them now."

"Freedom-loving, football-loving northerners, you mean?"

"Yes, Prime Minister."

"This is ridiculous!" interjected the Home Secretary. "How many deaths will it take before we act?"

"That's not the point, Home Secretary," said the Prime Minister.

"That is *exactly* the point. Our first duty is to protect the people."

"Fiddlesticks! Our first duty is to protect freedom," corrected the PM. "The British people have fought for centuries to secure the freedoms that we take for granted. To encroach on individual freedom is, may I remind you, an affront to the democratic principles that we all adhere to, including people from the north, although perhaps not from Scotland." The PM could never understand why the voters of Scotland didn't vote Conservative in larger numbers. "I therefore think it is right and proper that we keep the situation under careful review and be ready at a moment's notice, indeed in a twinkling, to act decisively. As I said, now is not the time to fight an unseen enemy, now is the time to make sure that we have all the tools we need so that, in due course, and at the right moment, we can begin to fight the virus, if necessary street by street."

"Dear God," muttered the Home Secretary under her breath, but then became aware of a strong smell of sulphur, and Derek

Goings' eyes upon her (although he could have been looking anywhere), and the realisation that her position in government might not be as secure as it had been a few minutes beforehand.

"In which case, now that we are in total agreement," said the PM, "*Vade in domum tuam et parare prandium.*"

This was too much Latin for the Health Secretary to remember, so he couldn't interrogate his Latin-English translation website, and therefore never found out that the Prime Minister was simply telling them all to *go home and prepare for lunch.*

*It was left to Culture Secretary Oliver Dowden (***Note**: not his real name*) to tell the BBC, in relation to the Cheltenham Festival, that there was "no reason for people not to attend such events or to cancel them at this stage." The Liverpool match also went ahead, with many fans travelling from Spain, where football matches were by then being played behind closed doors. Also, according to modelling from Imperial College and Oxford, Spain had 640,000 infections compared to a more accurate estimate of 100,000 in the UK.*

On 12th March, on the issue of banning major public events such as sporting fixtures, the Prime Minister said that 'the scientific advice as we've said over the last couple of weeks is that banning such events will have little effect on the spread.' A day later, the government said that mass gatherings would be banned from the following weekend.

Edge Health, which analyses data for the National Health Service, estimates that 41 deaths were caused by the Liverpool match going ahead and 37 because of the Cheltenham Festival – and those were just the fatalities recorded in local hospitals.

The Wuhan Institute of Virology had become a very obvious scapegoat as the creator of the new coronavirus. After all, China had been the source of the SARS outbreak and, with Wuhan having a virology laboratory that studied coronaviruses right at the heart of the Covid-19 outbreak, not a few fingers had begun to point in its direction. The science, after all, did seem to suggest that the Wuhan laboratory might have been involved, although the science also suggested that the virus most probably originated elsewhere. This didn't stop the President of the United States from laying the blame squarely on China saying that "the world is paying a very big price for what they did." The President's stance in March was at stark variance to his comments in February when, according to CNN, he praised Chinese President Xi Jinping's response to the crisis on at least 12 occasions. President Trump's change of heart possibly had something to do with the growing Covid-19 crisis in the USA, his inept handling of it, and a dawning realisation that he was up for re-election in November, and therefore had to shift all blame elsewhere.

Timothy Raambo, Secretary of State for Foreign and Commonwealth Affairs and First Secretary of State, had already asked the Secret Intelligence Service for its assessment of the source of the virus. MI6 didn't know but would, of course, dispatch its most resourceful agents. However, in its Top Secret reply, the agency did helpfully say that *Wuhan is the capital city of Hubei Province in the People's Republic of China. It is the largest city in Hubei and the most populous city in Central China, with a population of over 11 million...*

Timothy Raambo's credentials for the job were impressive. Not only had he been abroad on several occasions, Kevin Kock was right, he had also worked on secondment for a human rights NGO, and had done useful things for the World Bank in the Middle East. He had also been captain of his university kickboxing team. This last fact, coupled with his unfortunate surname and athletic physique, made him somebody to be reckoned with.

"May I ask what Cabinet decided?" asked his Permanent Secretary, Tony Bond, when Raambo returned from Downing Street, and was safely back in his office, back behind his desk, and with his feet up on the table.

"Precisely nothing," he replied.

"But it must have decided something." Like all permanent secretaries, who were generally identical clones from some distant humanoid source, Tony Bond was both efficient and suave, and always suspicious of meetings to which he hadn't been invited.

"We are still in a wait-and-see phase, Tony. However, the good news is that the PM says that we have world-leading scientific experts, and we should listen to them. It's called following the science, and it's now our mantra, apparently."

Raambo took his feet off the desk and looked at the pile of papers in his in-tray. How, in just a few hours, could so much have accumulated? He picked up the first file that came to hand, looked at it, then chucked it back onto his pile.

"But what about the Health Secretary's action plan?"

"It wasn't discussed, Tony. In any case, the Health Secretary's action plan, as you call it, is merely a long list of things we could do, entirely copied from countries who are already doing them. Except that it isn't an action plan, because the PM only wants action when he feels it is appropriate."

"So, while other countries lock down, we do nothing?"

"Quite so, Tony." Raambo looked at his permanent secretary more closely, realising that if he passed Tony Bond on the street, he would fail to recognise him. With his grey hair, grey suit and copy-and-paste smile, he was simply a test-tube copy of the mandarin super-class that ruled Whitehall, and perhaps had always ruled Whitehall. Raambo also realised that he knew nothing about him while he, Tony Bond, knew *everything* about him. Was he married? Did he have children? Did he actually live in a house? Or did he belong to a colony of mandarins that perhaps lived in a dense woodland somewhere outside London, and to which they all retreated every night to hang upside down from branches. Raambo stood from his desk, suddenly depressed, and crossed to a window overlooking Whitehall. There were tourists grouped around the Cenotaph, tourist buses edging up and down towards Trafalgar Square or the Palace of Westminster. It was a scene he'd watched yesterday, and a scene he would no doubt watch tomorrow. In the surreal world of Covid-19, everything was the same and yet nothing was the same.

He sat back at his desk, looking again at his bulging in-tray, and then around the room, letting his eyes rest for a moment (metaphorically) on the large mahogany conference table that dominated one side of his ornate office. Around it would have sat generations of diplomats and politicians, poring over maps, determining strategies to protect the Empire or win wars in countries that none of them had ever set foot in. Now, with email and group conferencing, Raambo couldn't remember if he'd ever sat at that table, or ever would.

"You seem distracted, Minister."

"Well, yes, now that you mention it, I am a little distracted. It's this lab in Wuhan, Tony. Might there, perchance or maybe, be any truth in the speculation surrounding it? That it could have, inadvertently of course, created this virus, purely for research purposes, and then accidentally released it?"

"We don't have reliable intelligence on that, Minister."

"Yes, I know we don't, which is why I've asked our friends in the Secret Service to look into it. Secretly, of course."

"You should have told me, Minister." His Permanent Secretary's voice was still unctuous and precise, its tone still grey and bland, but still containing the smallest frisson of disapproval.

"I'm telling you now, Tony. The trouble is that I've also had a report from the American Ambassador. While US intelligence doesn't believe that the Wuhan lab is implicated, the US President, perhaps for purely political reasons, says that it is."

"That much I do know, Minister. Also, that President Xi Jinping denies it."

"But what you don't know is that the US Ambassador also phoned me this morning. The State Department wants us to back the President's claim. They assume, I assume, that now we don't take orders from Brussels, we will now take orders from Washington."

"To pave the way for a bilateral trade deal?"

"The ambassador was careful not to suggest as such, while making it abundantly clear it was precisely what he was offering. He also reminded me that Trump's inflammatory comments on China were tantamount to tweaking the dragon's tail."

"Meaning what precisely, Minister?"

"That while China comes out of lockdown, having successfully implemented the measures that *we* should be taking now, the Western world is entirely paralysed by Covid-19 and unable to do anything." The Foreign Secretary realised that it was nearly lunchtime and that he'd achieved nothing so far with his day. "He suggested that China may use this opportunity to impose its will on Hong Kong and that, like it or not, Great Britain will inevitably become involved in the China blame game."

"Which could easily escalate, Minister. Perhaps alarmingly."

"The ambassador also said that they believe the president to be mad."

"Xi Jinping?"

"No, Tony, their president."

While the Foreign Secretary was grappling with issues of world significance, in particular worsening relations between the USA and China, Kevin Kock was rubbing sanitising gel between his fingers and wondering why he was now putting more alcohol onto his hands than into his mouth. No sooner had he placed the bottle back into a drawer than Sir Roger knocked softly, entered without receiving a response, and settled himself into a chair at the Health Secretary's desk. Unusually, he was carrying both a notebook and a small bundle of files, which was never a good sign. "A fruitful Cabinet meeting, Minister?" he began.

"That would depend on your definition of *fruitful*, Sir Roger."

"I therefore take it that nothing was decided."

"The Home Secretary did make a forceful case for closing down large gatherings. The Prime Minister and several Cabinet members made a strong case to the contrary."

"Well, the PM *is* going to Twickenham this weekend," said Sir Roger who would also be attending, albeit as the guest of a cosmetics company who wanted to fast-track a new eyeshadow range into the UK market now that it had been extensively tested on a wide range of animals, mostly against their better judgement. "I doubt that he would want large gatherings closed down until at least next week."

"Liverpool are playing Atletico Madrid next week."

Football was, of course, one of the few subjects about which Sir Roger knew nothing. "In that case, until the week after next," he observed.

"But are all those large gatherings safe, Sir Roger?" The Health Secretary had a brief vision of sentient and intelligent viruses communicating – well, virally – and deciding that west London and Liverpool would be ideal places to meet up.

The Permanent Secretary consulted one of his files. "The Chief Scientific Advisor says that large gatherings actually don't make much difference. He says, and I quote, that 'there's only a certain number of people you can infect. So, one person in a 70,000-seater stadium is not going to infect the stadium. They will infect potentially a few people they've got very close contact with.'"

"So, nothing to worry about, Sir Roger?"

"Absolutely nothing at all, Minister."

"We're just following the science."

"In a nutshell, Minister," said Sir Roger, "because the science is never wrong."

The R number

On March 9th, after another COBRA meeting, the Prime Minister said that efforts to contain the virus were unlikely to succeed on their own. He said that measures would have to be introduced, that he would follow the scientific advice, and that he would act when he judged it to be right. Three days later, he told the nation that "this is the worst public health crisis for a generation....many more families are going to lose loved ones before their time."

However, only just over a week earlier, he had described the virus as a "moderate illness."

In following the science, it wasn't that the science was wrong, it was simply that there was only so much science the government could rely on. Covid-19 was only just getting into its stride and most scientific advice, without good data, could only be given on the basis of broad assumptions and a bit of guesswork, fancily dressed up as empiric observation. For example, a US modelling group said that by August the UK could be looking at over 66,000 deaths. On closer inspection, this turned out to be a wholly useless average of their estimate range which was between 14,572 and 219,211 deaths. It was like holding a finger up to test the strength of a hurricane, or adding two and two together and coming up with whatever number you think of.

Despite reports reaching ministers that were often based on flimsy and unscientific assumptions, the government continued to rely on its domestic advisors, without looking to countries such as New Zealand or, closer to home, Greece or Croatia. These countries, Whitehall collectively decided, were perfectly fine for a summer holiday, but not as a source of world-beating science in which, of course, the UK excelled.

In Downing Street, the Prime Minister first smelled sulphur and then realised that his chief advisor, in jeans and T-shirt, was sitting on his office sofa. "Dee, good gracious, I didn't hear you come in!"

If Derek Goings minded being called by a girl's diminutive, he gave no sign of it. "How was your weekend, Prime Minister?"

"Splendid, splendid! Another triumph for our gallant rugby chaps!"

The advisor's nose wrinkled, not at the pervasive smell of corruption, but at the mere mention of something as frivolous as sport. "You wanted to see me, Prime Minister."

"Yes, Dee, I did indeed want to see you." The PM waved at a tall and precarious stack of files on his desk. "These are reports from our special advisory group for emergencies. Quite why somebody couldn't have condensed them down into one report, preferably one page long, or indeed shorter, is beyond me. However, I assume that you have read all of them and, no doubt, memorised every word. I would therefore like you to advise me of their contents."

The advisor crossed his legs slowly, showing off his rather tatty trainers. Quite how he was able to dress like this at the very heart of government was a subject of widespread and unfavourable speculation, mostly from civil servants who believed, possibly correctly, that good advice could only be given by someone wearing a shirt and tie. "You'll appreciate, Prime Minister, that there can be, and often are, contradictions between different scientific disciplines. An epidemiologist won't always agree with a virologist, and the views of a public health specialist will often differ from those of a behavioural psychologist."

"Quite so," said the PM, without having the slightest notion what Derek Goings was talking about.

"It means, that epidemiological advice tells us to go for an immediate lockdown because that will save the most lives. That's what many other countries are doing."

"Then, Dee, that's what we must do!" the PM exclaimed. "The good of the people must always come before their liberty," he added, notwithstanding that he'd argued the opposite in Cabinet the week before.

"*However*," the advisor continued, visibly irritated at being interrupted although, inscrutable behind dark glasses, it was hard to tell whether it was indeed irritation or merely trapped wind, "other advisory reports set out the likely impacts on physical and mental health and, not least, the devastating consequences of shutting down the economy."

"The economy is rather important, Dee."

"Of course, Prime Minister, and the strategy we seem to have adopted by default, in the absence of having adopted an *actual* strategy, is to allow large parts of the population to become infected and therefore to develop large-scale immunity. That would, at the very least, allow us to better prepare for a potential second wave of the virus later in the year."

"I see," said the PM, and nodded thoughtfully several times. "Why?"

"Because if most of us catch the virus, it means the virus will inevitably die out."

"But what about the sick or elderly?" The PM had never shown much empathy for such people, but recognised that everyone had a vote, however inconveniently they might sometimes use them.

"We tell the sick or anyone showing symptoms of the virus to self-isolate and, as far as possible, we shield the elderly."

"But not to self-isolate every household?"

"Your Chief Medical Advisor says that we shouldn't start doing that in advance of need."

"Old Whittle actually said that?"

"Word for word, Prime Minister."

"Well," said the PM gesturing to his stack of files. "I don't suppose that I need wade through those now. As always, Dee, a most illuminating briefing and some excellent advice, thank you."

"I haven't actually given you any advice, Prime Minister," said the advisor.

"But you have, because I had old Whittle on the phone to me this morning. Interrupted breakfast, would you believe! Kept wittering on about the R number."

"The number that estimates reproduction of the virus."

"Is that what it stands for? For some reason, Whittle assumed I would know. Quite why I *should* know, I don't know."

‘If R is above one, the virus spreads,” said Derek Goings, trying to keep things very simple. “If it’s below one, the virus dies away.” After his stint as the PM’s chief advisor, Goings sometimes felt that he would be perfectly trained as a primary school teacher.

“Whittle says that R could be above two.”

“Two, Prime Minister?”

“R two, Dee. Two.”

The PM never watched anything as low-brow as sci-fi films, leaving his advisor to conclude that he was, as always, simply being an idiot.

On 15th March, a professor of the evolution and epidemiology of infectious disease at Harvard University, writing in The Guardian newspaper about the UK Government’s herd immunity plan, said that ‘when I first heard about this, I could not believe it... my colleagues here in the US... assumed that reports of the UK policy were satire...policy should be directed at slowing the outbreak to a (more) manageable rate. What this looks like is strong social distancing...all this and more should have started weeks ago.’

The one strand in the government’s strategy that did make sense was its commitment to community testing, to better identify those infected, and quantify the spread of the virus. Kevin Kock was particularly pleased that his ministry had been the first to introduce such a testing regime before realising that only the Health Ministry had any jurisdiction in the matter, and that no other ministry was in the race to follow suit. He sometimes also felt that his ministry was bearing an unfair load, and that he should be able to devolve bits of his health remit to other government departments. Culture, for example, which did very little, or anything that was remotely important or, indeed, useful. The Health Secretary knew that his counterpart in the Department for Digital, Culture, Media and Sport spent most of his day wearing large earphones and listening to opera, while simply ignoring the digital, media and sport parts of his departmental functions. It was unfair, thought the Health Secretary, that the country's health should be the sole responsibility of the Health Ministry. In those dark days, in the first two weeks of March, it was a responsibility that weighed down heavily on him: that the British people needed his leadership and relied on his understanding of alien life-forms to formulate world-class policies.

His bad mood that Monday morning was in part the result of a dinner party that he and his wife Minty had attended the previous Saturday evening. It had been a small gathering with only two other couples, close friends, in north London and hosted by Janice and Ian Montgomery-Stuart-Rappaport (***Note**: surname changed for privacy and confidentiality*). The Montgomery-Stuart-Rappaports lived within walking distance of the Kocks, and Kevin had been looking forward to the evening; he liked Ian and Janice, which was why they were close friends, despite Ian working in advertising, and it would be a welcome distraction from his ministerial day job. Also at this elite gathering were Dot and Pete Jones (***Note**: surname unchanged because Jones is pretty common*).

It was the three husbands who were the oldest of friends, having met at Oxford. Kevin had studied (what else?) politics; Pete and Ian, English. They'd met in their first term, all having an interest in the performing arts. Kevin often thought that his masterful performances at the Despatch Box were all down to his Hamlet and Othello at DramSoc. (Not that Kevin had actually *played* Hamlet or Othello, merely such roles as Third Spear-carrier or Disease-ridden peasant). The three became friends, and Ian and Pete did actually get to play Hamlet and Othello, with Kevin either bounding on stage in a toga and carrying a long stick, or lying in the background and dribbling.

But Kevin's hopes of a dinner party away from the conversational clutches of Covid-19 were soon dashed. No sooner did he have a gin and tonic in one hand and a vol au vent in the other, than Pete Jones, who was a builder, albeit a builder who employed over 25,000 people, asked him for "all the gossip, strictly between ourselves, of course."

This put Kevin in a difficult position as Pete was the second most indiscreet person in the world, only bettered by his wife

Dorothy, a journalist on *The Sun* newspaper, and who would trade her mother in for a good headline.

"I'm not sure that there is any gossip, to be honest," he'd parried back.

"But you're a government minister," Pete responded, making Kevin feel momentarily proud. He cast a glance at his wife who, instead of smiling proudly in the warm glow of his achievements, was staring resolutely at the ceiling. "You must know what's going on."

"We're following the science," said Kevin in a firmer voice.

"But that's bollocks," said Ian. "How can you be following the science if other countries, presumably also following the science, are doing things completely differently?"

"We do, I suppose, have different scientists."

This blindingly obvious answer seemed to temporarily satisfy Ian who retreated to the kitchen for a refill, and who returned a minute later holding a white wine bottle. He replenished Minty's glass, and plonked himself back on the sofa.

"But the science must be the same, surely?" he persisted. "After all, the virus is the same here as elsewhere, isn't it? Either our scientists are giving you bad advice or you're not listening to them." He took a swig of his drink and winked at his wife.

"As I said, Ian, we're simply being guided by what our scientists and medical advisors are telling us. Can't do anything else, can we?"

"Well, yes, you could," chipped in Dorothy, wife to Pete, leaning expectantly forwards, and who might as well have had a reporter's notebook in front of her or be holding a microphone, or both. "The PM says that we'll have to introduce further measures. But why wait? The longer we wait, the more people become infected."

"It's not that simple," Kevin replied, looking to his wife who, at such moments could always be relied upon to change the subject away from the confidential nature of her husband's job.

"Good point, Dorothy. Darling, why the fuck *are* we dithering about?" she asked.

Over dinner (thankfully not rare beef), there were a few more half-hearted attempts to prise information from Kevin, which he batted away by saying that SAGE and Public Health England would be providing updated assessments after the weekend, and the government's chief medical and scientific advisors would then recommend what the possible next steps should be. "It's about balancing the science with other considerations," he concluded.

"But you said you were simply following the science," said Ian.

"You didn't say anything about *other considerations*," added his wife, Janice.

"For a start, the economy," replied Kevin. "People need livelihoods."

"People also need life," said Janice but, when Kevin looked sharply at her, she looked away.

After dinner, Kevin, Ian and Pete continued to sit at the dining table drinking Ian's best brandy (which was also his only brandy, bought at Tesco) while the three wives moved to the living room to discuss a mutual friend's marital woes, a subject to which their husbands were naturally excluded.

"Listen, I've got a coronavirus joke," said Ian. "Five people are on an aeroplane. President Trump, the Pope, Winston Spragg, Chancellor Merkel and a small boy. Then, suddenly, the captain announces that the plane is about to crash."

"That makes six people," Pete pointed out.

"Seven if you include a co-pilot. What about cabin crew, Ian?"

Kevin Kock was only half-listening, holding his mobile phone under the table and checking for any urgent updates. There was only one, from Derek Goings: *Don't tell Dorothy Jones anything*. His first thought was: how the *hell* did the PM's advisor know he was at a dinner party with a journalist? His second thought was: it's his job to know everything about everybody. He put his phone away with a small shudder.

"Okay, okay," said Ian, refilling his glass and passing the brandy bottle to Kevin who also poured himself a generous measure. He deserved, he thought, time off from being responsible. "These five people are flying on an entirely autonomous aeroplane that's being remotely flown by a pilot on the ground. Does that make sense to everyone?"

"Not particularly," said Pete, "but I assume it's not an integral part of the joke's punchline, if we ever get to one." He smiled broadly at Kevin, who had been grinning inanely at nobody in particular, still trying to work out how the PM's advisor knew both his whereabouts and who he was having dinner with. Was the electronic diary that Sir Roger kept for him also connected to Downing Street? Maybe so, but it wouldn't have included the names of dinner guests. Did that mean that he was being followed by MI5? Was he suspected of something?

"Anyway," continued Ian. "Five people are on the plane but there are only four parachutes. So, President Trump grabs one and says that he's the leader of the free world, the smartest man in the USA, and that he's desperately needed to fight this new disease. He puts on the parachute and jumps out the aeroplane. The Pope then grabs a parachute and says that, with disease and misery ravaging the world, people need the Catholic Church more than ever and a Pope to lead it. And he jumps out the plane. Then our very own prime minister grabs a parachute and mumbles inarticulately about Great Britain and the Commonwealth, and how he's absolutely needed to fight Covid-19, and he too jumps out the plane."

"Let's hope they're not mid-Atlantic," said Pete.

"That leaves only Chancellor Merkel and the small boy," continued Ian, speaking loudly over Pete. "Chancellor Merkel kneels down by the small boy and says that he must have the last parachute as he's young with his future ahead of him, while her life is mainly behind her. But the little boy tells Merkel not to worry as there are still two parachutes left because 'the smartest man in the USA just put on my schoolbag before jumping out the plane.'"

Kevin and Pete dutifully laughed, but it seemed like a joke with a sting to it. The three of them chatted some more; how Pete was due to play golf the next day, how Ian was taking his wife shopping ("while we still can") looking pointedly at his politician friend. Then Pete said that he needed the loo, got up, stretched and tottered away.

"About your joke," began Kevin.

"Good wasn't it?"

"Well yes, but why cast Merkel as the good guy?"

Ian's glass, which had been travelling towards his mouth, stopped on its journey and then reversed back down to the table. "You really don't know, do you?" he asked.

"No, Ian, I really don't know."

"Because, Kevin, she's actually doing something to help her people. Locking her country down. Maybe helping to save lives." He raised his glass again and pointed it at Kevin. "In contrast, you lot are doing precisely nothing."

It was therefore with some satisfaction that Kevin had presided over the creation of a contact testing programme that would better inform government policy options so that, while the Prime Minister still believed that the virus could be repulsed from the beaches – despite having bypassed beaches and being palpably evident across most regions of the British Isles – his department was actually doing something useful. It was a programme that aimed to test and then trace others who might be infected, and had long been in the UK's health armoury. It had eradicated smallpox and was still routinely used for vaccine-preventable infections such as measles or sexually-transmitted infections such as HIV and novel infections such as SARS-CoV, SARS-CoV-2 and Covid-19.

It was also the weapon of choice of many advanced, and some not-so-advanced, countries, from Singapore and South Korea to Germany (Ian was right), and a policy driven by the World Health Organisation, whose director general, Tedros Adhanom Ghebreyesus, had said that 'test, test, test' was the place to start.

But it was with mixed emotions that the Health Secretary strode into his ministry on the Monday morning. Yes, he was proud of what his ministry had achieved, but he was still unsettled by the weekend's dinner party, and the distain expressed about the government's strategic policy of inaction. Ian could generally be counted upon as a weathervane of public opinion – Kevin trusted his judgement over that of his own wife, who generally thought that hanging people was a good solution to most political issues, and had often confided in him for political advice over the years.

To make matters worse on Monday morning, his ministerial car was late and, on a busy road into the city, developed a flat tyre. To make things worse, he was then held up by a small road traffic accident, making him absolutely late for his start-the-week meeting with his Permanent Secretary. Sir Roger, in thrall to an inner biological clock that made tardiness a cardinal sin, could not stand being kept waiting, which he made abundantly clear to the Health Secretary when the latter did eventually make it to his office.

"I feared that you were indisposed," he said, looking pointedly at his watch.

"Traffic delays and a flat tyre," replied the minister, noting that Sir Roger was writing something in his notebook and would no doubt be checking with the departmental driver that his car had indeed suffered a puncture.

"It's just that I have other meetings to attend," said Sir Roger, "and a hold-up at the start to the day can have far-reaching consequences for the rest of the day."

The Health Secretary, as far as he knew, didn't have such an onerous day ahead, so didn't feel that he could sympathise with any credibility.

"I do, however, have some rather bad news to impart, Minister. It's about our community testing programme." Sir Roger had the good grace to look momentarily embarrassed. "We're scrapping it."

"What! On what grounds?"

"Because, with infections growing, we no longer have the capacity. What capacity we do have is being switched to testing in hospitals. After all, we have to protect the NHS, Minister."

The Health Secretary was black affronted that something of such importance could have been snatched away behind his back. "I should remind you, Sir Roger, that issues such as community testing are political matters over which you have no jurisdiction."

"It *was* a political decision, Minister."

"By whom?"

Sir Roger raised a finger and pointed it skywards.
“By God?”
“No, Minister, one rung down.”

Lockdown?

On Friday 13th March, Sir Patrick Vallance, the government's chief scientific advisor, said that the government's aim was "to build up some degree of herd immunity." He later quantified that by saying that herd immunity meant 60% of the population contracting the virus, some 40 million people – of whom some 1% were likely to die, based on data from China and Italy, and meaning that up to 400,000 British residents could die. However, herd immunity requires long-term antibody resistance, and whether that happened from Covid-19 infection had not been established. The government also denied that it was following a policy of herd immunity. Over 200 scientists and academics signed a letter condemning this delay policy. In evidence to a parliamentary committee four days later Sir Patrick modified his forecast by saying that 20,000 deaths would be 'a good outcome.'

Derek Goings was shown into the Prime Minister's apartment where the PM, without getting up, gestured him to a chair. Winston Spragg was sprawled across a cream settee, with a glass of red wine within easy reach, and a half-empty bottle next to it.

"I'm a libertarian, Dee," began the PM, "I therefore value freedom and liberty above all else and believe that the British people share that sentiment. Please tell me if I'm wrong." The PM, clearly already inebriated, looked rather beseechingly at his advisor, in much the same way as Dilyn, his Jack Russell, was looking up from the floor at the PM.

"Could I ask what has brought about this mood of introspection?"

"It's just that people keep dying."

"That is, I agree, rather inconvenient, Prime Minister."

The PM merely grunted and then sloshed more red wine into his glass. "I have been sent a draft report from some university-or-another that says that we must go for immediate lockdown. Another report, which I believe that SAGE intends to discuss next week, suggests that there could be over one million deaths in the USA."

"What happens in America is not our concern, Prime Minister."

"Well, no it isn't. But they are, however, following a similar strategy to ours."

"It's called containment, Prime Minister." Derek Goings still had no idea why the PM had summoned him to his apartment on a Saturday night, when he had meticulously planned to read Leo Tolstoy's *War and Peace* and rearrange his sock drawer.

"Is that what it's called, Dee? As always, your wise counsel is invaluable. But I must confess to now feeling somewhat conflicted. My heart still beats to the drumbeat of liberty and freedom, but my head keeps suggesting that our strategy of…containing…the virus hasn't actually done anything of the sort."

"It is rather a conundrum, Prime Minister."

"The real question I therefore have to ask myself, Dee, is whether it is better to temporarily curtail the public's right to absolute liberty and freedom, or save the lives of many thousands of people."

The PM's advisor gave an almost imperceptible shrug. "That is not for me to say, Prime Minister. I am primarily your political advisor and therefore most concerned about your popularity in the country."

"Yes, I do appreciate that. But, for example, if I stop people going to the pub, will I be lauded for my humanity or lampooned as a killjoy?"

"Preliminary evidence suggests, Prime Minister, that the virus is most lethal to those who are elderly, fat or diabetic."

The PM took another swig from his glass. "Your point being, Dee?"

"Are those the kind of people who vote Conservative?"

"I have absolutely no idea. You're my political advisor, you tell me."

Derek Goings had over previous months sent numerous reports to the PM, detailing the public's attitudinal responses to key messages, their likely voting intentions if a general election were to be held, and all meticulously broken down by age, gender and location, and filtered by educational achievement, category of employment and income. He wondered, not for the first time, why he bothered. "Polling data from the last election found that the elderly generally have no idea who to vote for and, when they do, often can't remember who they have voted for. The same data found that fat people and diabetics, often the same people, can't be bothered to vote."

"So, although the virus does seem to have a Darwinian element to it, and while I absolutely value every life equally, I needn't lose any sleep over that lot?" The PM seemed much happier, downing the contents of his glass and then refilling it.

"No, Prime Minister."

"Did you know, Dee, that *dilyn* in Welsh means *follow*?" For emphasis, the PM leaned over the side of the couch and scratched the Jack Russell behind its ears. Dilyn growled, perhaps remembering another occasion when the PM had been drinking red wine.

"I did know that, yes."

"Of course, you did, Dee. How silly of me to even consider otherwise! It just seems to me that, as this country's leader, I should strain every muscle and sinew to follow my instincts of liberty and freedom, instincts that I absolutely know will get us over the finishing line and beat this virus. If I do that, unstintingly and unwaveringly, then the British people will continue to follow me."

"Except those who are dead, Prime Minister."

"Yes, but they don't have a vote, Dee."

Derek Goings left the PM's apartment shortly afterwards, concluding that, with so much of his evening having been eaten up, he would only have time to read *War and Peace*. He'd have to leave the sock drawer for another day. However, with the Prime Minister wholly inebriated, he had taken the opportunity to secure his agreement to the closure of public testing, and primarily limit it to those being admitted to hospital. There simply wasn't the testing capacity to do anything more, he had advised. The argument he put forward was that the public loved their health service, that it was incumbent on the government to do everything in its power to protect those working in it and, in any case, hospitals needed to know who had the virus and take the necessary protective measures. The public would expect nothing less of us, he had said, to which the PM had mutely nodded, accidentally spilling wine over the dog which then barked and bit the PM's hand. Dilyn then licked off the wine and fell asleep. Derek Goings was surprised by how loudly a Jack Russell could snore. The PM's advisor also made it clear that if the Health Secretary had been remotely serious about test, test, test he would have done something to increase testing capacity weeks beforehand.

Before leaving the PM, and in line with government protocol, Derek Goings did try to contact the Health Secretary, to inform him of this change of policy, only to find himself connected to a very chatty babysitter who not only told him where the Health Secretary and his wife had gone, but who they were having dinner with, and hence his rather abrupt and menacing message to Kevin Kock not to say anything to Dorothy Jones. Instead, he then phoned Sir Roger Smallwood who, being a civil servant, could be assumed to have few friends and therefore to be at home on a Saturday evening.

While the government did agree in principle on 13th March that lockdown would be a good idea, it also decided not to do anything very much, and lockdown wasn't announced for another ten days. With countries such as Italy, Spain and Greece in lockdown, the government was asked whether similar measures could be imposed in the UK. The PM's official spokesman said that "we will be led by the advice from public health and medical experts and will take steps which they feel are required to best protect the British public. We are well prepared for UK cases, we are using tried and tested procedures to prevent further spread and the NHS is extremely well prepared and used to managing infections." On 16th March, SAGE called for the introduction of social distancing "as soon as possible," noting that the virus was accelerating faster than previously estimated, and calling for a significant increase in testing.

"I assume the PM is still shaking hands with everyone?" asked Tony Bond, The Foreign Secretary's Permanent Secretary.

"He was even boasting about it," replied Raambo, feet up on his centuries-old desk, and admiring his new brogues – bought over the weekend to complement his new tweed suit, bought from his Bond Street tailor. Raambo was pleased that he could refer to someone as 'his Bond Street tailor' – rather than have to admit like most people that he'd bought it at Marks & Spencer or, much worse, from a charity shop. He was, he often told himself, not like other people. He was super-fit, relatively intelligent, and had a beautiful wife and children. He could also snap someone's neck with the merest flick of one foot, both of which were safely encased in brogues costing the best part of £1,000, more than enough to bring running water to several sub-Saharan African villages. "At a hospital, no less. A hospital in which, I believe, there were Covid-19 patients."

"We can only hope that our Prime Minister remains healthy," said his Permanent Secretary blandly, "as I hope we all remain healthy."

"Indeed, Tony. Where would the country be without him?" Raambo was careful not to allow any inflection to enter his voice; he knew how the Civil Service mandarin club worked and how just a hint of ministerial treachery could spell doom, even for a relatively intelligent minister in ridiculously expensive shoes.

"Well, it was a nice photo op of him at a primary school the other day. Showing the kids how long to wash their hands by singing 'Happy Birthday to You' twice over."

"Did you actually watch it on the news?"

"I must confess that I sadly did not, Minister."

"Then you wouldn't have seen that he sang it rather badly. And, however hard he tried, *beatus natalis tibi, beatus natalis tibi* just didn't fit the tune. I also don't think that Latin is on the curriculum for primary schools."

Tony Bond raised his eyebrows while Raambo, removing his feet from the desk, picked up a file, opened it, closed it, and put his feet back up on the desk. "Tony, is there anything happening…I mean, anything, however remotely unimportant, anywhere in the world, that I should know about?"

"No, Minister."

Raambo sighed loudly. "Nothing from the State Department about supporting Trump against China?"

"No, Minister. Trump has decided to blame everything on the World Health Organisation instead. However, the State Department does hint that the President's mental acuity may be impaired." Tony Bond opened a file and flipped pages. "Apparently, Minister, he's taking a drug called hydroxychloroquine as a Covid-19 medication. It's mainly used to treat malaria and arthritis," he added.

"Does it work?"

"Probably not, Minister. But the President does have a small financial interest in a company called Sanofi, a French drug maker that produces a brand-name version of the drug. The State Department is worried that this medication may be blurring his judgement on what constitutes politics or business or, indeed, what is and what isn't true." Tony Bond consulted another file. "For example, he's also claimed thirteen times that the USA has conducted more coronavirus tests than the whole of the world combined."

"Is that true?"

"No. Minister."

"He's also blamed the Obama administration for limiting laboratory testing."

"Is that true?

"No, Minister."

"He also said that Google is building a website to help Americans determine if they need a coronavirus test."

"Is that true?"

"It was news to Google, Minister. Do you want me to go on?" Tony Bond waved an alarmingly thick file at the Foreign Secretary who, with a last admiring look at his new brogues, reluctantly took his feet off the desk and shook his head.

"Leaving aside the President's mental health, important and fascinating as it is, I believe I am to make a statement to the House."

"You are indeed, Minister, on the advisability of UK residents travelling abroad, and the risk of foolhardy travellers finding themselves stranded overseas should travel restrictions change."

"I appreciate the sense of it, Tony, but what about travellers coming to the UK?"

"What about them, Minister?"

"Well, we have to protect our borders."

"Indeed, we do, Minister. However, travel is a matter for the Transport Ministry."

"Guided by the needs of the economy?"

"In the capable hands of the Ministry for Business, Energy and Industrial Strategy."

The Foreign Secretary narrowed his eyes. "Tony, just how many people *are* coming into the UK?"

Tony Bond, sensing that one of his minister's feet might be twitching, quickly flipped open a file, having run out of ministries to blame. "By the end of this month, Minister, we expect that just over eighteen million people will have entered the UK this year."

"Without being screened?"

"That is a matter for the Home Office, Minister."

"But isn't that a bit risky?" asked the Foreign Secretary. "Shouldn't we be doing something? Screening? Quarantining?"

"That's a matter for the Health Ministry, Minister," said the Permanent Secretary, finally remembering that, in a health crisis, there was one other obvious ministry to blame.

On 4th March, the director of a UK company that made protective equipment said that it was exporting all over the world but hadn't had orders from the UK government. 'We actually offered our services [to the UK Government] when this first happened and unfortunately our services weren't taken up.'

It was later estimated that, out of all visitors to the UK between January and March, some 20,000 of those travellers would have been carrying coronavirus and that, with a transmission rate above two, some 50,000 people in the UK would have been infected.

However, the issue of foreign travel was not on top of the Health Secretary's agenda, if indeed it ever had ever been on his agenda at any time.

"I thought we weren't going to have any shortages? Christ, that's what I told Derek Goings only the other week!" The Health Secretary was as angry as his Permanent Secretary could remember.

"I do agree, Minister, that hospitals do seem to be using their protective equipment rather faster than expected."

"And why is that, Sir Roger?"

"Largely because they are seeing more hospital admissions than expected."

What with community testing being cut to support hospital testing and protective equipment shortages dominating the headlines, it was turning out not to be the Health Secretary's best week. "Then what can we do about it?" he demanded. "There must be something we can do?"

"Much as I would like to, I can't just wave a magic wand, Minister. However, we are, of course, looking at our supply chains and determining ways in which supply can be increased, as well as seeking new supply partners. But these things take time. There are forms to be completed, criteria to be met, sample products to be assessed for quality. Minister, if I may say so, much of this could have been avoided."

"I suspect that you're about to blame me," said the Health Secretary, knowing that he'd done nothing wrong at any stage of the pandemic, before realising that he hadn't actually done anything.

"There was an EU meeting in February, Minister, when officials were updated on the procurement of PPE by the European Commission. The UK was invited, but did not send a representative. In late February, the EU launched the start of joint procurement of PPE. The UK wasn't one of the twenty member states involved. Earlier this month, that procurement scheme was extended to include another five member states, again without the UK."

"Okay, okay, Sir Roger. Why didn't we join?"

"The EU says that it sent us an email, but that we didn't respond."

"An email? An email!"

"At least one, Minister, and perhaps a second one as well. I am, of course, looking into it."

"Dear God!" said the Health Secretary, fervently hoping that the errant email hadn't been sent to him. "What else are we doing?"

"Well, you have agreed to the creation of several new Nightingale hospitals across England and Wales. That may help to ease pressure on existing hospitals and intensive care units. However, until those hospitals are up and running, we also need to free up additional capacity." Sir Roger pushed a memorandum across the table. "I would therefore request that you sign this."

"What is it?"

"It's for the discharge of fifteen thousand elderly patients from hospitals and to return them back to their homes or care homes."

"Sounds reasonable enough," replied the Health Secretary and scrawled his signature along the bottom. He was more than used to signing things that he hadn't read, on the principle that his civil servants knew more about health policy than he did and could therefore be relied upon to have thought everything through.

If he had read it, he might have noticed, and only might, that there was no requirement for those elderly patients to be tested for coronavirus before discharge.

It was a week of growing panic, although the government still couldn't bring itself to announce a lockdown. Instead, on the 16th March, the government advised people to work from home, despite the fact that most who could were already doing so, and to avoid pubs or wine bars which many people working from home were spending most of their days in.

On the 18th March, the government also announced the closure of all schools, although that wouldn't happen for another two days, the same day as cinemas, restaurants, pubs and gyms were to close. That weekend infections were close to an estimated 800,000.

However, others were taking a more sensible approach, among them the Islamic State (ISIS) terrorist group, not hitherto much known as a source of good health advice, which issued a travel advisory in its *Al-Naba* newsletter telling its operatives to stay clear of Europe, describing it as 'the land of the epidemic.'

On 23rd March, the government finally gave way to the inevitable, and announced a complete lockdown, with UK residents only allowed to shop for essentials, exercise once a day and to only travel to work if it was 'absolutely necessary.'

Press conferences

On 23rd March, the deputy chief medical officer said that problems around protective equipment had been 'completely resolved' - although, in the first half of April, the Health Secretary was also urging NHS staff not to overuse PPE: "We need everyone to treat PPE like the precious resource it is. Everyone should use the equipment they clinically need, in line with the guidelines: no more and no less."

However, UK government stockpiles containing protective equipment for healthcare workers in the event of a pandemic had fallen in value by almost 40% over the previous six years, and an analysis by the Guardian newspaper found that £325 million had been wiped off the value of the Department of Health and Social Care's emergency stockpile, reducing it from £831 million in 2013.

While there was widespread support for the government's decision to lock down the country and impose restrictions on individual freedoms, there was also a growing clamour demanding to know why lockdown hadn't been introduced before, and why the country hadn't been better prepared. It was difficult for the government to admit, as minutes of a SAGE meeting record, that the government didn't want to overreact to the coronavirus epidemic, as it had done with the swine flu epidemic of 2009. But the general public, as naturally libertarian as the Prime Minister, also had a pragmatic streak: quite frankly, it didn't want to die. The government mantra that it was following the science and that everything was under control seemed at odds with a mortality rate that was rapidly becoming the worst in Europe. Against that fast-rising death toll, the government was on the back foot.

It was an uncomfortable position for the government to be in, as Derek Goings well understood. A functioning sociopath, able to read every government report, minute, memorandum and email before breakfast, Derek was not only a master of every fact, he was able to process and distil those facts into perfect clarity. His gift, like Sherlock Holmes before him, was to see both the big picture and the fiddly little details. It was a gift that, under his stewardship, had won referendums and elections.

Some critics said that he had an instinct for politics or, at least, an instinct for winning. They were wrong on both counts. Derek Goings was devoid of instinct, because instinct was a muddled gut feeling that held too many imponderables; the PM's advisor was never wrong because, being in possession of every fact, statistic and estimate, he only ever came to empirical conclusions. Like a computer with all the facts, Derek Goings was never wrong, and was therefore used to winning.

But his mental gifts offered little contentment, forever having to deal with ministers who hadn't bothered to read every government report, minute, memorandum and email before breakfast, and whose thought processes often led to decisions that could be muddled at best or, at worst, simply incompetent. His forensic conclusion was that, while the Chancellor and Foreign Secretary had some meagre intelligence, the Prime Minister was a buffoon in perpetual search of his legacy, and the Health Secretary was simply out of his depth. But sadly, against that incoming tide of mediocrity, there was only so much that Derek Goings could achieve.

Of course, he did try: a chastising comment here, a coruscating email there. His few friends had sometimes suggested a more encouraging approach, even to praise ministers when they did get something right. But that wasn't his style: all Derek Goings could see were the palpable failures of government, not its occasional successes.

As the PM's advisor, his role was primarily to ensure the continued popularity of his government, its re-election, and secure the PM's legacy as one of the UK's greatest peacetime leaders. Normally, that limited role could easily have been achieved, except that Covid-19 was throwing everything off-track. He was well aware that, while he personally didn't much care about the thousands of people who were dying, others did. He was also well aware that, once immediate grief had faded, anger would replace it. This would only compound the government's falling popularity and, perhaps, once the crisis was over, inexorably lead to a general election that the government would lose. Now that Labour had got rid of their previous loony leader and replaced him with someone vaguely credible, the Conservatives were no longer unassailable. In the middle of the worst health crisis for a hundred years, led by an idiot and with a bigger idiot in charge of health, it was a situation purpose-built for the talents of a functioning sociopath.

Derek Goings' other talent was to understand the electorate and, possessed of great mental powers, to recognise their innate need for clear leadership. In a crisis, people looked for leaders, people like Churchill or Thatcher: leaders who could inspire sacrifice and persuade the country that it was a nation of lions, led by lions.

He also understood that the nation was largely comprised of people who watched TV programmes such as *Love Island,* read down-market tabloid newspapers, and drank pints of lager in quaintly-named public houses. It could not therefore be trusted with complicated facts or, far less, inconvenient truths. Things had to therefore be couched in terms that the man on the Clapham omnibus could readily understand and wholeheartedly agree with, even if he was returning from a quaintly named pub after several pints of lager. Derek Goings' message strategy of Stay Home, Protect the NHS, Save Lives was therefore masterful. It was simple to the point of simplistic, while making the point, even to a single mum living in a small inner-city tower-block flat, that it was her patriotic duty to starve to death rather than go out unnecessarily to buy food.

But still the government's popularity was slipping. What he needed was a big idea to get the government back on the rails again, and one was forming in his mind.

Standing in the way of Derek Goings and his plans to boost government popularity was the Health Secretary, who was due to front that afternoon's Downing Street press conference. This was another of the PM's advisor's good ideas – that the country not only needed leadership, but had to be reminded of it on a daily basis. It would at the very least, he advised, show people that their government was taking everything very seriously, that everyone was in it together, and that nobody was metaphorically taking the day off to play golf. The problem, of course, was that these press conferences had to be fronted by a government minister, and few of them could be trusted to say the right thing.

"Are you sure that you're fully prepared, Health Secretary," he asked Kevin Kock in his stage whisper. They were in the Cabinet Room, surrounded by its aura of history and, thankfully, socially distanced from one another. Kevin Kock didn't like being in close proximity to the PM's advisor, not because he thought that Derek Goings could be infected – he was probably immune to Covid-19 – but mainly because of the smell.

"Of course, of course, Derek. I have read your briefing notes which are, of course, both lucid and persuasive."

"Then what are our key messages, Minister?"

This threw the Health Secretary, but only for a few moments. "We continue to follow the science, Derek."

"That's only one message, Minister. You must also emphasise how the government is doing everything in its power to protect our gallant health staff and care workers."

"Well, yes, I was going to say that as well."

The PM's advisor handed the Health Secretary what looked like a small pink snail. "This is a discreet earpiece, Minister. After a journalist asks a question, I will simply tell you a number. That number corresponds to a list of answers in this folder" – which he then handed over. "Acquaint yourself with what I have written, Minister, so that you can be even better prepared."

"But how do you know what the media will ask?"

"Because I do," said Derek Goings.

Not only was it part of his job to know what the media was thinking, even before it thought of it itself, it was also that the news agenda was tediously predictable. In the midst of a catastrophic PPE shortage, questions about what the government might be doing about it could be predicted. What was less predictable was the performance of government ministers in answering those wholly-predictable questions. On this occasion the Health Secretary would be flanked by Brian Whittle, to lend a bit of scientific credibility, and the chief constable of a regional police force, to answer questions on lockdown and the police's discretion to enforce it, which had included dying a lake in the Peak District black to make it less of a beauty spot, to encourage less visitors.

The Health Secretary, armed with Derek Goings' briefing notes and his DramSoc experience, felt in total command of proceedings. He welcomed everybody, although everybody was there only by Zoom video link. It felt a little like being on stage, but with no audience. Kevin Kock ran through statistics for the previous day, primarily how many had died, and then invited questions.

Dave Trotter, The Daily Telegraph's chief economic virus correspondent: "The government has announced a furlough scheme for workers laid off because of the virus. How much will this cost, and how can the government afford it?"

(Voice in ear: "Number three.")

Secretary of State for Health and Social Care: "Because of prudent fiscal policy, and because we've followed the science, the government's finances are in good order and we are well prepared to ensure that hard-working people are able to care for their families. While we are working on the details of the scheme, the overall cost could be as much as £14 billion per month."

Dave Trotter, again: "That's as much as the government spends on the NHS."

(Voice in ear: "Make something up.")

Secretary of State for Health and Social Care: "Good gracious, is it?"

Lauren Hindenburg: BBC chief political and virus editor: "The government's preparedness on PPE is being questioned, Minister. Does the government really believe that it is doing everything it can to protect NHS staff and everyone in the care sector?"

(Voice in ear: "Number five.")

Secretary of State for Health and Social Care: "I'm glad you asked me that, Lauren, because we have been following the science on this. I can assure you that veterinary surgeries are still able to care for sick pets, but only if you have a pet, and only if it's sick."

Lauren Hindenburg, again: "That's not really the question I asked, Minister."

(Voice in ear: "Number FIVE. Christ! NOT number twelve.")

Secretary of State for Health and Social Care: "Sorry, Lauren. When you said *PPE* I thought you said *dog*. However, now that's clear, we are putting a protective shield around care homes and making sure that this shield not only follows the science but offers complete and total protection for everyone working in the NHS or the care sector, or for that matter anywhere else."

Dominic Grieve, The Daily Mail's crime and virus correspondent: "Chief Constable, do you think that the police have been proportionate in dying the Blue Lagoon black to discourage visitors and following hillwalkers by drone?"

Chief Constable: "Yes."

Dominic Grieve, again: "Just yes, Chief Constable?"

Chief Constable: "Yes."

Bert Bloggs, The Sun's economics, environmental, health and virus editor: "Professor Whittle, is the government following the science?"

Professor Brian Whittle, Chief Medical Officer for England: "There are a number of different aspects to take into consideration when following the science. For example, our SAGE behavioural experts warn that there will no doubt be a rise in domestic violence, child abuse and mental health issues. Following the science does therefore require a balanced approach being taken to weigh up outcomes that may only be associated with Covid-19 but not, of themselves, be symptomatic of coronavirus illness."

Bert Bloggs, again: "With respect, Professor Whittle, was that a yes or a no?"

Professor Brian Whittle, Chief Medical Officer for England: "There are a number of different aspects to take into consideration when following the science. For example, our SAGE behavioural experts warn that there will no doubt be a rise in domestic violence, child abuse and mental health issues. Following the science does therefore require a balanced approach being taken to weigh up outcomes that may only be associated with Covid-19 but not, of themselves, be symptomatic of coronavirus illness."

Oddly fuzzy image of elderly man: "Is that the Nepal Spice? I'd like to order two chicken kormas and an onion pakora, please."

(Voice in ear: "Fucking hell!")

Secretary of State for Health and Social Care: "That's not a number, Derek."

Lauren Hindenburg, again: "Are you just reading out prepared answers, Minister?"

Secretary of State for Health and Social Care: "No of course not. In any case, we don't offer a food delivery service."

The British Medical Association said that PPE supplies in parts of England "are running at dangerously low levels and "that some pieces of equipment are no longer available – forcing doctors into impossible situations, and ultimately, putting their lives at risk."

After the press conference, the Health Secretary returned to the Cabinet Room to find Derek Goings looking oddly pensive. He poured himself a glass of water from the ever-present array of bottles, culled from sources across the United Kingdom, then removed his earpiece and chucked it over the table.

"I shan't be needing that for a while," said the Health Secretary, "although it did go rather well, don't you think? Good teamwork, Derek!"

"Certainly, no worse than usual," replied the advisor, which Kevin Kock took as a compliment and blushed happily. It was rare to receive a compliment from Derek Goings, and rarely one so effusive.

"You are, however, looking a little peaky, Minister."

"Probably just working too hard!" The Health Secretary gave a small chuckle and sat in a chair opposite. It took him a few moments to realise that, from luck or out of habit, he was sitting in the chair he normally inhabited at Cabinet meetings.

"No, you're not, Minister." The PM's advisor was still looking intently at the Health Secretary, or perhaps at the fireplace or the ceiling. His dark glasses, sparkling from the overhead lights, seemed to be signalling danger and his voice, his usual throaty whisper, also now seemed to contain a hint of menace. "Definitely peaky."

"I am?"

The PM's advisor placed his forearms on the table and leaned forwards. "Minister, I have some very bad news."

After his brief de-brief with the Health Secretary it took the PM's advisor only a few moments to locate the PM himself, who was in his apartment upstairs and spooning the contents of a carryout container onto a plate. "Watched the Health Secretary on the news," began the PM, "and for some reason it put me in the mood for a curry. I would, of course, offer you some but I suppose I'll have to keep some for the missus."

"She won't be joining you for supper, Prime Minister."

"Wonderful! I can eat hers as well!" The PM spooned more curry onto his plate then carried it to the kitchen table on which also sat a glass of red wine and half-empty bottle. With a contented sigh he sat on one side of the table and gestured Derek to a chair on the other side. "Do you happen to know, not that you should know, where she might be?"

"She's moved back to your home, Prime Minister."

"What home? This *is* our home."

"Your other home, Prime Minister. The other London home you both lived in prior to you becoming prime minister."

"Yes, yes, Dee. It's just that it's not like Claire to up sticks without even leaving a note. My wife is usually punctilious about notes. Not that I usually bother reading them, of course, what with being prime minister and having lots of other notes to read."

"Her name is Caroline, Prime Minister, and she's your girlfriend."

"Of course, of course. Anyway, would you perchance have the slightest inkling *why* she's moved back to our other home, not that you should know, of course." The Prime Minister shovelled food into his mouth and drank the rest of his wine.

"Because your test came back positive, Prime Minister, and I advised Caroline to move out of Downing Street immediately."

"Test? What test? She's the one who got herself pregnant, not me."

"You have, I'm sorry to say, tested positive for coronavirus, Prime Minister."

The Prime Minister poured more red wine into his glass. "I think, Dee, that you must be mistaken because I think I would remember if I'd had a test."

"I personally gave you the test this morning." Derek Goings tried to look sympathetic. "One of the first signs of Covid-19, Prime Minister, is memory lapse."

"But I have the razor-sharp memory of a hawk!"

"The virus is no respecter of rank, Prime Minister."

The PM took another large mouthful of curry, washed down with another glass of wine. "I rather know that, Dee. Prince Charles, poor sod."

"Exactly, sir! Caroline has therefore left Downing Street so that you can self-isolate here. You will, of course, be well looked after by your downstairs staff. Food will be left outside your door, as will any papers requiring your signature. If you need anything, all you have to do is phone downstairs."

"So, I can eat whatever I want?"

"Whatever you want, Prime Minister."

"No more salads?"

"None whatsoever, Prime Minister. Unless you specifically request salad, of course."

"Which I won't be doing. And Claire need never know."

"*Caroline* need never know, Prime Minister. I have also brought you a small present, to help you cope in your temporary solitude." The advisor handed over a plastic bag containing a box of fat cigars and a plastic lighter.

"Cigars, Dee? But I don't smoke."

"Then maybe you should start, Prime Minister. There's growing evidence that smoking offers some protection against coronavirus. Medics in France are even being offered nicotine patches."

"Are they, by Jove! Jove, incidentally, is an old Roman name for the planet Jupiter, just in case you didn't know."

"Which I did know, Prime Minister," also knowing that, as soon as he was out the door and the prime minister had finished his curry, and Caroline's, he would be posturing in front of a mirror with a cigar in his mouth.

"Crikey! Thank you, Dee, for your kindness and consideration."

"However, sir, and getting back to basics - in terms of your workload, you'll appreciate that much of it can be carried out by phone, email and video conference. I will organise for your next Cabinet meeting to be conducted via Zoom."

It seemed an inappropriate moment for the PM to mention that he could barely switch on a computer, let alone organise a video conference, although he had recently mastered how to send and receive emails. "But I can still rely on your sage advice whenever I need it?"

"I am always at the end of a telephone," replied his advisor, trying to form his mouth into a semblance of a smile, but which made him resemble a psychopath rather than a mere sociopath.

"So, I am still prime minister?" The PM was strangely buoyed by the thought that he could eat whatever he wanted without his chubby and tedious girlfriend nagging him about it *and* smoke cigars at whatever time of day or night he chose. Having a deadly illness was turning out to be rather good fun.

"More than ever, Prime Minister!" The PM's advisor said this loudly and with conviction. "At a time of crisis, the country needs to know that their leader is experiencing the same trials and tribulations as they are going through. That by unstintingly and unwaveringly doing your job, and shaking hands with all sorts of unsavoury people, you have taken a hit for our country. A country that will thank you for it, Prime Minister. At the next election, the British people won't forget that their prime minister was prepared to put himself in harm's way so that they could enjoy the freedoms of liberty and justice."

"I'm not going to die, am I?" The PM seemed momentarily worried, then discovered there was more food on his plate and another glassful of red in the bottle.

"No, of course not, Prime Minister. You are neither diabetic nor overweight, and therefore have nothing whatsoever to worry about. Self-isolation is merely a precautionary measure to ensure that you don't inadvertently give the virus to someone else."

"Okay, but for how long must I not eat salad for? If, of course, I choose not to eat salad."

"Seven days, Prime Minister."

The prime minister then realised that he hadn't devoured an onion pakora, an omission that he proceeded to put right. "Shouldn't I see a doctor or someone?"

"You have merely tested positive, sir, and do not require medical advice. I should also add that the Health Secretary has, like you, tested positive and will also be taking time away from his office."

"Good Lord! Going down like flies, aren't we?"

"Professor Whittle is also displaying mild symptoms, and has voluntarily decided to self-isolate."

"Old Whittle as well? But that's the country's entire top team!"

"Ironic, isn't it," said Derek Goings, pleased that his plan was coming to fruition and even more pleased that he could now get on with running the country properly.

A report published in May said that three-quarters of coronavirus deaths in the UK could have been avoided if lockdown had begun a week earlier.

If the Prime Minister had taken little persuasion that he had indeed tested positive for coronavirus, the Health Secretary had taken no persuasion at all. Kevin Kock, consumed with the certainty that he had been suffering from coronavirus – and many other ailments - since birth, had taken the news with calm equanimity bordering on complete panic, phoned his wife, and then disappeared off home in a haze of disinfectant. Derek Goings didn't bother offering the Health Secretary any cigars or good advice. That was Sir Roger Smallwood's job and, with the PM and his top team out of the way, he had enough jobs to do.

Strangely, he had expected more resistance from Brian Whittle who, having some medical training, might have recognised that he wasn't displaying any Covid-19 symptoms. Derek therefore chose another route, suggesting to the professor that, after his robotic and ill-conceived performance at the Downing Street press conference, he should perhaps take a few days off otherwise, perhaps, the country might consider appointing a new chief medical advisor, with all the associated reputational damage that would involve. Derek had also chewed several sulphur tablets (which he took for dandruff but that, being bald, he didn't need, but which he knew other people, particularly Brian Whittle, found threatening and unpleasant). "Perhaps you could put yourself in self-isolation for a few days," he'd suggested. "Purely precautionary, of course, but a personal demonstration of your absolute good sense and your total responsibility to the country. You can't, after all, give health advice while not following it yourself."

His various tasks complete, Derek cycled home to find Moira, his wife looking sweaty in their living room. A children's author by profession, Moira didn't often get sweaty anywhere, and never to his knowledge in their living room. Beside her on the settee, looking equally miserable, was their small daughter Lucy. Wags insisted this was short for Lucifer, but who, disappointingly, was named after the Latin masculine name Lucius, meaning light, because Lucy had been born at daybreak. Moira also spoke Latin, a fact he had found out prior to asking her out, and which had been an important prerequisite in any of his (few) relationships.

"Derek, I'm not well," she told him, then coughed.

"You don't look in particularly good form," he agreed. "Perhaps I could get you something?"

"Derek, you know fine what I think I've picked up."

Momentarily, he wondered if he'd given his wife a coronavirus test that morning, alongside the Prime Minister and Health Secretary, then realised that he'd tested none of them. It was sometimes difficult to tell fact from fiction despite, or because of, working at the heart of government.

"I'm sure you haven't," he said. "Probably just a passing cold, or something." Derek, who had never been ill in his life, was a little vague about illness in others. In his encyclopaedic knowledge of virtually everything, an understanding of illness was missing, an omission that he would put right at the earliest opportunity, and just after rearranging his sock drawer.

"But supposing you've caught it from me, Derek? Suppose we've both now got it? What happens to Lucy?" On cue, their toddler child looked at her mother and burst into tears. "I've been thinking about it all afternoon, and I think I have a solution."

It was usually Derek who had solutions to virtually everything, from diagnosing a malfunctioning dishwasher and then mending it, to completing *The Times* crossword in under five minutes, on a bad day.

"The only thing we can do," she continued, then paused to cough, "is to drive to your parents in Durham. They've got an empty holiday cottage, haven't they? Almost next door. Then if we both get too sick to look after Lucy, they can step in."

"But suppose Lucy gets sick?" he asked, trying hard to think of an alternative to a long-distance drive, and with his poor eyesight.

"Small children are almost immune," his wife told him.

"Then what about my parents? Suppose they catch it from her?"

"Your parents are of little concern to me against the wellbeing of my child." His wife glared at him, daring him to disagree.

"But I've got a country to run," he complained, then caught a withering glance from his daughter. Her eyes seemed to be boring into his, although she could actually have been looking anywhere. He was also sure that her breath carried with it a distinct smell off sulphur although that was surely impossible. His tablets were in his pocket. "Although it is probably an idea worth exploring," he conceded.

"Good, then that's decided."

In Derek's world, things usually took a little longer to decide. "It is?" he asked.

"Your parents are looking forward to seeing us tonight, socially-distanced of course, and I've packed your bag."

No sooner had all of Derek's plans for complete domination come together, than they were all now falling apart.

Durham days

Towards the end of March, the editor-in-chief of the Lancet *medical journal said that the government's response to the pandemic was 'a national scandal.' At the start of April,* The Guardian *newspaper said that hospitals across England were running out of the surgical gowns needed to treat patients with Covid-19 and did not know when fresh supplies would arrive, according to two secret NHS memos. These contradicted repeated assurances by ministers.*

By the start of April, the graveyards were fast filling up with indispensable people, and quite a lot of other people as well. In the week to 17th April, when deaths from the virus reached their peak, nearly 40% of all UK deaths were caused by Covid-19 and, despite the government cheerily repeating that it was making herculean efforts on all fronts, the UK was fast becoming the worst-hit country in Europe, or the 'sick man of Europe' as several newspapers put it.

The Health Secretary was certainly making herculean efforts to make himself understood to his wife.

"Kevin to Minty, over."

Static hiss.

"Kevin to Minty, over."

More static hiss.

The walkie-talkies had, of course, been her idea now that the Health Secretary had become a health hazard. From now on, 'either until the end of time or the end of your quarantine' he would live upstairs, confined to the spare bedroom with its en-suite bathroom, and which handily doubled as his study. He was not to venture downstairs, unless emergency circumstances dictated it. Those circumstances included death, but not much else, according to a piece of paper that she'd shoved under his office door. Their children, Tom and Tim, were barred from seeing him under any circumstance, including death. It meant that Minty would have full and free access to all their home's primary amenities – including living room, kitchen and garden -

which he didn't think was an entirely fair division of their property. She could watch TV on their large plasma-screen downstairs; he had to make do with his laptop or the smallest of small TVs in his study. She had all the benefits of a well-stocked fridge; he had to make do with a defective walkie-talkie.

His wife then shouted up the stairs. "Minty to Kevin, were you trying to get hold of me?"

"Yes," he shouted back, leaning over the bannisters.

Long silence. "Well?"

"Well what?"

"Minty to upstairs idiot, what did you want me for?"

"A cup of coffee, please."

"Kevin, you do know that you must only communicate with me by walkie-talkie, don't you?"

"I do know that, yes."

"Kevin, your walkie-talkie has only one knob. One fucking knob! You press it when you want to speak, okay?"

"I'll remember from now on, darling," he promised loudly, still leaning over the bannisters.

"In which case I will make you a cup of coffee, immediately after I finish an article I'm reading, and once I've done a few other things as well. But let me therefore remind you of a few rules that we agreed last night, just after I had shown you how to use your walkie-talkie. First, I will leave your cup of coffee outside your office-cum-bedroom, the door to which I expect to be firmly closed. Second, I will then knock on the door to alert you to the fact that I have, at some inconvenience, not only made you a cup of coffee but carried it upstairs as well. Third, you will then wait for ten seconds to give me time to retreat down the stairs *before* you open your door. Later, at a precise time to be agreed, to ensure social distancing at all times between us, you will leave your empty cup outside your office door, which should once again be firmly shut, prior to my removing your cup wearing plastic gloves and placing it in the dishwasher. Any infringements of these rules will have consequences."

"Consequences?" To the best of his knowledge *consequences* hadn't been mentioned when he'd arrived home the evening before and explained about his positive test. To be fair, when she'd run through the new rules, he'd been standing at the French window leading onto their patio, while his wife had been at the bottom of the garden, shouting their new house rules for all their neighbours to hear, while simultaneously searching Amazon on her laptop for hazmat suits.

"For a start, no unscheduled coffee breaks outside of agreed mealtimes."

"I'll remember from now on."

"In future, just use the fucking walkie-talkie!"

Sir Roger was as pleasant on the phone as he usually was in person, in contrast to his wife from the bottom of the stairs, with her fridge, plasma-screen TV and large patio, complete with outdoor gas heater.

"I trust you are feeling okay, Minister?"

"Fine and dandy, Sir Roger."

"And still in good spirits, I trust? Self-isolation must be a terrible bore."

"My wife is looking after me admirably," he replied.

"Such a comfort," said Sir Roger, "to have an understanding wife, particularly at times like these. Still, Minister, it won't be much longer before you'll be back in person at the heart of government and keeping us all on our toes." His Permanent Secretary gave a short laugh although, even to Kevin, it did seem to lack sincerity.

"Quite so," he replied, "although I'm sure the department is managing perfectly well without me. However, given how quickly everything is moving, is there anything going on that I should know about?"

"Nothing at all, Minister."

"Nothing at all," he echoed. "There must be something, surely?"

"Well, you will be making a small announcement on testing, Minister."

"The programme that we abandoned?"

"Well, we didn't so much abandon it as switch testing capacity to meet demand from the NHS. At the time, there didn't seem much point in testing more widely because hundreds of thousands of people were already infected. However, as those people didn't work in the NHS, it was agreed that they weren't really very important."

"I do remember, Sir Roger."

"You'll also then remember that SAGE said, back in mid-February, that Public Health England only had the capacity to trace the contacts of just five Covid-19 cases per week, Minister."

The Health Secretary cleared his throat. "You said that I had a small announcement to make?"

"Did I? Oh yes, on the orders of the Prime Minister himself, who also seems to be doing absolutely splendidly in self-isolation. I had Derek Goings on the phone. You're going to be announcing that, from the end of this month, we will be testing 100,000 people a day. Isn't that wonderful news, Minister?"

Kevin couldn't immediately decide just how wonderful this news was and whether, as Health Secretary, he shouldn't have been the one to have decided on increased testing. It was, after all, what the WHO had been advising all along. Or, if his role as Health Secretary wasn't actually to *make* decisions, shouldn't his officials have been making them for him? It surely hadn't needed the intervention of the Prime Minister to decide something that he, or somebody, should already have decided.

"Sir Roger, shouldn't we have announced this weeks ago?" he asked.

On 2nd April, the chair of council at the British Medical Association, said they had heard concerns from doctors in more than thirty hospital trusts about personal protective equipment shortages. The Guardian *newspaper said that 'reports have been rife of shortages and large variations in the level of PPE available. Pictures of healthcare workers who have created their own makeshift protective equipment out of bin bags and other materials have proved embarrassing for the government and NHS leaders. Staff have also improvised masks out of snorkels, bought kit from hardware stores, and used school science goggles to protect themselves.*

Derek Goings had driven north the evening before in a fog of conflicting thoughts. Normally, he didn't have foggy thoughts;

his brain was generally only capable of registering facts and, like Spock, coming only to logical conclusions. But that evening was different because, due only partly to bad eyesight, the road ahead was also foggy and that mistiness had somehow infiltrated his brain, rendering it difficult to separate fact from fake news, or to see the lorry in front of him. Not that this stopped him from driving fast, the M1 giving him lots of lane options and, with national lockdown, there was less traffic on the road. He was therefore able to concentrate for long periods, reading reports and memos on his laptop which was perched on his left knee, read and compose texts on his two smartphones, held in either hand, while steering perfectly well using his right knee. His wife slept silently beside him, still looking a little sweaty, while his daughter slept silently behind him. It wasn't until York that he phoned the Prime Minister, who informed him that he was now eating a Chinese carryout, on top of his earlier curry, to make up for all the salad he was usually subjected to. "Someone downstairs ordered it from Deliveroo," said the PM. "Damned stupid name for a Chinese restaurant."

Derek merely informed him that testing capacity had to be increased, and that he would inform Sir Roger Smallwood immediately. He didn't, he told the PM, want to disturb the Health Secretary himself who might be displaying early-stage Covid-19 amnesia and might have forgotten all about testing by the morning.

"As always, a wise course of action," said the Prime Minister, his voice muffled as he chewed on something Asian and crunchy.

"You are also chairing a Cabinet meeting tomorrow morning, Prime Minister," said the advisor, swerving around a large truck that had suddenly materialised from the darkness, a manoeuvre he was pleased to have safely accomplished with the sole use of one knee.

"In my apartment, impossible!" said the PM. "Or am I allowed downstairs as this is *casus inusitati consili*?"

"It might be an unprecedented circumstance, Prime Minister, but you cannot afford any of your top team to break lockdown or self-isolation rules."

"Even you, Derek? You seem to be driving somewhere."

"I am merely driving home, Prime Minister." In his world, a lie was as good as the truth, and sometimes better, and often difficult to tell apart. "However, to answer your earlier concern, you will be chairing the Cabinet meeting remotely. That will involve using your computer, so that you can see them and they can see you. To reassure them and, through them, to reassure the country that you are fully in command of national events."

"Good gracious!"

"Someone from IT will be up in the morning to make sure you are fully appraised of the technology," he said, although the PM only made crunching noises in reply.

But the fogginess would not dissipate. He had managed, with considerable ease, to dispose of the Prime Minister, Health Secretary and chief medical advisor but he was now also hurtling away from the seat of power. That's where his plan required him to be: to not only be the figure in the shadows but the puppet master holding all the strings. With the best will in the world, puppet strings didn't extend from London to Durham.

His decision to take over the reins of government and do what the PM and his ministers should have been doing weeks before was therefore faltering before reaching the first hurdle, although his decision to increase testing capacity had been a useful first step in the right direction.

Surprisingly, Derek and his family reached Durham in one piece and, while he unloaded the car, his wife put Lucy to bed. With his wife potentially suffering from Covid-19, he would have to sleep downstairs on the couch although, having spent several hours with her in the cramped confines of his car, he did feel that to be an unnecessary stricture, although her dry cough did seem to be getting worse.

His parents had, as they promised, left a large plastic bag of essentials on their doorstep although, being elderly, had mostly filled it with Werther's Originals. His parents lived a few doors down from their Airbnb holiday flat and he went to see if they were still up, and to thank them for the caramels, but their house was in darkness.

Derek then poured himself a large whisky, and drank it in the small kitchen of his temporary command centre, still tormented by mental fog and the length of puppet strings and whether, with the country's heroic prime minister in quarantine, the popularity of the government would finally see an upturn.

He was soon to be sorely disappointed.

On 5th April, the news agency Reuters *reported that the UK had carried out 195,524 tests, in contrast to at least 918,000 completed a week earlier in Germany. Two days later,* The Guardian *newspaper said that a lack of personal protective equipment continued to be a critical issue. 'It is heart-breaking to hear that some staff have been told to simply 'hold their breath' due to lack of masks,' said the president of the Doctors' Association UK.*

If the Health Secretary was having trouble ordering a cup of coffee from his uncooperative wife, the Prime Minister was having a worse morning. Some bright spark in the Downing Street public relations department had decided that the PM, to show solidarity with other countries affected by Covid-19, should start the day by eating what they ate for breakfast. Why he couldn't just start the day with a traditional English breakfast was beyond him. He was the prime minister of the UK, after all, not Egypt, but which was why he was now supposed to be eating *foul mademas*, a dish made from fava beans, chickpeas and garlic, topped with olive oil, cayenne, tahini sauce and a hard-boiled egg. An Egyptian chef had been brought in to prepare it, he was told by the unsmiling secretary in plastic gloves, mask and face shield who brought it to him. The Egyptian president would also be informed, she said, which will help to form stronger bonds in the Middle East.

The Prime Minister merely deposited his foul *foul mademas* in the bin but, when he searched through the kitchen, could find neither beans nor bacon – nor anything edible, or nothing he recognised, having thrown away all traces of lettuce, cucumber and spring onions the previous evening.

Tomorrow, he also knew, he would be served *menudo*, a Mexican soup popular for breakfast, made from tripe and a cow's head. He was not looking forward to that either, or whatever other culinary delights might await him on succeeding mornings.

Instead, he phoned downstairs and demanded that someone bring him lots of things that would fit into a large frying pan, "and some bread," he added.

"I'm afraid that we cannot do that, Prime Minister," replied a lilting Irish accent. "Your girlfriend was on the phone earlier."

"Claire? What did she want?"

"*Caroline*, Prime Minister, wanted to find out what you'd been eating in her absence. She was rather…um…disappointed that you had ordered both an Indian and a Chinese takeaway."

"Look, I am the prime minister," said the PM in his most commanding voice. "I therefore demand that I am fed with things that I can actually eat."

"A range of salads will be delivered later today, Prime Minister."

"What! But I don't want salad."

"Caroline was most insistent, Prime Minister."

"However, I rather think that I outrank her."

"Of course, you do, sir, which is why we thought it best to follow the science."

"The science? What bloody science! All I want is a decent breakfast!"

"We therefore consulted with the Downing Street doctors, Prime Minister. They agreed that the nutrients in salad would be ideal in helping your immune system to fight off the infection."

The Prime Minister was about to mention that he felt absolutely fine and that, to continue to feel fine, he needed the comfort of eating something that came from England and not Egypt. "Am I at least allowed bread?" he asked.

"Of course, Prime Minister, and I'll ensure a loaf is immediately sent up. But no butter, I'm afraid."

"Marmalade?

"I think not, sir."

The PM sighed, outmanoeuvred as always by his chubby and meddling girlfriend. Who the hell had had the temerity to tell her what he'd eaten the night before? And how was it possible to be the leader of one of the most powerful nations in the world, and not eat what he wanted for breakfast? "I'm also chairing a

Cabinet meeting this morning. So please also send up some custard creams," he said, and hung up before anybody had the further temerity to say that he couldn't have those either.

On 3rd April, the new Nightingale Hospital in London was opened by Prince Charles, to provide up to 4,000 beds for Covid-19 patients. Other Nightingale hospitals were being constructed in other parts of the country. On 5th April, John Hopkins University reported that the number of global confirmed cases had passed 1.2 million, with 64,753 deaths. On the same day, the UK reported 621 deaths, a total of 4,934.

It was the first time that the Prime Minister had conducted a Cabinet meeting on his computer and, given the inconvenient spread of Covid-19, he rather doubted it would be the last time. He was also rather taken with the idea of not having to be in the same room as a bunch of people that he didn't much like, couldn't be trusted, and who didn't share his appreciation of the finer things in life, including, Latin, opera, the Second World War and breakfast. This latter problem was weighing heavily on his mind, if not his stomach, as he dressed in blue tweed suit, white shirt with bow-tie and lit his first cigar of the day. His fetching attire, entirely inappropriate to a centrally-heated flat did, however, slightly take his mind off hunger pangs.

The Irish matriarch had indeed brought up a loaf of bread, loudly knocking on the front door to announce its presence although, with nothing to eat it with, he had resorted to rummaging in the kitchen bin to retrieve some shreds of lettuce. While this might have perfectly suited a rabbit, it didn't do much for the leader of a nuclear power.

"Welcome, gentlemen," he began, as his screen filled with lots of postage-stamp pictures of his Cabinet, as always ignoring the Home Secretary and other Cabinet members of the wrong sex, and puffed on his cigar. "I rather think, colleagues, that technology now offers a way for us to *facere quae sunt meliora*, don't you agree?" – with only Mick Gore nodding in agreement and everyone else merely making indistinct animal noises. "Top of the agenda must be, as it's our most pressing issue, and the one thing I am determined that we get right, this disease thingy. Health Secretary, perhaps you could update us on progress."

As soon as Kevin Kock began to speak, he was presented full-screen to the PM – and, presumably, other Cabinet members – so that everyone was able to admire the Health Secretary's blue curtains, a floral print of some daisies behind his head, and quite distinctly hear a loud knocking noise followed by female voice shouting from nearby that *you're not getting another fucking cup of coffee until lunchtime.*

"Well, Prime Minister," said the Health Secretary, looking rather alarmed by this off-camera intrusion, "we have issued guidance that 'family and friends should be advised not to visit care homes, except next of kin in exceptional circumstances.' We must of course ensure that in following the science we erect a protective shield around the most vulnerable in our society."

"Quite so, Health Secretary," replied the Prime Minister, "and if I'm not mistaken, we also brought in lockdown in care homes ahead of the general lockdown, a fact that this government should be proud of and which I will emphasise to the House in due course."

The Prime Minister did indeed do so, although it wasn't until 15th April that all patients discharged from hospitals would be tested for coronavirus. By then, more than 5,700 care home residents in England and Wales had either died in their care home or in hospital.

The Home Secretary then piped up who, the Prime Minister saw, had distinctly second-rate beige curtains. "Nevertheless, Prime Minister, on 15th March, this government's official advice was, and I quote, that 'it remains very unlikely that people receiving care in a care home will become infected.' Now that we are beyond false optimism, could I urge the Health Secretary to do everything he can to ensure that adequate supplies of PPE reach the care sector and that a robust programme of testing is introduced for those in care homes, staff and residents, as well as everyone working in community care."

"Yes," said the Health Secretary, and wrote something on a piece of paper in front of him. He then held it up to the screen. YOU HAVE GREEN STUFF ON YOUR CHIN, it read. Kevin

Kock, as new to Zoom as the PM, was oblivious to lots of little postage-stamp faces leaning forwards to see what kind of green stuff the PM had on his chin, although it was quite hard to discern as the PM was now almost completely hidden behind thick smoke.

"Well, that seems to take care of health," said the Prime Minister, peeling a shred of lettuce from his chin and popping it in his mouth.

"Not quite, Prime Minister," interjected the Home Secretary, obliging everyone to have another look at her beige curtains. "We are all still playing catch-up on this, and it's simply not good enough. Let's not forget that President Trump said just last month that the virus would 'miraculously' go away by April. Well, it hasn't disappeared there, and it hasn't disappeared here."

"Your point being, Home Secretary? Incidentally, why are you working from home? You're not ill, are you?"

"My point is that medical staff and care workers are now dying, Prime Minister, and we owe it to all those who are risking their lives to save others that they have access to the required protective equipment and regular testing. As for being at home, we're all working from home this morning. It is, *apparently*, to show solidarity with you and the Health Secretary and to demonstrate to the country that working from home need not be a hindrance to modern business practice. It is, *apparently*, to show everyone that, if an entire nation can be governed remotely, then so can a small business." The tone of her voice made clear that the idea had not been hers.

The Prime Minister could no longer bear to look at her curtains, and puffed mightily on his cigar to blot everyone, including her, out. "Well, I suppose we should all be setting a good example. *Ponere exemplum*, and all that. Anyway, as to what you also said, did you get all that, Health Secretary?" then realised that the postage stamp that should have been the Health Secretary contained only blue curtains and the fetching daisy print. "Health Secretary?"

Kevin Kock reappeared on the screen holding up a mug on which was written IDIOT in what looked like black marker pen. "Sorry about that. Just getting a cup of coffee, Prime Minister."

"Excellent idea! Nothing like a spot of caffeine to bolster one's mental faculties." For emphasis, the Prime Minister also held up his mug, and drank from it, safe in the knowledge that his colleagues wouldn't know that it actually contained Merlot. "Foreign Secretary?"

"President Trump, I am told, now wants to freeze payments to the World Health Organisation," said Raambo, seemingly unaware that behind him was a poster of a young women playing tennis, but without wearing knickers and scratching her bottom. The PM momentarily thought that this should be compulsory dress code for all women tennis players, or for those below a certain age and dress size, and made a note to contact the Lawn Tennis Association. Raambo, speaking from his teenage son's bedroom, went on: "He believes that the WHO is largely responsible for the spread of the virus and wishes to take action again it. That will likely involve freezing payments to the organisation, and in all likelihood making a bad situation worse."

"But is he wrong?" asked the PM, whose instinct was to keep in with the Americans now that the UK was no longer friends with anyone in Europe.

"The WHO declared the virus to be a public health emergency at the end of January, Prime Minister. The President, however, continued to hold rallies, play golf and compare coronavirus to the common flu. He's also now delaying relief cheques to the hardest-hit in his country because he wants his name printed on them." Raambo paused. "There is also the small matter of China, Prime Minister."

"What about it?" asked the PM, who could still taste prawn balls, beef chow mein, Singapore noodles, spring rolls, prawn toast, sweet and sour chicken and several other things that he couldn't now be expected to remember.

"Our ambassador says that China may use the pandemic to bring in new security laws in Hong Kong and tie our former colony closer to the mainland. If so, Prime Minister, we may have to calibrate a response. The Hong Kong people won't like it, and we can expect further large-scale riots."

"Our ambassador, you say? Sir Humphrey Maddox, Foreign Secretary? I thought I had given instructions for him to be terminated." Raambo raised his eyebrows, along with most

Cabinet colleagues, except the Home Secretary who was shaking her head which was entirely covered by her postage-stamp hands. "Of course, when I said *terminated*, I meant reassigned to other duties. He no longer has my confidence, Foreign Secretary," said the PM, remembering the boyish Sir Humphrey's dexterity with a wet towel.

"You didn't mention it to me, Prime Minister. However, if that is your wish, I will see what can be done."

"Excellent!" said the Prime Minister. "In which case, let's move onto Brexit." A number of small heads looked left or right, as if looking at other small heads, and deciding who was the right person to answer.

After a long pause, Mick Gore decided that he was the right person, despite wearing a green dressing gown over peach-coloured pyjamas. "We got Brexit over the line, Prime Minister."

"Yes, but that was just the political bit. Don't we have to agree a trade deal or something?"

"Yes, we do, Prime Minister, and I am in close contact with our former colleagues and former close friends in Europe about that very thing. We have to agree that trade deal by the end of this year, which is the final deadline before we all fall over the edge of a cliff, or *consequi per pactum*." Nobody quite knew whether he was being serious nor, being unable to speak Latin, what he was actually telling them.

"Excellent" said the Prime Minister, who could speak Latin and who therefore had full confidence in Mick Gore, minister for something-or-other, to secure an agreement entirely advantageous to the UK. "Now, is there anything else?"

"Yes, I've still to receive two chicken kormas and onion pakora," said an oddly fuzzy elderly man.

Cabinet over, the Prime Minister had merely to press one button on his computer to make all the postage stamps disappear, including the oddly fuzzy elderly man, without the need to make small talk with any of them, or enquire after their offspring in whom he had no interest, or discuss what might have happened to two chicken kormas and an onion pakora, which the Prime Minister would at that moment have gladly eaten. Food denied, he was left instead to move to the sofa in the living room and switch on to Netflix.

On 10th April, the UK reached a new high of 980 recorded daily deaths from coronavirus from those tested in hospitals, a higher number than any daily maximum recorded in Italy or elsewhere in Europe, and which placed the UK's per capita death rate from Covid-19 as probably the highest in the world.

Derek Goings was not having a good day, although he had been able to eat a bacon and sausage roll. His wife was still coughing and spluttering and, rather to his alarm, he too had developed a slight dry cough. However, having never been ill in his life, he wasn't going to start now, meticulously reading the deluge of government reports and emails that constantly filled his various inboxes. Most, of course, simply contained self-serving twaddle designed to give the impression of action rather than the reality of it, and mostly from the health ministry that was so palpably failing at virtually everything that it was turning its hand to. He also sat in on the morning's Cabinet meeting, narrowing his eyes at the Home Secretary's rather sarcastic comments about working from home which, he thought, had been one of his better ideas. He then watched the lunchtime news, with Raambo being interviewed on Britain's place in the world after Brexit and the pandemic, which was rather overshadowed by a woman's bottom in the background. Mick Gore was also interviewed on the government's PPE fiasco, but had forgotten – accidentally or on purpose – to change out of his pyjamas. Both, however, kept to the script that he had prepared for them but, as always, it was the things that were out of his control that kept going wrong. Why hadn't Raambo looked at the wall behind him? Why hadn't Mick Gore changed into a suit and tie?

But why, he thought, should those things have been out of his control? Normally, he would have phoned the Foreign Secretary and pointed out that women's bottoms and foreign policy don't usually go together, except in certain circumstances. He would have phoned Mick Gore and reminded him to look sombre for an important interview on an important subject. He hadn't spoken to either, a transgression that he had never before been guilty of, then realised that on top of mental torpor he was also becoming a little sweaty.

His worried concentration was broken by one of his mobile phones that, rather fittingly, was playing the theme from Star Wars.

It was the chief executive of Ipsos MORI, one of the few people that Derek could count as a friend, being also acquainted with the dark arts of public opinion and the subtle, and not so subtle, ways in which it could be manipulated.

"Derek, I have bad news."

He listened, quickly concluding that he would have to make another tedious, and secret, trip to London, despite his bad eyesight, and to put Plan B into action.

Twilight tales

On 11th April, a leaked letter from the Association of Directors of Adult Social Services to the Department of Health and Social Care noted that the handling of PPE for care workers had been 'shambolic' and with delivery of equipment 'paltry' and 'haphazard.' On 13th April, the Alzheimer's Society, Marie Curie, Age UK, Care England and Independent Age sent an open letter to the Health Secretary: 'We urgently need testing and protective equipment made available to care homes...we're seeing people in them being abandoned to the worst that coronavirus can do... A lack of protective equipment means staff are putting their own lives at risk while also carrying the virus to highly vulnerable groups.'

Twilight, and a silence only broken by the measured tread of someone who could only be wearing very expensive brogues. It had been a troubling day, for reasons he couldn't quite fathom, although his wife shrieking in laughter when he'd appeared on lunchtime TV had been temporarily embarrassing. Why hadn't he checked the wall behind him? Why hadn't Derek Goings phoned him after that morning's Cabinet meeting?

As a designated keyholder and Secretary of the Chelsea and Kensington Karate, Kickboxing, Martial Arts, Self-Defence, Latin American Dancing and Fitness Club, Raambo had a key, which he used to let himself into the rather spartan interior of his club and change into shorts, T-shirt and bespoke kickboxing shoes. He was rather pleased with the shoes, which made a discreet and exclusive squeak when he walked, bought from a specialist supplier in Japan, where his chosen sport had originated.

He was often asked why he'd elected to take up kickboxing as a sport rather than, say, jogging or just boxing. In reply, he'd simply say that he hadn't chosen kickboxing but, rather, kickboxing had chosen him which didn't, of course, mean anything. However, it did add to his charisma as someone deeply thoughtful, imbued with Eastern mysticism and able, if he so chose, to kick someone's teeth in. It was also a sport in which he must have excelled having risen to the captaincy of his university kickboxing team, despite it having only three members, a fact that Raambo always glossed over. In a government of the inept and overweight, he was the shining example that proved that he was *fit for government*, a phrase that he'd used with journalists on several occasions.

Raambo limbered up with a quick jog around the main training room, dodging between various pieces of gym apparatus, and then did a series of stretching exercises, after which he faced the club's punchbag, attached to the ceiling by a lengthy chain, and gave it an experimental kick. The punchbag gave an expensive thud noise, while his other shoe squeaked happily on the wooden floor.

Then, overcome with an emotion he couldn't immediately place, he sat down on a wooden bench and, elbows on knees, placed his head between his hands. He felt soporific and listless, as if all his boundless energy had seeped from the soles of his shoes. He struggled to locate the cause of this unbidden lethargy. Was it something he'd eaten? But he'd eaten only what he ate every day, generally a fruit drink at breakfast, some mixed nuts at lunchtime and, in the evening, something wholesome and nutritious like tofu or lentils.

Or was it something to do with his job? Yes, Trump was a constant worry, with his infantile Tweets and puzzling pronouncements, but they were no more puzzling than his own prime minister's, who, thankfully, didn't use Twitter. Or China, with the threat of draconian laws on Hong Kong or, worse, possible military invasion, although Sir Humphrey Maddox thought otherwise, and who didn't yet know that, fluent in both Mandarin and Cantonese, he was being posted to Ghana. But China wasn't a real worry – a country on the other side of the world, with problems that could safely be kept on the other side of the world except, of course, for Covid19 which proved that what went on in one place couldn't always be kept in one place.

So why hadn't Britain carried out health checks on people arriving into the country? Why hadn't we insisted on them going into quarantine? Why hadn't we closed down the country weeks beforehand? Why was the care sector in such crisis? Why was PPE such a shambolic mess? The list went on and on and on.

As he posed these most obvious questions, energy began to seep back from the floor, through the soles of his bespoke kickboxing shoes, and into his body. It wasn't all down to the failures of the Health Secretary, who also had thousands of civil servants to do his thinking for him. Or the failures of other ministers, who had thousands of other civil servants to actually do things. It all came down to the leadership of one man, who should have been setting the national agenda but who, generally, wasn't known for reading anything as detailed as an agenda.

What the country needed was a new prime minister, he decided, giving the punchbag one last almighty kick, which dislodged one of his shoes and sent it flying skywards to smash an overhead length of strip-lighting.

Be careful for what you wish for, whispered a small voice in his ear, which was mostly drowned out by the clatter of broken glass hitting the floor.

Twilight, although not particularly silent, as Derek Goings drove south at breakneck speed, his car lit up from inside in various and shifting hues of blue. He had one laptop on his left knee and another, now that he was alone, on the passenger seat, and mobile phones in both hands.

But he too was filled with a lethargic absence of energy, an inner emptiness that Derek was unacquainted with. His day-to-day life involved making a myriad of decisions every minute of every hour, having assessed every shred of evidence, distilled every pertinent fact and, like an infallible computer, coming to conclusions that were never, ever wrong. Now, he was having trouble reading a report on possible variations in the R number across Britain, while also reading a separate report on wheat production in the USA. This latter report wasn't entirely necessary to his advisory role, but he liked to intersperse work with light reading. His mobile phones were also in constant use, spewing vast numbers of terse emails and texts across the machinery of government.

In his defence, there was a lot or organise.

Twilight, and a silence broken only by the crystal-clear sound of the plasma screen TV downstairs, loudly reminding him that he was a prisoner in his own house. Actually, worse than that – a prisoner of his spare bedroom, although it did have an en-suite bathroom, rather fetching blue curtains and a daisy picture on the wall facing his laptop. But it didn't have access to the kitchen or the garden or any of his home's other amenities, including his children.

"Are you dying?" one had shouted through the door earlier.

"Are you dead?" the other had shouted a little later.

He'd reassured them both that he was, in fact, still alive and in good health – to which they hadn't replied – while also asking if someone could bring him a gin and tonic. His entreaties over the walkie-talkie had not been answered.

Perhaps oddly, the Health Secretary wasn't worried about his own mortality. He was in good health, had no Covid-19 symptoms, and rather felt that his positive test may have been a mistake. Nor could he remember having been given a test by Derek Goings, although the PM's advisor had no reason to make up something like that. In any case, he was a practical man and, if he should get sick, he could easily call for medical assistance. His bedroom-cum-office had a functioning outside phone line, unlike his semi-functioning walkie-talkie. He settled down to watch TV, each programme tediously interspersed with advertisements from supermarkets telling everyone how well they were looking after their staff and customers, banks telling everyone how important their impoverished and unemployed customers were to them, and online casinos telling everyone to make things worse for themselves.

Twilight, and a silence broken only by the sound of a bottle of red wine being opened. *Game of Thrones* was on pause, and the Prime Minister's dinner of tuna salad lay untouched on the table in front of him. During the day he had also watched several episodes of *Outlander*, and signed several official papers. He liked it when he was called upon to show a bit of leadership, or to append his name to the bottom of a piece of paper. It instilled a sense of purpose, he thought, puffing on yet another cigar and pouring Merlot into a glass. He was, after all, the lynch-pin around which everything else revolved, the pinnacle of the pyramid around which other things revolved, and the big peg from which the fate of the country dangled.

Caroline had phoned, of course, making sure that he was eating only what she had determined was in his best interests and pleased that he was enjoying his tuna salad so much and that, once he was recovered, she would prepare it for him more often. Several ex-girlfriends also phoned to enquire after his health, including a rather brash American woman whose voice he dimly remembered, and who introduced herself as Jennifer, as if that should mean anything to him, and several of his children, whose names he absolutely couldn't remember.

The Prime Minister prodded his tuna salad one last time, perhaps hoping that it might suddenly be transformed into a lamb bhuna, before consigning it to the bin and chewing instead on a piece of bread.

On 5th April, Lord Bath of Longleat died after contracting Covid-19, as did a nursing assistant and five London bus workers, bringing the total number of deaths to 4,934, a rise of 621 in twenty-four hours. The number of confirmed cases had risen from just over 5,000 on 21st March to nearly 50,000. Some NHS staff in England said they were wearing bin bags for protection. The Health Secretary announced that sunbathing was banned.

The door to Number 10 Downing Street was opened by an Irish matriarch before Derek Goings had even reached it, the approaching smell of sulphur having alerted the PM's assistant that his advisor was close by and getting closer. She insisted that he wore a Perspex face shield and surgical mask before she allowed him upstairs to the PM's apartment, joking that "we can do without the Prime Minister, but where would we be without his advisor?" – although, by the sour expression on her face, it may not have been a joke.

The PM was both surprised and happy to see his advisor, although disappointed that Derek Goings wasn't carrying anything that could have contained food. He felt in a garrulous mood having talked to nobody of importance all day, except his Cabinet, several ex-girlfriends, one current girlfriend and several children, who might have been his or someone else's.

"Derek, my dear fellow. How is the outside world?"

"Still outside, Prime Minister, where it usually is." The advisor removed his face shield and surgical mask, wondering why any sane person would choose to wear them.

"Quite so, but what news from the outside world?"

"Prime Minister, in this room you have command of the most advanced communications technology in the world," he reminded the PM. "You hardly need me to repeat news that I assume you must already know."

The PM chose not to respond to this, remembering that he hadn't summoned his advisor and that, ergo, his advisor must have summoned himself. He must be here, the PM decided, for a reason. Rather than ask Derek outright, the PM poured himself a glass of red wine and plonked himself on the sofa.

"You do not look well, Prime Minister," began his advisor, solicitously enough.

"Neither would you on a diet of bread and tuna salad."

Derek, whose diet did mainly consist of bread and tuna salad (with only the very occasional bacon and sausage roll) merely nodded. 'Not at all well, Prime Minister," he said with some emphasis.

"Look, if I give you some money, perhaps you could slip out and..."

"I would say that your condition has deteriorated considerably."

"My condition? What condition?"

"Your health, Prime Minister, as I am sure you will agree, is of paramount importance to us all."

"Well, yes, and especially to me."

"I was thinking about the country, Prime Minister."

"I suppose that my health does have a certain wider importance," the PM conceded. "Look, Derek, is there a point to all this waffle?"

"You must be admitted to hospital, Prime Minister. A precaution, I assure you, but a precautionary measure that follows the science and which must therefore be taken to better ensure your speedy recovery."

The PM's mouth opened, closed, then opened again. "But I'm not really feeling ill, Derek." He said this in a stage whisper, in case Downing Street's walls were bugged, which perhaps they were. "To be honest, tuna salad excepted, I am in rude good health."

"That may be so, Prime Minister, but the fact is that you're not ill enough. IPSOS Mori have found that people merely think that you're taking a bit of a break."

"A break? Me? With the weight of government on my shoulders?"

"Hard to believe, I agree, Prime Minister. However, with your worsening health, admission to hospital is our only course of action."

The PM rose unsteadily from the settee, pottered to the wine bottle and refilled his glass. He then relit a half-smoked cigar that sat in a large ashtray.

"When you say hospital, Derek, what precisely do you mean?"

"I mean hospital, sir."

"What, a real hospital, with actual doctors and nurses?"

"That pretty much describes it, Prime Minister. I have taken the liberty of booking your room."

"A room? You make it sound like a hotel!"

"A VIP room that can be secured for your protection, with access limited to designated and essential personnel only, which will include me but not, I'm afraid, your girlfriend."

"Excellent!" said the PM. "I mean, how disappointing not to be able to see Claire. But we can't be too careful with coronavirus about."

"Exactly, sir."

For a few moments, the PM paced up and down in front of the settee then, perhaps realising its purpose, sat down on it, spilling only a small amount of wine over a cream cushion. "But suppose, Derek, if I say no your plan."

"Sir, you are ill and in need of immediate medical attention. My plan, as you term it, is merely to ensure that you receive it. However, and although it's not in my thinking, the British people need a commanding leader who has led them from the front, someone who has charged into machine gun fire, and been slightly and heroically wounded in the process. That's you, sir," added the advisor, relieved to see that the PM had drawn himself up to his full height, jutted out his chin, stuck his cigar firmly into his mouth, puffed out his chest, and shoved one Churchillian hand into his jacket pocket. "Together, Prime Minister, we can be the few earning the gratitude of the many. In other words, your worsening health and low public opinion rating mean that we must take action."

"Put like that, Derek, how could I possibly refuse."

"In which case, sir, best to pack a small bag with some overnight essentials because the ambulance is due here any moment."

The intercom buzzed. "There's an ambulance downstairs. Would that be for you, sir?" The Irish matriarch didn't sound very concerned.

Derek watched as the PM filled a very large bag with a large number of essentials, mainly from the wine rack. "Well, Derek, time to face the machine guns."

There wasn't much time to chat in the ambulance, what with the noise from the siren above their heads, and behind them from the police escort, and the fact that St Thomas' Hospital was just across Westminster Bridge and only a few hundred yards away. The Prime Minister was unloaded into a wheelchair and pushed into the building by his advisor, who was again wearing his face shield and mask, with the PM waving airily at medics who recognised him, and less airily at anybody who didn't.

His room, at the top of the building, had a commanding view over the Thames to the Houses of Parliament. It was also surprisingly comfortable for a hospital room, with a large TV and small bathroom, and all finished in cheery pastel colours. There was even a jolly picture of some daisies on one wall, uncannily reminding him of the picture on his Health Secretary's wall. The

PM unloaded bottles from his bag which he carefully secreted into his small wardrobe, and put a pair of pyjamas under his pillow. His overnight bag didn't contain much else.

"What is this room, Derek? Looks much too good to be used by an ordinary sick person."

"It's for VIPs, sir. In case, for example, a visiting head of state should fall ill. We wouldn't want such a person to be treated on an ordinary hospital ward."

"Crikey, no!" The PM looked approvingly round his new quarters. "How long do you think I will be here for, Derek? Until I fully recover and can resume my duties."

"No more than a few days, sir, and then we'll have you back across the river where you really belong. In the meantime," said his advisor opening the door, "these two nurses are here to ensure your stay is as comfortable as possible." Two medical-looking people in scrubs stood smiling at him although, wearing face shields and surgical masks, it was difficult to tell. "This is Jenny from New Zealand, and this is Luis from Portugal." The advisor gestured to each one in turn.

"Well, nice to meet you," said the PM, and shook hands with Luis and the other one. Both were wearing surgical gloves. "Do you speak English?" he asked Luis.

"Of course, sir," replied Luis.

"And do you speak English?" he asked the other one from New Zealand.

"Of course, sir. A requirement to speak English is a prerequisite for employment in the NHS."

The PM looked at her blankly. "Nope, didn't get a word of that. Maybe it's Māori or something. Look, Luis," said the PM reaching for his wallet. "Do you know a Chinese takeaway around here called Deliveroo…?"

Both nurses then left, Luis clutching a £20 note, and the PM couldn't help but notice that a very large and sturdy-looking police officer was also standing outside his door and carrying a very large and equally sturdy-looking machine gun. "Is he really necessary, Derek?" The PM didn't like machine guns, or guns generally, unless he was metaphorically charging into them.

"*She*, Prime Minister, is there for your protection. We wouldn't want you being disturbed unnecessarily, would we?"

replied the PM's advisor, happy that Plan B was now firmly in place and going without a hitch.

Dominic Goings left soon afterwards to walk back across Westminster Bridge, retrieve his car and make the long journey back to Durham. He hadn't reached the main hospital entrance before the fire alarms sounded and supposed, rightly, that the Prime Minister had lit a cigar.

Raambo received the phone call from Downing Street shortly after he'd swept up all the broken glass and changed into his brogues. The Prime Minister, he was informed by a Downing Street aide, had taken a turn for the worse and had been admitted to St Thomas' Hospital. This was a precautionary measure only, and should not be interpreted as anything serious. However, with the PM now unable to perform the duties to which he had been elected, it now fell on him, Timothy Rennie Raambo, as First Secretary of State, rather than as Secretary of State for Foreign and Commonwealth Affairs, which was irrelevant, to step into the PM's shoes, as it were, and carry the can.

"Do you have any questions, sir?"

"None I can think of," replied Raambo, putting the broom back in its cupboard and shutting the door. "But thank you for phoning."

"Then goodnight, Prime Minister."

Last resort

On Sunday 5th April, Italy recorded 525 new coronavirus deaths, the lowest number since 19th March. Spain recorded 674 deaths, the lowest since 26th March. In the UK, there were 621 deaths, with fatalities still rising. A tiger at a zoo in New York also tested positive for coronavirus, perhaps the first case of human to wild animal transmission. In an address to the nation, the Queen said that 'we join with all nations across the globe in a common endeavour, using the great advances of science and our instinctive compassion to heal. We will succeed - and that success will belong to every one of us...We should take comfort that while we may have more still to endure, better days will return: we will be with our friends again; we will be with our families again; we will meet again.'

Early morning, and Raambo had a new job to do, his lips pressed firmly together in an expression of steely determination although, as nobody had been drafted in as Foreign Secretary, he presumably had his old job to do as well. This conflicting thought made him ask his driver to drop him at the end of Downing Street where he stood for some time wondering whether to go into his Prime Ministerial office in Downing Street or the more familiar surroundings of the Foreign Office on The Mall. He decided on the latter because his Permanent Secretary would be in need of his leadership, and which was where his kale and avocado smoothies were kept.

Raambo quickly dealt with the contents of his inbox, referring several reports to other officials, requesting further information from other officials, and sending on a particularly troublesome report on climate change to the Prime Minister, before realising that he was the prime minister. This thought was both satisfying and alarming as he knew virtually nothing about climate change. He therefore sent the report to the environment secretary who, presumably, would know where to file it and, with Whitehall efficiency, to then forget all about it.

No sooner had he dealt with the many issues requiring his attention than there was a deferential knock on his office door. Tony Bond sat himself in the chair opposite Raambo and opened his notebook. "Good morning, Foreign Secretary," he said, "or should that be Prime Minister?"

"Perhaps you could enlighten me on the protocol, Tony."

"It's a tricky one, sir," his Permanent Secretary replied, "because we don't have a written constitution to make such issues clear. Nothing to refer to, you see, and it's always easier to have something to refer to, as I'm sure you would agree?" A rising intonation at the end of the sentence suggested that Tony Bond was asking a question. The Prime Foreign Secretary Minister chose not to answer. "You are certainly *acting* prime minister, but the Prime Minister is still the *actual* prime minister, until such time as he ceases to be prime minister."

"And when might that be?"

"When, or if, he becomes permanently incapacitated, Minister, at which point the Party would have to elect a new prime minister which, I regret to suggest, might not be you."

The idea that his Party might not elect him to the lofty role of Prime Minister was absurd, although they had done just that not long beforehand. "We must, of course, hope and pray for the Prime Minister's recovery from this terrible illness," said Raambo, as if reading from a prepared script, which he was, having jotted down a few answers to likely questions at that afternoon's Downing Street press conference.

"Indeed, Minister, and I know that many millions of people up and down the country are doing just that."

"Doing what?" asked Raambo, who had rather forgotten what they were talking about.

"Praying for the Prime Minister, Minister."

"As are many millions of people up and down the country," replied Raambo, making a mental note to add that into one of his media answers, and put his feet up on the desk to better admire his footwear. "So, I'm only a temporary and *sort of* prime minister?"

"Precisely, Minister! However, you are in a position to execute every one of the duties of prime minister, except for some which might not be appropriate."

"Inappropriate?"

"Well, for example, launching a pre-emptive nuclear strike, for no reason, against a friendly nation."

"As Foreign Secretary, I can tell you, Tony, that we no longer have any friends."

His Permanent Secretary merely sniffed in a meaningful way, although Raambo had no idea what he was meaning. "In your capacity as First Secretary of State you have therefore assumed the responsibilities of prime minister, but without the particular and unique powers that the office commands. For example, to launch an unprovoked missile strike against another country, for no reason whatsoever. If you did that, you would probably be overstepping the mark. You do, however, have the power to authorise a military response if this country is attacked."

The Foreign Secretary had read all that morning's gibberish from embassies around the world. "Alas, Tony, I just can't see the likelihood of war, at least for the foreseeable future."

"Disappointing, I'm sure, Minister."

"But what if somebody launches a nuclear strike against us? Can I authorise the use of nuclear weapons in response?"

"Each new prime minister must write *last resort letters* to the commanding officers of our ballistic missile-carrying submarines. Those letters are only opened in the event that the chain of command is disrupted from a nuclear strike on the UK."

"But suppose one last resort letter says, bomb Moscow; and another says, bomb Edinburgh." Raambo liked things to be absolutely clear and, like the Prime Minister, didn't much like how the Scots were a bit iffy about remaining in the United Kingdom. "I mean, shouldn't I be writing new last response letters?"

"I don't think that will be necessary, Minister, as the prime minister remains the Prime Minister."

"Even though he's in hospital?"

"Quite so, sir, and if you should fall ill, there is a chain of succession that starts, first, with the Chancellor, then Home Secretary, then Cabinet Office Minister, then Justice Secretary..."

The Foreign Secretary held up a hand. "Enough, Tony! What you're saying is that I'm Prime Minister but not prime minister?"

"As acting prime minister, you are merely the first among equals. That means that your new role comes with a consequent requirement to seek greater consensus among Cabinet colleagues for any action that you might propose."

"What, *talk* to them?" The First Foreign Prime Minister looked suitably appalled. "So, what can I do?"

"Well, sir, you can make recommendations to the Queen on appointments to the senior judiciary."

"Does the judiciary need any senior appointments?"

"Not that I am aware of, Minister. You can also advise Her Majesty on high-ranking positions in the Church of England."

"And does it need any?"

"With churches closed, Minister, it's rather difficult to tell."

Having got nowhere in determining the limits of his new powers, or if he had any, Raambo moved on to another consideration. "I suspect that the Prime Minister will have received a great many documents and reports since his admission to hospital. Am I allowed to deal with those?"

"Absolutely, Minister. Correspondence to the Prime Minister always requires immediate and urgent attention. That is now a duty which falls to you."

"And how do I give such correspondence my urgent and immediate attention?"

"That primarily, but not exclusively, requires access to the Prime Minister's computer which, in turn, requires access to his passwords."

"Which are?"

"Downing Street wouldn't give them to me, Minister."

"Kevin to Minty, over."

Static hiss.

"Kevin to Minty, over."

More static hiss.

The Health Secretary sighed loudly, having been in confinement for what seemed like weeks and denied the very basic of human rights, such as a cup of coffee and a digestive biscuit. How was he to execute his duties as a minister of the Crown without having nutrients and stimulants? He was also running low on bacteriological aerosol spray, hand sanitiser and wet wipes – all of which were in plentiful supply in the top drawer of his desk at work, which he no longer had access to.

He tried again, but with fading hope. "Kevin to Minty, over."

Static hiss.

"Kevin to Minty, over."

More static hiss, which suggested that his wife couldn't be bothered picking up her walkie-talkie or that she was out. Kevin looked into their garden, with its patio and patio heater, but devoid of his wife, and concluded that she was out, no doubt making an absolutely necessary trip to the supermarket to buy essentials. The Health Secretary didn't like to think that his wife could have just nipped out to buy an ice cream or tube of toothpaste, which led him on to think about what actually *did* constitute a necessity. Was cat food a necessity, particularly if you didn't own a cat? Or was it a necessity if you did own a cat? Was toothpaste a necessity if you didn't have any teeth? Was buying dog food a necessity, if you didn't own a dog, but did eat dog food yourself? If hen's eggs were essential, were quail's eggs a necessity? Having looked out the window, the Health Secretary sat at his desk and composed an email to his Permanent Secretary, suggesting that the government should better define what was a necessary purchase, and what unnecessary purchases should carry a prison sentence.

Email sent, Kevin contemplated the empty plate on one side of his desk on which, at breakfast, had been one slice of toast and marmalade. Having been married for nearly twenty years, or which felt like it, didn't his wife know that he *always* had two slices of toast? Didn't she also know that he *always* had a glass of orange juice? And didn't she know that he needed many cups of coffee throughout the day, to ensure that he remained at his razor-sharp best? Not only was his plate empty, but so too his coffee cup.

"Kevin, to my wife. Where are you, over?"

"Static hiss."

"Kevin to wife, if you don't answer I shall be forced to come downstairs."

More static hiss.

The Health Secretary took a deep breath and opened his bedroom door a small crack. It was enough of a crack to hear only silence from downstairs although, he thought, you can't really hear silence, and enough of a crack to be able to see out the window on their half-landing and confirm that his wife's car was not in their driveway. Ergo, his wife had taken it out, because his children were too young to drive, or consider stealing their mother's car. (Their father didn't, of course, require a car, having access to a ministerial limousine which, this week, had been a second-hand Skoda. His posh Jaguar had been impounded by the police for road tax offences).

Suitably emboldened, Kevin made his way downstairs and into the kitchen, feeling like a prisoner must, after a long stretch inside, to find himself in the unaccustomed company of a breadbin. He quickly made and ate a ham sandwich, washed down with orange juice, and was just waiting for the kettle to boil when he heard a key turn in the front door. Kevin, instead of being a prisoner legally released from captivity, felt immediately like a prisoner who has sawn through bars in his cell, dug a long and improbable tunnel, and crawled through endless sewers to taste freedom.

But knowing his wife's capacity for unreasonable behaviour, and that he had broken her absolute rule to remain upstairs until hell freezes over, the Health Secretary did the first coherent thing he could think of.

He hid in a cupboard.

The Foreign Secretary, or whatever he now was, was having better luck in Downing Street, being saluted by the policeman on duty at the door, and welcomed inside by an unsmiling woman with an Irish accent, who introduced herself as the Prime Minister's personal assistant.

She showed him to the Prime Minister's book-lined study, whose shelves were mostly devoted to ancient Rome or the Second World War and, with obvious reluctance, wrote down the PM's highly confidential password, although B-O-R-I-S didn't seem particularly secure. The First Secretary, as he now considered himself, sat down in the Prime Minister's chair, switched his computer on, and was rather alarmed to see that his inbox contained 8,754 items, the oldest of which dated back several months and which hadn't been opened.

Raambo started to randomly go through the PM's emails, to see which ones needed attention, or which could be deleted or sent elsewhere for attention. Some didn't need a reply.

From: His Excellency, the President of Mexico

Hombre

I am informed that you will be eating *menudo* for breakfast tomorrow. Do not eat it! It is revolting. It was invented by mistake.

From: President Donald Trump

Hey

Hear that you're a bit poorly, so my sincere condolences. I have Tweeted about it so that everyone in your country should now know that you're ill.

Some, frankly, were too personal for Raambo to reply to.

From: Jennifer (**Note:** *Surname redacted*)

Hi Babe

Missing you! Bruises have cleared up! Can I have another $10 million, please?

Others could wait until the other PM returned to work.

From: (*Name too fuzzy to redact*)

Prime Minister

I ordered two chicken kormas and an onion pakora, and neither has been delivered. I am at my wit's end.

From: Chancellor Merkel

Prime Minister

Now that the UK has left the EU, please do not even think about a ground invasion. This isn't 1944, much as you would like it to be.

Others were simply too old to require a reply.

From: Caroline (*or maybe Claire*)
Winston
I'm pregnant. You're the father. Be happy.

From: Defence Secretary
Prime Minister
In the event of this country being the subject of a nuclear attack, the TOP SECRET code for our nuclear response is BORIS.

After several hours, Raambo gave up on what was an unequal task, having only dealt with about a hundred emails, and having read only a couple of attachments. It was a reminder to him that the highest office carried with it a burden of toil that few would wish for unless, of course, it was their destiny. Raambo put his feet up on the PM's desk, wiggled happy toes inside another pair of exquisite shoes, and contemplated what destiny might have in store for him.

The Health Secretary was also thinking about destiny, although in more immediate terms, and how he seemed destined to be forever denied a cup of coffee, now that his wife and two children had returned from their shopping trip. He knew it had been a shopping trip from the sound of heavy bags being plonked on the kitchen table and of things being removed from bags and then plonked on kitchen surfaces.

He was in a cupboard that he hadn't really known existed. He had, of course, seen the door but, unlike Alice, had never actually opened the door to see what might be inside. Others might climb mountains to admire the view, or dive into the deepest oceans to discover new creatures, or venture into space to discover other new creatures, but Kevin Kock was simply happy to inhabit a limited number of places – his office, bedroom, bathroom, kitchen, living room, patio and garden. Everything else was an irrelevance, including downstairs cupboards, whether or not they might contain a gateway to Narnia or a hoover. Feeling around, the Health Secretary couldn't discern either a hidden portal or anything very much, except that he seemed to be in a padded cell. He was surrounded on three sides by packets of squelchy stuff which, being a kitchen cupboard, was probably important for food preparation. How raw ingredients became food was another mystery to him. He was also slightly worried about the cupboard's hygienic standard, having failed to bring hand sanitiser downstairs with him.

"Shall I check on Daddy," one of his children asked.

"No." His wife seemed sure about this.

"Should I make him a cup of coffee?" asked his other child.

"No, absolutely not." His wife seemed equally sure about that as well.

It simply didn't occur to the Health Secretary that, being a kitchen cupboard, his wife might want to put something into it so he was unprepared for the door being thrust open and his wife screaming loudly. This so unnerved him that he fell backwards onto the squelchy stuff, rebounded onto the kitchen floor, and was then entirely buried under a great many toilet rolls.

"What are you doing in my kitchen?" yelled his wife.

The Health Secretary extricated himself from his immediate predicament, only to be hit rather painfully on the head by several jumbo-sized packets of pasta and a tin of tomatoes.

"I was looking for my pen," he said with as much dignity as he could muster, while his wife and child cowered on the other side of the kitchen, his wife trying rather ineffectually to cover his children's faces with kitchen towels. He rather groggily ascended the stairs to the spare bedroom and, this time, heard a key turn in the lock.

The prisoner had once again been incarcerated, leaving the Health Secretary to wonder why they needed so many packets of pasta when they never ate any.

Not a million miles away – 260 miles to be precise - Derek Goings was also a prisoner, but a captive only of his tormented genius, having decided, after careful thought and weighing up all the evidence, to actually *do* something useful. While his main task was to make the government look good – a phrase that his job description actually contained, while not containing much else – it wasn't a task easily accomplished with the Covid-19 epidemic running riot.

Derek's genius lay in his ability to absorb information and make sense of it, remembering every fact and statistic and coming to empirical conclusions in which error was never an option. However, he recognised only too well that there were rare occasions when he was wrong because, in his scheme of things, if X and Y happened, then Z was the only logical conclusion. However, in the well-oiled machinery of government, Z was usually only possible if a minister or senior civil servant made an all-too-obvious and logical decision. With ministers such as Kevin Kock and a prime minister with the attention span of a rather dim gnat, X + Y could add up to anything. Simply, he couldn't make the government look good if it was patently being run by individuals who weren't functioning sociopaths.

His decision to do something useful was therefore borne, not from sympathy with all those who were dying, needlessly in his view, but from his rather precise job description. Not that Derek didn't care about people, but his feelings were more nuanced than most. He saw other people, not as bits of humanity but as little jigsaw pieces that, with a bit of time and effort, could be slotted together to vote Conservative at the next election.

But that didn't mean that he was oblivious to suffering because he did understand pain and loss and the raw emotions they could unleash. His limbic system was fully functional; unlike a crocodile, he was not without emotion or empathy. It was just that his emotions, and his empathies for strangers, were deep down and his conscious mind rarely came across them. Derek Goings was therefore a caring sociopath but, mostly, a caring sociopath who didn't much care.

But the pandemic had shifted that small disconnect. The illness of his wife, and his own possible illness, had focused his attention on his child. He cared about them both. His wife was pretty, highly intelligent, funny and possessed of both insightful intuition and a functioning vagina. In her, he had found a soulmate; a jigsaw piece that slotted into his jigsaw piece. Their daughter made the picture complete. In caring for his family, Derek was therefore able to understand how other people must feel about their families, however stupid, fat or ugly. He had learned, from his own family, to feel what other people feel. Or, at least, to understand what other people must feel. His family had taught him how to be human and, while he despised the frailties that went along with being human, he was prepared to accept that other people mattered.

In short, Derek Goings had a job description that solely involved making the stupid look wise. But that couldn't be achieved without making the stupid act wisely. In the middle of the worst health crisis for a hundred years, the government had acted with complacency and incompetence. That now had to be put right. Derek Goings, hunched over their kitchen table, the light from several laptops illuminating his face in ghostly hues, set about terrorising the machinery of government into doing something.

Despite not being in London, and not being able to terrorise in person, his plan was coming along quite nicely.

The Prime Minister, insulated from the world by a closed door and a person of the wrong sex carrying a gun, had little to do except stare out of his window at the Palace of Westminster and contemplate its long and illustrious contribution to the nation and the wider world. Its corridors had felt the footsteps of Disraeli and Gladstone; its meeting rooms had witnessed noble compromise and shady deals; its debating chambers had echoed to grand oratory demanding peace or war; its very fabric was steeped in the history of a nation. It was a reminder, he considered, of permanence: a symbol that, while some things change, other things don't change - framing his thoughts into a draft speech: a speech he would never make because he never wrote down his thoughts, such as they were, and a thought forgotten was an idea lost forever.

He had little to do because, being properly ill and in hospital, Derek Goings had removed his official phone and laptop, although Derek was unaware that the PM had never used it because he hadn't yet located the 'on' switch and had been too embarrassed to ask anyone.

The PM wondered if he could have done things a little differently: perhaps, for example, taken the coronavirus a little more seriously. But, of course, looking back didn't change anything. Of course, in retrospect, he might have made other decisions, but that was true of everything that anybody ever did. Which one of us, with the perfect gift of hindsight, wouldn't go back and change things? He certainly would. Like the evening when he'd been particularly drunk and Claire (or Caroline) was being particularly alluring. Having sex had been on the agenda; getting her pregnant had not been, and he entirely blamed her for this biological lapse for which, of course, he was entirely blameless.

The genius behind Derek Goings' plan was to make the country forget that everything was entirely the fault of the Prime Minister and his government and to instead focus their hopes and fears onto the PM's illness and recovery. To forgive the dither and ineptitude and recognise that the country's leader was a fighter who could be relied upon to fight the virus on the beaches or, at least, from his hospital bed. It was a strategy to restore the popularity of a stricken PM in the middle of a national crisis, pave the way for a snap election before the end of the year and ensure that Conservative governments would rule from the Palace of Westminster for another hundred years, or so Derek Goings thought.

During the day, various people had phoned the PM on his personal mobile phone. Derek, of course, had phoned several times to reassure the PM that focus groups were already predicting the end of the 'Winston wobble' and that an upswing in the polls was inevitable. But when you come out of hospital, he was advised, you must act humble and contrite; your illness should have made you more of a man, more of a leader: a leader able to look his people in the eye and say, I was there. The PM had merely grunted, not sure what he was being advised but sure that, coming from Dee, it had to be sensible. In any case, he still felt perfectly fine, despite being in hospital and despite not having seen a doctor.

His two companions, Luis and Jenny, were cheerful enough, making sporadic visits to his room and bringing him a surprising range of delicious food which, Luis explained, he cooked himself in the hospital's kitchens. Luis said with a wink that, for security reasons, the Prime Minister was only allowed to eat meals prepared specially for him and that it would be his pleasure to cook whatever the Prime Minister wanted, which was quite a lot of things. The PM wasn't sure about the other nurse as, try as he might, he was entirely unable to understand a single word she said. He really must have a word with his Health Secretary, he thought. NHS staff really should have some kind of English proficiency test before being allowed to practice. If, indeed, they were nurses, he also thought, because they didn't carry stethoscopes. But if not nurses, who were they? Close protection officers, just in case the large police officer of the wrong sex with the gun should be overpowered? He suspected that they must be something to do with Derek. After all, when he'd arrived, it was Derek who had introduced them to him. The PM also knew that it would be pointless asking Dee about them; in some things, his advisor worked in mysterious ways best not questioned.

His chubby girlfriend phoned at regular intervals to ask him how he was, to which he would simply reply that he was exactly the same as on the previous occasion when she'd rung, as well as interrupting him from important matters of State. To which, irritatingly, she would laugh, for some reason thinking that he was joking.

On one occasion, to be chatty, he told her that, during the night, he'd had a strange experience. That he'd woken up and seen a light, and had got out of bed and followed the light.

"My goodness, Winston, were you all right? An out-of-body experience?"

"No, I'd just left the bathroom light on," he'd replied, making her laugh again, although he hadn't been joking. At the time it had been rather scary, waking in a strange bed, with a strange light, and having an out-of-bed experience. Women could be so tiresome, he thought, and should take more care about their reproductive systems.

Winston Spragg resumed his place by the window and looked once again at the Palace of Westminster, his popularity on the ascendant, and the British people rightly reassured that their country was in the best hands possible.

Rather than simply stare into space, or at old buildings with large clock towers, Derek Goings' day was filled with phone calls, emails and texts. Some were, for him, rather unctuous; most were terse and abrupt, others downright rude. He didn't always mean to be rude - his detractors were wrong about that - he simply wanted to convey information and ensure that his instructions were understood. Rudeness didn't come into it, because that implied an intention to be rude. Derek was rarely rude on purpose; he simply did his job as efficiently as possible because, even for him, there were only so many phone calls he could make, only so many emails and texts he could send, and only so many computer screens he could look at. His time was limited: necessity made his emails, texts and phone calls short and to-the-point. Some people thought that, not taking the trouble to ask after their wives, children or golf handicap, was rude. But Derek Goings was always busy, and didn't have time for unnecessary distractions, even if he was remotely interested in their wives, children or golf handicap. Derek Goings was therefore rarely, intentionally rude.

Sir Roger Smallwood was the exception; the one person to whom Derek would like to be very rude, but the one person who – at that moment – needed to be wheedled rather than needled.

"My department is working well beyond its capacity," Sir Roger was saying, thinking proudly of all those civil servants who were toiling downstairs, or from home or, for some, from their second homes in Devon, Cornwall or the Canary Islands. "We cannot be expected to do more than that, Derek."

It was the usual refrain that he heard a thousand times every week from the Whitehall apparatus. "I wouldn't expect otherwise, Sir Roger," said Derek, hoping that he sounded conciliatory although, to the Permanent Secretary, he merely sounded menacing. "My point is that we have to think and behave in new ways. The old normal is no longer good enough for the new normal."

"As I said, Derek, my department is working flat out to deliver on the promises that my Health Secretary and this government have made. We are building a protective shield around the care sector, we are sourcing more PPE than ever before and we are putting in place world-class testing capacity which, with a bit of luck, might be up and running by the end of the month."

"With a bit of luck, Sir Roger?"

The Permanent Secretary bit his lip in frustration. Derek Goings had the unholy knack of making him start a sentence in perfect civil servant terms, then lapse stupidly into honesty. "We can't do more than proper procedures allow us to do," he said, then took a deep breath, steeling himself against inadvertently letting anything remotely true seep out. "In delivering on service quality, which includes the development of increased testing, and the procurement of additional supplies of PPE, we have certain protocols that have to be followed."

"Protocols, Sir Roger?"

"Protocols to ensure that public money is spent wisely, Derek. Protocols to ensure that the PPE we source is fit for purpose. Procedures to ensure that testing targets can be met, while generating useful and actionable data that this department, SAGE and other government departments can use to make assessments, forecasts and generate policy options."

"Then do more and do it faster," suggested Derek, now tired of this waffle from the health ministry. In the same space of time as this phone call had taken, he could have rearranged his sock drawer except, he had to remind himself, he was in Durham and the sock drawer was in London.

"That is simply not possible, Derek. As I have repeatedly emphasised, this department is working at well beyond capacity, cutting corners where we can, but making sure that everything that *can* be done *is* being done."

"I said to do more and do it faster, Sir Roger."

"Look, Derek, I don't answer to you. I answer democratically to the Health Secretary and, through him, to the Prime Minister."

"Both of whom are *in absentia*, as it were."

"That's not the point. I take my orders from them, not from you."

"Oh, but you will," said Derek, all trace of civility now removed from his voice, and replaced with chilly precision. "You see, Sir Roger, I know your secret."

Sir Roger Smallwood sat for a long while after his phone call with Derek Goings, his hands shaking and his mind in turmoil. How the hell had he found out about *that*? Who could possibly have told him? There again, as he well knew, it was the PM's advisor's job to know everything about everybody, even a small public discretion that he bitterly regretted and wished, with the benefit of hindsight, that he hadn't committed. But, he admitted, what was done couldn't now be undone. The only question was: would Derek Goings tell anyone? If so, *who* would he tell?

After a while, once his hands had stopped shaking, he began to track down members of his staff, one of whom was at home and asleep, and to lay down the law. He ordered, he shouted, he demanded. This was a new Sir Roger Smallwood to all of them; a man with steely purpose and in whose hands, if they didn't jump to it, their gilt-edged pensions might no longer be safe. Sir Roger couldn't risk anyone finding out his secret.

Derek Goings sat in the gathering twilight, noting with approval the vast numbers of texts, emails and phone calls that were now emanating from Sir Roger's office. He had one computer on permanent link to the Permanent Secretary's communications devices, an easy enough task with his contacts at MI5, an organisation almost entirely staffed by functioning sociopaths, and which was therefore entirely supportive of Derek Goings' activities.

Of course, Derek had no idea what Sir Roger's secret was. But he did know one thing above everything else. Everyone has a secret.

Intensive care

'Public Health England did not increase testing for Covid-19 as quickly as was needed to control the spread of the virus,' the Government's Chief Scientific Advisor suggested in mid-April. His comments echoed those of England's Chief Medical Officer, who said a week previously that Germany 'got ahead' in testing people for Covid-19 and that the 'UK needed to learn from that.' Interviewed on BBC Newsnight, Clare Wenham, Assistant Professor of Global Health Policy at the London School of Economics, said 'I don't know why the UK Government haven't been listening to the guidance coming from the World Health Organisation, whose guidance was test, test, test. She said that 'the countries we have seen getting out of this situation and the lockdown sooner than others, or in fact never going into a full lockdown...they have followed a very simple strategy of testing, isolating those who are infected, and then contact tracing who they have been in contact with.'

Vijay Patel, the Chancellor of the Exchequer, was proud to be holding one of the four Great Offices of State and, as someone who actually had worked in the financial sector, did know how to run a whelk stall, unlike the Prime Minister who wouldn't know what a whelk was. His actual experience in finance therefore made him a natural ally of the First Foreign Secretary Minister who also knew his stuff, having been abroad. They had agreed to meet in Raambo's office, a short stroll from Horse Guards' and the Treasury.

The two men liked one another, despite Vijay's interest in football and cricket, and his complete disinterest in shoes or kickboxing. Both men were also young, fit, personable, able, and extremely ambitious. In the scheme of things, Vijay knew that one day he would have to kill Raambo or, if he let his guard down, be killed by him. Such was the way of the Conservative party, which behaved in many ways like a quasi-religious sect in which only the fittest could aspire to the top job. But, with no leadership contest in sight, Raambo's feet were on top of his desk and Vijay was leaning back in his chair.

He took a sip of Raambo's rather fine whisky. "I just think, Timothy, that the Health Secretary really must go."

"I agree that he's incompetent, but since when has that been an impediment to ministerial office?" Now that he was quasi-prime minister, Raambo was being unusually defensive about a colleague whom he usually disparaged. "He also has some qualification to be Health Secretary."

"He does?"

"Apparently, he once had measles."

"Measles? I didn't know that," said Vijay thoughtfully, who had also suffered childhood measles, and who didn't regard it as being a qualification for the highest health job in the country. "The trouble is that Kock cock-ups have rather become a rather too-familiar refrain in the media." Vijay looked at Raambo's shoes, noting that they were made from soft leather, and therefore useless for playing football in. "A mantra that reflects badly on the government, and therefore us."

"But that's why he must stay," suggested Raambo, also now sipping from his glass. He had been planning a couple of hours in the gym, but now felt too tired, what with the strain of holding down two jobs. "After all, when this whole virus thing is over and done with, someone will have to take the blame for it. To carry the can, so to speak. The person who most fits the bill is the Health Secretary."

"The person responsible for health," mused Vijay aloud, "and therefore the person responsible, at least on paper, for getting us out of the mess. The person who should be digging us out of the hole, rather than digging us in deeper."

"That certainly is the way I see it, Vijay."

The Chancellor waggled his head, not looking convinced. "But won't the electorate blame us anyway? They might think that, if the Health Secretary was so incompetent, why didn't we replace him? After all, Timothy, a lot of people are dying. Sticking by the Health Secretary when we should have got rid of him might not stack up with the voters."

"I agree up to a point, but removing a minister from office isn't our job, is it?" Raambo paused to allow this thought to infuse the Chancellor's brain, alongside his 15-year-old Speyside malt. "Quite simply, when that time comes, we blame the Prime Minister."

"So, the Health Secretary carries the can for being incompetent, and the Prime Minister carries another can for not doing anything about that incompetence?"

"That's how I see it, Vijay."

This time, the Chancellor smiled, leaned over the desk, and clinked glasses with Raambo. The top dogs in the quasi-religious sect were in agreement on something, although that something might require there to be bloodshed at some point between them, despite their friendship, and both men knew it.

"What do you mean he's in intensive care!" yelled Derek Goings into the phone.

"I mean he's in intensive care, guv'nor," said Luis, who might or might not have been a nurse. He had also dropped his Portuguese accent and was speaking broad Cockney.

"But I didn't give orders for him to be ill!" replied Derek reasonably enough.

"Difficult to Adam and Eve it, I know."

"In any case, who authorised a move to Plan C?"

"Circumstance, mate. Moving to Plan C would have required your specific authorisation."

"Which I didn't give," the PM's advisor reminded him.

"His move to intensive care was done by a doctor," Luis said, trying to keep his voice down. In the background were hospital sounds, such as squeaking trolleys and machines making beep noises.

"What? A real doctor?"

"A real doctor, mate. I'd just been for a pony and trap, see?"

A door slamming next door to Derek's Airbnb had momentarily drowned Luis out. "Say again, Luis. Missed that."

"Was in the Gary Glitter for a French kiss and Eartha Kitt, mate. That's when I found him, all gaunt. First, I thought he was just Schindler's List, what with all them bottles of Calvin Klein that he brought. Then I thought he was having a Meryl Streep."

"And what alerted you to the suspicion that he might not be pissed or asleep?"

"He was, like, having trouble breathing. So, I called the docs."

"You also broke protocol."

"No option, guv. We don't want the geezer Father Ted, do we?"

"Look, Luis, I want you and Jenny to stick close to him, understand? I want regular updates."

"Intensive care wasn't in our contract, mate. What about my Bugs Bunny?"

Derek Goings found talking to Londoners almost as tiresome as speaking to Prime Ministers. "Don't worry, you'll get your Gregory Peck. In US dollars, into your Swiss ham shank. But remember, Luis, if there's any change in his condition, any change whatsoever, you call me immediately, understand? On the dog and bone."

"The dog and *what*?"

"Just phone me, you imbecile!"

"No need to be rude, mate. I could go to rusty nail for this, you know."

"No, you won't, Luis. Not if you do precisely as I say. Is that understood?"

"Crystal, mate."

Luis took a deep breath, wondered briefly if he could nip down the apple and pears and outside for a quick Harry Wragg, looked instead at the dickory dock on the other side of the river then, thinking himself back into his other persona as a nurse from the Algarve, walked quickly to the Intensive Care Unit to resume his medical and other duties, whatever they were.

The Chancellor was just finishing his whisky and about to leave the august surroundings of the Foreign Secretary's office when Raambo's phone rang. The Foreign Secretary listened intently, made a few grunting noises, then put the phone down. Then he put his feet back up on his desk and stared into space for a few moments.

"That was the hospital," he said at length. "The PM's been taken into intensive care."

"Intensive care!"

"It's where they take you if you're very poorly."

The Chancellor sighed inwardly. The Foreign Secretary might have been abroad, but that didn't make him qualified to be patronising except, perhaps, to people from abroad. "The prognosis?"

"He's being well looked after, that's all I know, and been assigned two particularly experienced nurses to be with him at all times. The next couple of days, so I'm told, are likely to be critical."

The Chancellor swilled what was left of his whisky around his glass. "I supposed that makes you even more of the de facto prime minister."

The Foreign Secretary removed his feet from the desk, planted his elbows on his blotting pad and rested his chin in the palms of his hands. "I will merely and temporarily be carrying out the duties of the prime minister until our great leader is fully fit and able to resume his duties."

Both men tried to look sombre, then couldn't help it, and laughed. The Foreign Secretary fetched the whisky bottle, and they clinked glasses again in a silent toast for the Prime Minister's speedy recovery, or to something else entirely.

Derek Goings was delighted with the Prime Minister's rapid decline in health, although troubled by the way that events had intervened to usurp his carefully laid plans. Plan C was only to be deployed if the opinion polls didn't show a rise in Conservative popularity, and not before then under any circumstances. However, as Derek well knew, it would not have been an easy plan to deploy with the PM being in such robust good health. Intensive care units, he supposed, would be filled with properly ill patients, not people sitting up in bed smoking cigars and drinking red wine. Getting the PM into hospital had been the easy part, because his VIP room was a limbo area, with medics and administrators assuming that the PM had his own doctors, and that he wasn't therefore their responsibility. Luis and Jenny had been working on variations of Plan C, but had yet to put forward anything that would stand even basic scrutiny.

That the PM had actually contracted coronavirus and was in intensive care was very good news, because the opinion polls still showed that Conservative fortunes were slipping, and that he need no longer worry about Plan C. He therefore opened up his most secure laptop, with passwords that didn't contain anything as insecure as BORIS, and then into a heavily encrypted programme that detailed the exact workings of Plan C. Plan B could now be ignored, having been successfully completed.

However, the notes that contained Plan C were rather sparse, even by Derek's minimalist standards, because what happened during Plan C wasn't really under his control. Either the PM could die, in which case Plan D would kick into operation, or he could get better, in which case there was Plan E. Plan D was rather more complex, involving both a funeral, with all due pomp and ceremony for a deceased leader who had taken a hit for his country, although without much pomp what with social distancing, and a Conservative party election for a new leader. Derek had already mapped out who he believed should be the country's next PM, having had nothing to do with Winston Spragg's election, not being in government at the time. How the country could have elected Winston as PM was beyond him, and was a mistake he wouldn't make when the next leadership election took place. There were, of course, a couple of front-runners, but Derek had never been one for front-runners. They too easily could turn out to be their own man, or woman, and Derek didn't like anybody being their own person, when he should be that person for them.

Plan E was less problematic. The PM would recover, again having taken a hit for his country, but would be safely tucked away to recover in Downing Street or at Chequers, his country retreat, and therefore safe from pesky journalists asking intelligent questions. Plan E was, of course, his preferred option, because it was the easiest to carry out, having virtually nothing to carry out, and therefore virtually nothing that could go wrong.

But Derek Goings was also troubled by something else, although that something else didn't include a sick wife and his own troubling cough and high temperature. He now assumed that his whole family had contracted Covid-19, but what the hell. Death wasn't an option, at least for him, although what his wife chose to do was up to her. He would, of course, miss her, and would find it difficult at short notice to find a replacement with warmth, wit, intelligence and a functioning vagina.

No, what was troubling him was his ability to drive back to London, what with his eyesight. Getting back to London, and being able to threaten or cajole in person, was a priority. With the PM nominally in charge, he had been able to hold at least some of the reins of power. Now, with Raambo holding the reins, and with the PM's horse having bolted, it was incumbent on Derek to shut the stable door, so to speak. He needed to be back in Downing Street, only a short walk from the more important ministries, and where he could eavesdrop on whatever Raambo was telling people to do. That was his main worry. The actual PM had few original thoughts, leaving Derek to get on with things, including running the country. Now, an imposter was in Downing Street.

Derek's worry was that he might be developing cataracts, because he had begun to see the world rather differently. His world was becoming mucky, full of yellows and purples. He had, Derek believed, the same problem as the great Claude Monet, whose penchant for repeatedly painting water lilies made him properly famous. But Monet's perceptions of the world were changed by cataracts, so that vivid greens and blues were slowly transformed into muddier and yellowish tones. Monet even took to sticking labels on his tubes of paint, so that he could remember what water lilies (and other stuff) actually looked like, rather than the lilies (and other stuff) that he couldn't really see properly any more. Derek didn't have much of an interest in painting, and didn't therefore have tubes of paint to stick labels on, but he absolutely knew that his world of blue computer light was becoming dulled, an affliction that had nothing whatsoever with wearing dark glasses in the dark.

To test whether he was safe to drive, he would have to do what Monet would have done, and go and look at flowers that he knew should be blue, and to see whether they were blue.

The Foreign Secretary strode purposefully towards the lectern, his feet sighing with pleasure with every step, a bunch of notes in one hand, and a thoughtful expression on his face. As the most powerful person in the country currently not in hospital, it was his job to reassure the nation.

"Before we get on to the detail," he began "can I first give an update on the condition of the Prime Minister. I know a lot of people will be concerned about that. I can tell you he is receiving the very best care from the excellent medical team at St Thomas' hospital. He remained stable overnight, he's receiving standard oxygen treatment and breathing without any assistance. He has not required mechanical ventilation or non-invasive respiratory support. He remains in good spirits and, in keeping with usual clinical practice, his progress continues to be monitored closely in critical care."

"Can we expect the Prime Minister to die?" asked Lauren Hindenburg, recently promoted from the BBC's political editor to be virus editor. "If so, when?"

"I cannot comment on that, Lauren, except to say that, in terms of his treatment, his medical team is doing appropriate medical things to him, and not doing inappropriate things to him, particularly things that may not strictly follow the science which, as you know, is precisely what this government has been doing since long before the pandemic started, creating mountains of spare PPE and making sure that we had shields ready to throw around the most vulnerable in our society."

"That's not really what I asked," said Ms Hindenburg, in her almost-impenetrable Romanian accent.

"He's a fighter," said the Prime Foreign Minister.

On 7th April, the day the Prime Minister went into intensive care, there were a further 786 deaths among hospital patients suffering from Covid-19 in the UK, none of whom couldn't therefore have been fighters, and who joined the 6,159 other dead patients who presumably also couldn't be bothered not to die. The same laziness was evident in other countries. For example, the USA recorded 1,736 deaths, the most Covid-19 deaths in a single day, some of whom were serving or former members of the US military, and who could therefore have been described as fighters. In a press briefing on 7th April, President Trump said: "Even during this painful week, we see glimmers of very, very strong hope. And this will be a very painful week, and next week, at least part of next week, but probably all of it..."

Press conference over, Raambo strode back to the Prime Minister's office and, under the watchful eye of the Irish harridan, entered BORIS and waited for the PM's computer to open. His most recent emails were either a variation of:

Dear Prime Minister
Get well soon.

Or

Dear Prime Minister
Please never get well.

But there were a few others:

Hombre
I told you not to eat the menudo! Please don't think too badly of my country or my people, most of whom have tunnelled their way into the USA where menudo is not considered edible.

Dear Prime Minister
I don't want to go to Ghana. Remember what we got up to at school?

Darling
I'll do anything for that $10 million, as I did before many times, although my bruises have now cleared up, which I think I may have mentioned.

Winston

We all need to be distracted from what's going on because for us, and maybe for you, and I know you're in intensive care, this will be a very painful week, and next week, at least part of next week, but probably all of it...anyway what do you think about declaring war on North Korea? A predecessor of yours was quite happy to wage an illegal war on Iraq, so that's a bit of a precedent, and North Korea is further away than Iraq. Anyway, if you don't die, please let me know.

That night, or it might have been a couple of nights later, the Prime Minister had a vivid dream. Until then, drifting in and out of consciousness, his dreams had been fleeting; transient dreams that might have been memories of long ago, or of things yet to happen, or of things that hadn't yet happened and which would never happen. Normally, the PM was a good sleeper but, deprived of his girlfriend, red wine and decent food, his sleep was fitful, his brow slick with sweat. He was more than aware of how ill he was, and that he could therefore die, and tried hard to rouse himself to his full height, straighten his tin hat, and prepare to climb over the top and charge into machine gun fire.

He also wasn't used to not being in control. In his normal life, away from hospitals and doctors, he was the master of his own destiny and, being Prime Minister, the master of quite a lot of other people's destinies, some of whom he hadn't yet met, despite shaking lots of hands. He was used to making decisions, and having those decisions acted upon; he was used to being able to stand up and swing his legs over the side of the bed, rather than be confined within swaddling bedclothes with two nurses looking down at him. One of the nurses, who the Prime Minister remembered was Spanish, had a syringe in one hand.

"This won't hurt a bit," he said and stuck it in the PM's arm.

"Actually, that did hurt a bit," said the PM, wondering why medical people always said that something wasn't going to hurt, when they knew perfectly well that it was going to hurt rather a lot. "What was it?"

"Bleach," said Luis. "It's your last chance."

The Prime Minister then saw that the other nurse, the female one who couldn't speak English, was also holding a syringe.

“What’s in that?” he asked, nodding vaguely at her very large syringe.

“Hydroxychloquine,” she replied. “It’s your last chance.”

“What did she say?” he asked the other nurse.

“Hydroxychloquine,” said Luis, back in his nurse persona, and who couldn’t in any case think of anything to rhyme with hydroxychloquine. “She also said that it’s your last chance.”

“I thought you said that bleach was my last chance.”

Luis shrugged. “That’s the NHS for you, Prime Minister. One minute you get one chance, the next minute the American President recommends something else.”

One of his last chances did seem to work because, early the next morning, he woke to find that he had climbed out of bed and was walking towards a bright light. It didn’t feel threatening and he wasn’t scared. It just seemed to want him to walk towards it; to be embraced by its warmth. His bare feet felt warm against the lino floor and he walked slowly, while finding that new strength was filling his body. His arms felt less weak; his legs were working; his lungs were filled with air and he sucked new breath in eagerly, tasting the sweet aromas of a hospital and London SE1 7EH. The bright light had grown close; he could almost touch its luminescence.

“What are you doing out of bed?” asked Luis.

“Just switching the bathroom light off,” replied the PM.

The peak

On 12th April, a UK survey by the Royal College of Surgeons of England found that 'a third of surgeons and trainees say they do not believe they have an adequate supply of PPE in their trust, enabling them to do their jobs safely.' Three days later, the former Chief Scientific Advisor, told LBC Radio: 'It seems like we were unprepared and we didn't take action. We didn't manage this until too late and every day's delay has resulted in further deaths.' Of NHS staff who downloaded the Doctors' Association UK app to track the availability of PPE in the NHS, 38% reported no eye protection, and only 52% reported having a gown for high-risk procedures.

"Derek, I have prevailed."

"I am, of course, delighted, Prime Minister. As will be most of the country, I am almost certain."

"Touch and go, Dee. Touch and go. At one point, I didn't think I would make it. Still, no point looking back, is there? Eyes to the fore, and backbone steeled for the challenges ahead, eh?

"I take it, sir, that you're back in your old hospital room?"

"Indeed, I am, Dee, with the same two nurses taking care of my every whim. Not that I have many whims, you understand. Just feel damnably tired."

"Understandable, Prime Minister," said Derek Goings, who had noted that the PM hadn't asked after his health, or his wife's, or his daughter's. "Best take it easy for a very long while."

"That I shall do, Dee, at least for a couple of days. The country needs a prime minister like it needs air to breathe, or stuff to eat, or other stuff to drink."

"Quite so, sir."

The PM was quiet for a few moments. "When perchance will I have the chance to avail myself of your advice in person, Dee? I've missed you," he added in a small voice.

"I am in quarantine until tomorrow, sir. After that, I will be at your beck and call." He only had a small thirty-mile journey to make, and all would be well, hopefully.

"*Splendidus*! I have sorely missed your *consilium sapiens*."

"As I have missed giving it, Prime Minister."

Derek Goings put down his mobile and contemplated one of his many computer screens. The document that was open was headed Plan D and Derek was rather proud of it, what with all the meticulous planning that had been involved. The PM's coffin lying in State in the Great Hall at Westminster, with a soldier each from the Coldstream Guards, Welsh Guards, Scots Guards and Irish Guards at every corner of the coffin with heads bowed, and representing the four corners of the Kingdom. Filing past would be socially-distanced dignitaries paying their respects, and then a horse-drawn procession to Buckingham Palace, with more red-coated soldiers from the Blues and Royals as mounted escort. Then, a moment's silence, broken only by a clip or a clop from a horse then, as the last notes of the Last Post faded away, played mournfully from the roof of the palace by an equerry in fancy tailcoat, the Queen would drop lilies and poppies from the palace balcony, a tear discernible in her eye. Then back to Westminster Abbey for a funeral ceremony conducted by the Archbishop of Canterbury, in the presence of the PM's girlfriend and his immediate family, but excluding his ex-wives and numerous children, to comply with new government regulations on the conduct of funerals. (Even Derek Goings was uncertain how many children the Prime Minister had, and suspected that the PM had no idea either). The Abbey ceremony, the last bit of the formal jigsaw, had been of most concern to the PM's advisor, as he didn't think that *Abide With Me* sung by about six people in a very large church would sound very good.

Derek Goings placed a finger on the 'delete' button then reconsidered. Everybody had to die someday and who knew when Plan D might have to be resurrected.

No sooner had the Prime Minister finished speaking to his chief advisor when a very chubby woman came into his room carrying flowers and a box of chocolates. As she came in, the PM could still see the shape of a very large police officer standing outside and still carrying an equally-large gun.

"Winston, you look terrible!" Caroline, or Claire, kissed him on the cheek.

"I could say the same about you," he grumbled back, although this wouldn't have been true. For someone of rare intelligence, except for her penchant for overweight prime ministers, the PM's girlfriend looked quite normal.

"How do you feel?" she asked solicitously, signalling to a passing nurse to take the flowers, find a crystal vase in which to display them, and to preferably only use spring water. Luis took the flowers, left the room, and deposited them in a nearby bin.

"Probably just as bad as I look," he admitted. "Washed out, tired and not hungry in the slightest."

"Then you must eat, Winston! To regain your strength! To fortify you for the struggles ahead!"

"That's what the doctors have told me. Doctors, I ask you! What do they know!"

"They probably know as much about medicine as you do about running a country, Winston," she said reasonably enough, but which gave the PM a small panic attack. "You also look very pale."

"Probably the bleach they injected me with," he said, which made his girlfriend smile, thinking he was making a joke. "Anyway," he then said, waving his arms around, "look at all my cards. They've been arriving by the sackful! Even the Queen sent one to me!" He indicated a card pinned in pride of place above his bed.

Caroline retrieved it. GET WELL SOON, it read, AT LEAST IT'S NOT CHLAMYDIA. Inside it was signed Liz and Phil.

"I am, of course, profoundly grateful to Her Majesty," said the PM, "and the fellow she's married to."

"Winston, this is from our neighbours."

The PM subsided on his pillows. "Not the Queen?"

"No, Winston. Phil and Liz Dobson from next door."

"Damn cheek! I'd have sent her a card."

The Prime Minister emerged into the full glare of public scrutiny a day later, looking a little gaunt, and still without a card from the monarch. His first act on returning to Downing Street was to record a five-minute video, which was broadcast to the nation: "I have today left hospital after a week in which the NHS has saved my life, no question."

He also named and thanked nurses who had cared for him, including Jenny from New Zealand and Luis from Portugal, who the PM said had stood by his bedside for 48 hours "when things could have gone either way." He chose not to mention the episode with the syringes, although he did say that "the reason in the end my body did start to get enough oxygen was because for every second of the night they were watching and they were thinking and they were caring and making the interventions I needed."

The Prime Minister watched himself on the TV news and felt a small sense of purpose; he had walked towards the light and been gifted a new life. He had stepped back from death's door with the humility to thank Luis and Jenny.

"Winston!" screeched his chubby girlfriend. "We're going to Chequers! Right this minute!"

"Technically it's a second residence, and therefore…"

"You've been smoking cigars, Winston! The smell upstairs is terrible! Christ, and you don't even smoke!"

"*Temporibus numis…*"

"I don't care how desperate the times were! I'm not having my unborn child breathe your stale smoke."

The country, or most of it, rightly rejoiced that the PM was restored to good health, quite luckily, because an infusion of bleach could have made things a lot worse although, by the previous evening, the death toll in British hospitals from Covid-19 stood at 10,612, an increase of 737 over the day before. Not everyone was rejoicing.

While not exactly jumping for joy himself, the Permanent Secretary did look genuinely pleased to have the Health

Secretary back behind his desk, and looking as healthy as the day he left. Kevin Kock had risen at dawn, finally able to dress in a suit and tie and drink several large mugs of coffee before his wife got out of bed and long before his limousine arrived. In a sign that things were getting back to a kind of normal, the Skoda had been replaced with a gleaming Jaguar. He was therefore able to arrive in his office before virtually anyone else in the ministry, and make sure that his office was thoroughly disinfected, with every surface sanitised and sanitised again. He could, of course, have made it back to his desk sooner, except that his wife insisted that he remain in strict quarantine for a day or two longer 'just to be on the safe side' – although she really wanted a few more days without his company and to be able to watch whatever TV programme she chose.

It had therefore been a rather happy morning for the politician: from choosing his most fetching tie, to making two slices of toast and marmalade, to being whisked in style to his office in a car fitting his political stature.

"I must say that you have been through your ordeal rather well," said Sir Roger, now sitting in his normal place at the Minister's desk. "Better, certainly, than our dear Prime Minister who looked a little bedraggled on the TV last night."

"Well, he had been rather ill," replied the Health Secretary, who mercifully hadn't displayed any adverse symptoms during his incarceration, except hunger and boredom, and neither were recognised signs of coronavirus. "Much more ill than I was. That's the strange thing about this illness, Sir Roger. Some people hardly feel a thing, others die. I was, I suppose, somewhere in the middle."

"If I may say so, a very good place to be," replied the Permanent Secretary, who had spent his entire career somewhere in the middle.

"However, Sir Roger, enough small talk! What do you have for me today?"

Sir Roger opened his notebook and even Kevin Kock could see that he was looking at a blank page. "Well, we have been rather busy, sir."

"I would have expected nothing less!"

"I myself have been at my desk well after five o'clock on a number of occasions." This devotion to work was somewhat uncommon in the civil service, and the Health Secretary raised his eyebrows. "We have been doing our utmost to ensure that government commitments are met, and that hasn't been an easy task what with all the commitments the government has foisted on us." Like the Health Secretary, Sir Roger also secretly wondered why other ministries couldn't be drafted in to share the load. For example, the culture ministry, with all culture in lockdown, simply twiddled its thumbs all day.

"But has your hard work achieved results, Sir Roger?"

"Absolutely, Minister. First and foremost, we are well on our way to achieve the target of testing 100,000 people per day by the end of this month, probably."

"Probably?"

"Almost certainly, probably, Minister. But whether we reach that target or not, we do have contingency plans to cover any shortfall with meaningful and verifiable data."

"I see," said the minister, then shook his head. "Actually, I don't see."

"It's really quite simple, sir. There are different testing regimes, with different testing methodologies, so that metadata coming from one source may not be entirely compatible with information from other data streams, and cannot therefore be easily reconciled to generate one fully-integrated dataset."

"Do you have an English version, Sir Roger?"

His Permanent Secretary sighed, almost audibly, wondering as he often did at the inability of the political class to understand the administrative class. "Put very simply, Minister, one testing programme requires those who may be displaying symptoms, or who are asymptomatic but looking after someone who is deemed to be vulnerable under the guidelines or who may indeed, but not necessarily, be displaying symptoms, to have their test undertaken at a designated facility, a large number of which are being set up across the length and breadth of the country. The other programme just involves people giving themselves a swab at home and sending it back to us." The Permanent Secretary pursed his lips, clearly rather horrified by the simplicity of home testing. "You see, Minister, different testing methodologies and different sets of metadata, all of which will conclusively prove that we have met our 100,000-testing target."

"You're certain about this?" the Health Secretary asked, knowing the importance that was being placed on getting ahead of the virus, as he'd read in a memo from Derek Goings only a few days before.

"As certain as I can probably be," said Sir Roger, smiling his civil service smile, and knowing that blame would never fall on his head, particularly since he had worked beyond five o'clock on several occasions. That's why it was good to have the Health Secretary back at his desk, of course, so that any blame would inevitably fall where it was supposed to.

"The other bit of good news, Minister, is that we have been developing and testing an app to track and trace the spread of the virus within individual communities. This will, as you will appreciate, give us much better data at a micro level. It could, for example, allow the government to ease lockdown regionally rather than nationally and get the economy, or what's left of it, up and running."

The Health Secretary had no idea what an app was or what it was short for. "An apple, Sir Roger?"

"An *application*, Minister. It's something you download onto your smartphone. You then provide some basic health information on a daily basis. Very simple, and a highly-effective tool to enable statisticians to chart how the virus is moving between communities and within communities. The implications for easing lockdown are enormous."

"You said we were testing this app thing?"

"We chose to undertake a small and very secret test, Minister, as a proof-of-concept trial to assess its reliability, determine if there were issues of privacy involved and ensure that it was as user-friendly as possible. You will appreciate that it has to be made simple to ensure that a high percentage of the population actually downloads the app and enters their data, while not making it so complicated that only intelligent people can use it. We estimate that as much as 60% of the population will have to download and use it before we can generate useful and actionable data so, with that high percentage, we therefore have to attract a sizeable number of not-so-intelligent people. Of course, in so doing, the design beauty of the app is that it should subliminally discourage uptake from the elderly or very stupid people who might enter inappropriate or inaccurate information." The Permanent Secretary paused to take a sip of water, then dabbed daintily at his mouth with a handkerchief from his top pocket. "We have, of course, liaised fully with the Information Commissioner's Office on the amount of data that we collect, and have submitted a report to the House of Commons Human Rights Select Committee who will naturally be anxious about the use of locational data."

"And are we collecting, or will we collect, inappropriate data?"

"Certainly not, Minister!"

"I see, and where is this app being tested?"

The Permanent Secretary referred to his notebook, and found a page on which actual words had been written. "Erraid, Minister."

"Air raid?"

"*Erraid*, sir. It's a tidal island in the Inner Hebrides of Scotland. Lovely place, so I'm told by our research team. It may not be strictly relevant, but it features in the novel *Kidnapped* by Robert Louis Stevenson, which you may have read at some point, Minister. The hero, David Balfour, was marooned on the island for a while."

The Health Secretary couldn't remember whether he'd read the book or not. "And was the Scottish government informed about this?"

"No, Minister. We thought it best to conduct our research without the distraction of external interference."

The Health Secretary knew how badly secret tests in Scotland would go down with the government in Edinburgh. "And why was this place chosen, Sir Roger?"

"Because it's an island, Minister, and a place that has few visitors at this time of year. It is therefore a place that is absolutely self-contained and perfect for calibrating how the virus can move between people."

Kevin Kock didn't much like the idea of a virus moving between people, as if it had little legs although, he also remembered with a spasm of alarm, it might also be a living thing, and living things were capable of evolution.

"And was the test successful?"

"That would depend on your definition of successful, Minister. It was probably successful, although it didn't entirely provide us with all the empirical data we were hoping for."

"In which case, Sir Roger, could you tell me what the test results were?"

"Well, as in any scientific or statistical project we first modelled the size of the likely cohort of potential subjects within the testing area," replied Sir Roger, lapsing into gibberish. "That cohort had to include those who were able, as well as willing, to download the app, and exclude those who, for reasons of age, infirmity, laziness, stupidity, or without access to a smartphone, would be unwilling or unable to download the app."

"Cohort?"

"The island has four inhabitants, Minister."

"Four!"

"It did come as surprise to us as well, I have to say. Our projections on the likely size of the test cohort were, however, based on population size during the summer months."

"Four!"

"However, we were able to enlist the full and helpful support of the only person on the island in possession of a smartphone, a Dr Mhairi MacDonald, who is the island's postmistress, shopkeeper, special constable, landlord and GP."

"Four!"

"Well, one, if you include Dr MacDonald, but who was extremely generous with her time although, as she did admit, she does rather have a lot of spare time."

"Four!"

"You see, Minister, one of the sophistications we built into the app is that Dr MacDonald has a daughter in Madrid and likes to play poker."

The Health Secretary felt, as he quite often felt, that the briefing from his Permanent Secretary was now coming from a parallel universe. "Perhaps you could enlighten me, Sir Roger."

"Well, sir, one of our first duties as public servants is to ensure that we make best use of the taxpayer's money, or whoever is still employed to pay tax. We therefore decided that cost-efficiencies could best be achieved by forming partnerships between the public and private sectors. Our app doesn't just therefore appeal to its users' altruistic instincts, it appeals to their instinct for a bargain, giving them discounts on Ryanair flights and free spins on BetYourLife."

Sir Roger sat back with a triumphant beam on his face, having worked quite late on several recent occasions. "Lateral thinking, Minister, wouldn't you agree?"

"Lateral, certainly," replied the Health Minister, not entirely sure whether Sir Roger's plan contained an element of genius or was barking mad.

"So, on the basis of a limited trial that was both completely successful and only slightly disappointing I am recommending that we undertake a full-scale trial, now that we can possibly, or indeed probably, be fully or mostly confident of the app's success."

"Another island, I suppose."

"The Isle of Wight, Minister."

On 16th April, Dr Rachel Clarke, a doctor specialising in palliative medicine, said that the government responded to the threat to care homes 'absolutely woefully inadequately, I'm afraid,' on the BBC's Question Time. 'The point at which the Government decided to change its testing policy [on 12 March] so that every possible case was being tested, to one in which only cases in hospitals were being tested was the point at which residents of care homes and people receiving care in their own homes were thrown under a bus. They were being abandoned.'

Derek Goings, having driven south from Durham the day before, now drove north-west to Chequers, the 16th century country residence of British prime ministers since the early 20th century when it was gifted to the nation under the Chequers Estate Act 1917. A stained-glass window in its long gallery, commissioned by the house's last private owners, says that 'this house of peace and ancient memories' was given to England as thanks 'for her deliverance in the great war of 1914-1918 as a place of rest and recreation for her Prime Ministers for ever.' Derek Goings could have recited those facts, and many others, about Chequers, its grounds, and surrounding villages, as well as the number plates of the few cars he encountered on his journey. His brain, all neat files containing the important and the trivial, could be opened and closed on a whim. The policeman on guard duty at the gate waved him through.

He found the Prime Minister in his pyjamas and dressing gown and sprawled over a settee in one of the house's smaller living rooms. A log fire glowed in a large fireplace. Sombre pictures of former prime ministers glared down from the walls, as if disapproving of the current prime minister's attire and allowing a dog to sit on the furniture.

The Prime Minister scratched Dilyn behind an ear. "Damned close shave, Dee. I really thought that, having charged into machine gun fire, the machine guns might have got me."

"And yet here you are, sir."

"Indeed, I am, but not quite the chap I was before all this." The PM indicated a half-eaten plate of tuna salad that lay on the coffee table in front of him. "Until last week, I couldn't stand the stuff. Now, I actually quite like salad…but don't you dare tell Claire! I'm still hopeful that my normal appetite will be restored forthwith, and I don't want to eat like a rabbit forever."

"My lips are sealed, Prime Minister."

"I will of course be taking it easy for a while. Doctor's orders, Dee, so I can't rush back to Downing Street even if I wanted to, which I do of course, but which at the same time I don't, if you get what I mean."

"Perfectly, sir."

"Raambo must therefore continue to govern in my absence, Dee. It's now his job to steer a steady course, one hand on the tiller of State, a weather-eye on the far horizons…"

"…Was there anything you particularly wanted to see me about?" asked the PM's advisor, who had already wasted enough time driving up to Chequers and would have to waste more time driving back to London, having wasted a lot of time the previous day driving from the north of England, let alone driving to look at a bluebell field to determine if he was capable of doing all that driving.

"Not particularly, Dee. It just gets a bit boring having nobody to talk to except my girlfriend, and whoever it is who cleans, and whoever it is who cooks, and whoever it is who comes in from time to time, but I don't know what that person does." The PM looked fondly at the dog which looked up and growled. "I am also coiled like a spring, Dee, to leap back to London at a moment's notice."

"I'm sure that won't be necessary, Prime Minister. I'm sure that the Foreign Secretary has everything under control."

"I wasn't actually thinking about leaping aboard the ship of State, Dee, far less placing my hands on its tiller. No, it's this blasted baby thing."

"Of course, Prime Minister, Caroline must be due any day now."

The PM swung his legs to the floor and picked up a wine glass. "Pinot Grigio, Dee! Right now, I can't even stomach a decent red!" After a hefty slurp, he put the wine glass down, to Dilyn's visible relief, and swung his feet back onto the settee. "No, it's just that I have to be there at the birth. As if I hadn't had enough to do at the conception!"

"I'm sure it will be an enriching experience, Prime Minister, and an opportunity to show some support to Caroline."

The Prime Minister was shaking his head. "She wants to call the little blighter either Sue or Bob."

"Both perfectly adequate, sir, if a trifle short. Perhaps Susan or Robert might be more appropriate. I take it that you don't like her choice of name?"

"No, I do not, Dee. Other people call their children Sue or Bob. Other people! Not, however, prime ministers! I invited you here to ask your opinion, as your opinions are invaluable to me. What might a better name for a son be?"

"You might have a daughter, Prime Minister."

"Impossible, Dee! My chubby girlfriend will be delivered of a baby boy, I simply know it."

"She's actually quite thin, Prime Minister, and only looks chubby because she's pregnant."

"Well, we'll see about that, won't we?" The Prime Minister again took a slurp from his glass, watched with careful attention by Dilyn.

"I would suggest, Prime Minister, that you consider naming your baby after the two valiant nurses whom you praised so lavishly in your address from Downing Street."

"I can't call my son Jenny."

"You could call him Luis, sir, or an Anglicised version of it, and Jennifer only if he turns out to be a she."

"I seem to remember that I had a bit of a fling with someone called Jennifer. Blonde. Rather loud. American. Always badgering me for money. She might think that I was calling the boy after her."

Derek Goings sighed. "It would, however, be a visible demonstration of your affection and admiration for the doctors and nurses who are working so hard at this difficult time."

"Jennifer or Louis," mused the Prime Minister. "I'll think about it, Dee."

Research later established that coronavirus infections in England and Wales peaked several days before the lockdown was implemented, suggesting that lockdown restrictions were not responsible for the decline in deaths and Covid-19 cases from mid-April. Modelling at the University of Bristol demonstrated that the majority of people who died at the peak of the crisis would have been infected some five days before the lockdown was introduced. This conclusion is based on data that shows that the average death from coronavirus takes about 17.8 days from the initial onset of symptoms, which appear some 5.2 days after infection – to a total of 23 days. It means that the majority of people who died at the virus' peak had become infected around the 18th-19th of March. Had the government locked down the country a week earlier than it did, on 23rd March, many of those people would still be alive.

The Health Secretary was unusually thoughtful that evening, having worked to beyond five o'clock although, when he poked his head around the door of his outer office, Sir Roger was nowhere to be seen.

He largely ate supper in silence, although his wife chatted away to their children about what they had socially-distanced been up to and how, tomorrow, she would give them a maths lesson, followed by an English lesson, followed by PE in the garden, followed by a German lesson, then followed by breakfast. The German lesson would be tricky, as his wife didn't speak German. However, her pointed remarks about how busy she was being were, he knew, really aimed at him and whether, she was thinking, his recovery from Covid-19 had been a good or bad thing. It was as if she was trying to work out which persona suited her better: that of loving wife, or grieving widow, and having to put up with the former, for now at least.

"Are you proud of what I do?" he suddenly asked his children, when they were half way through apple crumble. They both looked at him, then looked at their mother.

"We all are," she reassured him, "what with you being on the telly so much."

It was true, he thought. I am a sort of celebrity, because only celebrities appear on TV and, logically, anyone who doesn't appear on TV can't be that important. But when it came to coronavirus, had he done the right things? Had his decisions been made from good scientific advice, or by libertarian dither from the Prime Minister?

Or am I doing the right thing now? he asked himself after supper, settled in front of the TV, with his wife watching some antiques programme. The TV remote control seemed to have vanished.

He was reading a scoping document from Sir Roger, outlining the development of the track and trace programme from the Isle of Wight to the rest of the country. The basic idea behind it seemed sensible enough – to test as many people as possible, and generate much greater intelligence of the spread of the virus nationally, regionally, locally, at community and street level, and within families. That kind of intelligence would get the country ahead of the virus, perhaps so far ahead of the virus that it would give up and go away. The Health Secretary fervently hoped so because he was running low on aerosol disinfectant, and his hands were almost bleeding from the constant washing regime he subjected them to.

However, it was Sir Roger's plan to involve the private sector that seemed fraught with political difficulty, not least when the app started to be unrolled across the British mainland. It didn't much matter when it was confined to the Isle of Wight, because nobody was remotely interested about what went on there. The islanders could access their cheap Ryanair flights or free spins to their hearts' content, without anybody noticing.

No, the problem would start when it was deployed more widely although, like any good plan, the strategy was to move slowly and stealthily. At first, this would simply involve all app users to be segmented by age and sex, so that young people would be offered KFC vouchers and old people given access to affordable funeral plans. Young men would be offered money-off deals for beer; young women would be offered money-off vouchers for makeup and sanitary products, which did seem useful, if a little sexist.

However, it was the next stage of the app's development that was causing him most concern because the grand vision was to secretly tap into every phone's communications and browsing data, so that if someone, for example, started to send inappropriate texts or emails to another someone who wasn't their husband or wife, that first someone could be sent details of marriage guidance counselling in their area, or recommended divorce lawyers. Even more clever, a picture of the mistress, preferably with no clothes on, would be sent to the first person's wife.

At its most basic, the Health Secretary could agree with its aims. For example, once the app began to know you, targeted advertisements would follow. If you were interested in music, Amazon would send you the latest deals on new releases; if you were interested in fashion, Amazon would send you images of all the latest ranges; if you were a functioning sociopath, Amazon would send you the front cover and buying options for Derek Goings' autobiography, when he got round to writing it.

But it all seemed a little intrusive and, even at this early stage, rather insensitive. For example, if you lived in Scotland and were interested in gourmet eating, the app would send you haggis recipes; if you lived in Hull, the app would send you reduced railway travel to anywhere that wasn't Hull; if you were suicidal, the app would send you reduced railway travel to Hull (the Foreign Secretary couldn't quite work that one out); and if you were a bibliophile interested in fast-paced action, Amazon would recommend buying options for the new Derek Goings thriller.

At the end of April, the coiled spring that was Prime Minister did have to leap into action if, indeed, a coiled spring can leap into action. By then, the PM and his girlfriend were back in Downing Street. The windows had been left open for several days and all soft surfaces sprayed with odour-eliminating products. The prime Minister was, of course, an enormous source of encouragement to his girlfriend. ("Push, push!" shouted the midwife. "I am," said the PM, "but it won't go back in.") The only sour note was struck when the baby was born and handed to the proud mother. "What the hell's happened to his face!" she shrieked. The Irish harridan who was the PM's assistant had made a little facemask from material dotted with shamrocks, but not little enough, so that the baby looked as if it had some Medieval disease.

The baby was named Wilfred Lawrie Nicholas Johnson, in memory of grandparents and as a tribute to doctors who had looked after the PM. Jenny and Luis didn't get a mention.

The Health Secretary said that, on 30th April, 122,347 Covid-19 tests had been carried out, well above the government's target of 100,000. However, it was confirmed by Public Health England that tests sent out to people at home were counted at the point they were sent, rather than when they were actually tested. The figures instead suggested that actual processed tests stood at 81,978, although experts also pointed out that 'significant numbers' of home tests were likely to have been 'void or unsatisfactory.' In addition, some tests would have been multiple tests on the same individual.

Mail

In October 2016, a three-day training exercise called Exercise Cygnus was carried out. It involved all government departments, the NHS and local authorities and was all about how to deal with a pandemic. While the report on the exercise has never been published, it did apparently show gaping holes in the UK's emergency preparedness, resilience and response plans. One senior government source who was involved said that the findings were 'too terrifying' to be revealed. An academic who was involved in Exercise Cygnus and the Covid-19 crisis said that 'these exercises are supposed to prepare government for something like this – but it appears they were aware of the problem but didn't do much about it.'

In September 2017, a National Risk Register of Civil Emergencies was published by the Cabinet Office, and noted that 'there is a high probability of a flu pandemic occurring' with 'up to 50% of the UK population experiencing symptoms, potentially leading to between 20,000 and 750,000 fatalities and high levels of absence from work.'

In July 2018: a UK biological security strategy was published, looking at the threat posed by a possible pandemic. That strategy was not properly implemented, according to a former government chief scientific advisor, who said that a lack of resources was to blame.

Derek Goings was mildly pleased that the government's popularity was on the rise, although his pleasure in that positive poll data was tempered by the fact that, despite his efforts, it hadn't really been down to him.

Plan A (giving the Prime Minister coronavirus and isolating him in quarantine) hadn't worked. Plan B had fared a little better (putting the PM in hospital), with only a mild upswing in government support. However, it was Plan C that had moved the government's rating up several notches although, technically, Plan C hadn't really been activated. The Prime Minister, true to form, had actually become seriously ill on his own volition.

Normally, the PM's advisor was able to balance the risks and benefits inherent in every plan, calculate the chances of external events impacting on that plan, and having contingency back-ups to ensure that the final outcome would never be in doubt. Recently, however, random and chance events had badly affected all his careful scheming, and that was simply intolerable. Derek Goings would have to look again at all his risk analysis spreadsheets and all his computer-generated methodologies to ensure that future plans were not derailed by things actually happening. Like his family *actually* catching Covid-19, and necessitating a trip to Durham; like the Prime Minister *actually* going into intensive care without authorisation under Plan C; and the Prime Minister having unauthorised sex with his girlfriend and getting her pregnant. Okay, Derek Goings had not been the PM's advisor when that act occurred, but he disliked having to create spreadsheets for events and scenarios that he had not approved and planned for.

What Derek Goings therefore hated most of all was that the positive shifts in government popularity had been nothing whatsoever to do with him. The PM's incarceration in intensive care, and his girlfriend subsequently giving birth – making him only the fourth prime minister in the last 170 years to have a child while in office – had been the main factors. Amid all the death, a new life to give hope; amid the poppy fields of Covid-19 a rose had been born. Seconding Luis and Jenny from MI5 had therefore been a waste of time and government resources; spending all that time driving north and south, then north and south again, had also been a waste of time, what with his eyesight.

But there was one unresolved piece of Plan C that had to be completed before that particular computer program could be permanently closed down, and that related to the vital question of who, and who had not, sent the PM a get-well card. Normally, if the PM merely had a cold or a particularly bad hangover, the issue of get-well cards was irrelevant. But in the febrile atmosphere of Covid-19, and with the PM in intensive care, the issue had taken on a new importance. It was a daunting task, with the PM having received many thousands of get-well cards (and a few never-get-well cards).

What Derek had to determine, now sitting in his cubby-hole in Downing Street, surrounded by sacks full of mail, was which minister and MP had sent a get-well card and who had not. Those cards had to then be assessed by handwriting (had the MP or minister written it themselves or delegated it to a minion) and for authenticity of message. Derek, something of a graphologist, could immediately tell insincerity from a looped letter or too-firm full-stop, turning a message of support into something more ambiguous and therefore suspect. Derek needed to know who was an ally and who wasn't because, at some point in the near future, there would have to be a political cull, and much better if the right people were purged.

It was going to be no easy task, what with sacks of mail filling his office and spilling out along the corridor, with each envelope having to be opened and its contents examined. Most, of course, coming from the British public, could simply be thrown unread into the recycling bin. Others, from ministers, MPs, chairmen of Conservative party associations and foreign dignitaries would have to be given more than a cursory glance. Derek Goings stood up from his desk and looked down the corner, knowing that the sacks also stretched up a flight of stairs and along another corridor. He sighed, but knew that a task begun was a task sooner ended and, moreover, a task that had been foreseen under Plan A, Plan B and Plan C.

However, it was still annoying to be diverted from other tasks that could offer him personal reward, what with the Isle of Wight trial about to begin and the health ministry's strategy of offsetting public expenditure with private sector income. Derek, of course, had known all along about the Erraid trial, and its likely commercial developments. He had therefore begun his autobiography – *Derek Goings: The Early Years* – and been working on a spy thriller – *Derek Goings Saves the World* – one hand on one keyboard, and the other on another keyboard. Hacking into Amazon's ridiculously-insecure system to ensure his books received due prominence had been easy.

With another small sigh, and a small emanation of sulphur, Derek opened the first envelope and looked at the first card.

Dear Prime Minister

I wish you the best for a speedy recovery.

Kind regards

Douglas Ross MP, Parliamentary Under Secretary of State for Scotland

Derek Goings awarded this card a full five stars for both its sincerity and brevity, and made a mental note to consider Douglas Ross as a candidate for promotion.

Winston

Don't ingest bleach. I was being ironic and can't understand why people take what I say seriously. Like when I said that the leader of the northern bit of Korea was a 'little rocket man,' I didn't expect to receive a letter from Elton John's lawyer alleging breach of copyright. Or bleach of copyright, or whatever the word is.

Donald, President of the United States

Prime Minister

We intercepted a communique from the warmongering maniac who occupies the White House. Do not declare war on my heroic country or I will rain fire down on you and your countrymen.

Kindest regards and warm best wishes

Supreme Leader Kim Jong-Un, the Democratic People's Republic of Korea

Dear Prime Minister

I wish you every sincere good wish for a speedy recovery.

Kind regards

Timothy Raambo, Secretary of State for Foreign and Commonwealth Affairs

Derek's eyes narrowed a little. Not only did the wording seem a little forced, as if Raambo had written several drafts, but the words 'every' and 'sincere' were superfluous and therefore not to be trusted. Derek made another mental note, on top of a filing cabinet of other mental notes, to have a word with his contacts in the Security Service.

Dear Prime Minister

We heard with considerable concern about your illness and extend to you our very best wishes.

Elizabeth R

This, like most cards, could be chucked in the bin. Derek Goings had never heard of an Elizabeth R, and disliked anybody who couldn't be bothered spelling out their surname.

Dear Prime Minister

I live a very quiet life and don't own a TV. I didn't know we was going through an illness until I saw it on someone else's TV. I had no idea the curry takeaway was closed and have cancelled my order for chicken korma and onion pakora.

(Name indistinct)

It was going to be a long night, what with all the mailbags, writing his autobiography, a novel, a *Cookbook for National Crises* and *101 Things to do With Pasta and Toilet Roll Tubes* – as well as preparing for the next morning's Cabinet meeting.

The Prime Minister (the real one, not the other one) had also been buoyed by his increased popularity in the country: a recognition, finally, that his government had followed the science, or bits of it, and was charting a safe passage through choppy waters. This bit of news had come in a phone call from his chief advisor who also wanted to know whether the Prime Minister would be chairing the morning's Cabinet meeting, or whether he should give the job to the other prime minister.

"No, no, Dee, I shall persevere. It's my job as leader of this great country to stand on the front line, even as the machine gun bullets fly. Fortitude and stamina, that's what this country needs, and which I have in abundance."

"Yes, Prime Minister."

Silence.

"Prime Minister?"

More silence.

"Prime Minister, are you there?"

This time it was Caroline who answered. "Is that you, Derek. He's gone to sleep, I'm afraid."

Night, and Vijay Patel, the Chancellor, lay on his back in bed and stared at the ceiling, not that there was much ceiling to see as it was dark. Like many people, darkness brought on dark thoughts in him. He knew the state of the British economy, he knew how many workers were now being paid by the State, and how many would likely become unemployed. The virus might now be receding, but not the economic mess it would leave in its wake. That was the next crisis, a crisis with human repercussions; in many ways, a crisis beyond solution; a legacy that would take years to blot out, if it ever could be blotted out.

As someone of Indian descent, and who could have sorted out the chicken korma crisis, he was also acutely aware that coronavirus was disproportionally affecting ethnic minorities. People of Bangladeshi ethnicity were around twice as likely to die of Covid-19 than white people. People of Chinese, Indian, Pakistani, other Asian, Caribbean and other black ethnicities were between 10% and 50% more likely to die from it. It had led to an enquiry, of course, by Public Health England and additional funding for scientific research. The stark disparity, he knew, was being most acutely felt in hospitals with medical staff succumbing to the illness in greater numbers.

There were various factors being put forward as contributing causes, such as economic disadvantage and living in areas of high population density. But could it also be that privileged white hospital administrators were disproportionately putting black and other ethnic minority staff onto the front line? If so, what would it take to make people sit up and realise that black lives matter.

Night, and the Health Secretary was also in bed and staring up at the ceiling, and perhaps should have been thinking about the disproportionate death toll among ethnic minorities. He was, however, thinking about the Isle of Wight trial and what minor tweaks, if any, he could propose to a programme of such ambition and national importance. Despite having stared at the ceiling for quite a long time, he hadn't come up with any suggestions. It seemed to him to be a joined-up vision of what the future could offer: good health and a wealth of financial and retail bargains. He was also wondering why on earth his wife had now bought yet another carload of toilet rolls, when the kitchen cupboard was now completely filled, and that precarious stacks of the stuff had now appeared along the downstairs hallway.

Night, and Derek Goings had only completed six of twenty mailbags, but had already identified twenty-four MPs whose cards demonstrated insincerity, four of whom had provisionally been on the Queen's birthday honours list, and who were no longer on the list. It didn't much matter, he thought, as the provisional list was confidential and the four MPs whose names had been deleted wouldn't have known that their names had been on the list in the first place.

Night, and the Foreign Secretary was also lying in bed and staring at the ceiling. His period of being in charge would, he knew, come to an end by the end of the month. The real Prime Minister would then be back in charge, offering his unique blend of patriotic dither, while delegating leadership to ministers incapable of making the tough decisions the country really needed. What was required was a real prime minister, not the *actual* real prime minister, but a different *real* and *actual* prime minister. Someone like Raambo: somebody able to bring the country together, to forge a new national consensus and, from the darkness of Covid-19, articulate a new vision for the future. The current, actual Prime Minister would be swept away after the virus had done its worst - once the country had looked for someone to blame and then realised that scapegoats usually sit on top of the pile. The country would then look for someone who couldn't be blamed: someone whose role - as Foreign Secretary, for example - made him a peripheral player in the Covid-19 response, and therefore someone to be trusted or, certainly, someone less untrustworthy.

There were few obvious candidates apart from him, and none who had also served as the *real* Prime Minister's *actual* understudy. Someone, therefore, with experience, without obvious political blemishes, and male. He didn't think that the country would stomach another female prime minister so soon after the last one, so that ruled out the pretty Lovely Rasool.

His lofty ambitions needed allies, of course, a lesson he had learned from the last leadership election and in which he had stood, very successfully getting to the second round before being eliminated. Allies throughout the party and, most importantly, allies in high places. He could probably rely on most of the various makeweights in charge of other ministries, but he absolutely needed one person's support above all others.

The Chancellor, the other big beast on the Conservative benches. Together they would make a great team; one with the financial ability to get the country moving forwards again; the other, Raambo, with the ability to inspire the country to believe that it was indeed moving forwards, rather than backwards or sideways. They would be like Batman and Robin, making Britain great again.

He would therefore have to have another chat with the Chancellor, a chat less ambiguous, a cards-on-the-table chat requiring the purchase of a ludicrously-expensive bottle of 50-year old Speyside malt whisky. If that failed, he would have to kill him.

Night, and the actual Prime Minister was lying on a settee and fast asleep. Dilyn, still slightly wet from white wine spills, was also asleep, and snoring.

Lockdown rules

According to the Office for National Statistics, nearly 50,000 care home deaths were registered in the eleven weeks up to 22nd May in England and Wales — 25,000 more than would have been expected at that time of year. Two out of five care homes in England were affected while, in the north-east, it was half. However, Covid-19 may also have had a more insidious impact. A study in the southern Île-de-France region suggested that confinement alone had catastrophic consequences. In long-term care facilities with excess Covid-19 deaths, researchers found that acute respiratory distress was not the primary problem — deaths were mainly due to hypovolemic shock, or fluid loss. Confined to their rooms in lockdown, with staff absences running as high as 40% and with a consequent reduction in the usual support, residents were dying of thirst. (The Spectator)

The high number of infections in care homes can partly be explained by the fact that, until 16th April, government guidelines allowed elderly patients to be released into care homes even if they had tested positive for Covid-19, or without any test at all, a move that some MPs said 'beggars belief.'

At the end of April, the Health Secretary announced that the deaths of all people who had tested positive for Covid-19 – in care homes, the community, as well as in hospitals – would be reported in daily figures published by government.

Morning, and the Prime Minister had shaved and was wearing shirt and tie and pyjama bottoms, this being another virtual Cabinet meeting, without anyone knowing what anybody else was wearing below their waist. The Prime Minister had given this some thought, wondering which of his Cabinet would also be wearing pyjama bottoms or, indeed, anything at all. Not that he cared. He was a libertarian, someone who had held the mayoralty of London through two elections, one of the most cosmopolitan and diverse cities in the world: he was a prime minister who was proud, so he said, to judge the person rather than their clothes, including the Foreign Secretary with his rather tasteless, but undoubtedly expensive, footwear.

Slowly, the little postage stamps began to appear on his computer screen, except for a square which should have contained Mick Gore, but which was blank. The Prime Minister quickly mussed up his hair before anybody saw that it was neat and tidy.

The Prime Minister opened the meeting by declaring that the UK was "past the peak" of the Covid-19 outbreak, and that "we should now be looking to getting the country back to normal."

"Nevertheless, Prime Minister," interjected the pretty Home Secretary, "in the past week there have been over 25,000 confirmed cases of infection and nearly 5,000 deaths."

"But that's excellent news!" said the Prime Minister, while noting that her curtains were still drab and not in the least pretty. It had been explained to him by his advisor that some of the little postage stamps were having a dress-down day, because they liked working from home.

"Excellent, Prime Minister?"

"Well, not so excellent for all those who have died. But excellent for the rest of us who haven't died, Home Secretary. In that respect, I should remind you that I could have died, but didn't die, so I know what I'm talking about."

"And what are you talking about, Prime Minister?"

"That the week before saw many more deaths. We're flattening the curve, and that's important to squashing the virus and wrestling it to the ground."

"However," the Home Secretary went on, "the UK now has a death toll of more than 30,000, and we are now the worst-hit country in Europe and second only to the USA."

The PM, who hated being second to America in anything, took a few moments to respond, and had closed his eyes to avoid looking at her curtains. "Your point being?"

"Frankly, that trends from other countries suggest that it is too early to tell whether the UK is past the peak. The R number is perilously close to one, and may be above one in some regions of the country. If we unlock now, new infections could follow, and we'd be back where we started."

The Chancellor coughed and put his hand up. "Yes, yes, Vijay, I see you," said the Prime Minister. "What is it now?"

"Merely, that I agree with your analysis of beginning to unlock the economy, while we still have an economy to unlock. Economic activity is not only vital for family income, it's also vital for the tax revenues on which we all depend, including the health service," he added pointedly, looking at Kevin's postage stamp. "The fact is, Prime Minister, that while old people have been dying in unprecedented numbers, the savings we are making on State pensions is nowhere near enough to set against other government expenditures, including health," he again added pointedly.

"The decision on whether or not to unlock restrictions has been one that I have been giving a great deal of thought to," said the Prime Minister, who had opened his eyes now that he didn't have to look at the Home Secretary's curtains in full-screen mode, "although I am alert to the concern that we must do so in a measured way and, of course, if we can follow the science." The PM paused for a moment, then wrote 'alert' on a piece of paper, thinking how profound it sounded when spoken, and how profound it looked when written down. "Talking of science, when's Brian Whittle's funeral?"

"He's not dead, Prime Minister," said the Foreign Secretary. "He's back at work."

"Is he, by Jove! Good old Whittle." The poster of the tennis-playing woman had been removed, to the PM's disappointment. "How would you know?"

"I bumped into him in the street," replied Raambo, in front of a blank wall, and who had been carrying a box containing the finest bottle of centuries-old whisky ever to have graced a box when he'd chanced upon the medical advisor. Not that it was just a box, the salesman had assured him in a whisper of hushed reverence. It was a container of great value, made solely for this bottle, and crafted from silver mined from an ancient Cornish mine and then worked upon by long-dead Celtic silversmiths. On its surfaces had been inlaid rubies, the stone of Krishna (apparently), lapis lazuli, to protect the box's owner in the afterlife (apparently), emerald, given by God to King Solomon (apparently), and diamonds, to signify love, because Cupid's arrows were topped by diamonds (apparently). It was a pedigree that couldn't be ignored, no doubt containing a liquor to entice, beguile and bend the Chancellor to his will. The Foreign Secretary hadn't realised that Aldi sold such alcoholic treasures and, rather foolishly, hadn't turned the box over to see that it was stamped MADE IN CHINA.

"Well, I never. Old Whittle, alive and still with us! After all this time!" said the Prime Minister, articulating a thought that none of them had been thinking, even if they knew what it was the Prime Minister had been thinking. "Perhaps, since we're talking about health, we could hear from the Health Secretary?"

Kevin Kock had been wondering what he'd done to annoy the Chancellor, then supposed that, with the nation's money now being spent on nothing much else except health, it was an eggs-in-one-basket fiscal policy that offended him. "Well," the Health Secretary began, "we have greatly increased the manufacture and distribution of PPE to front-line staff in the health and care sectors, and are developing new methodologies to manage our surge capacity – the ability to manage sudden or unexpected increases in patient volume that would otherwise challenge or exceed the capacity of a health facility or care home. You see, there were absolutely no commonly-accepted measurements to distinguish surge capacity from normal day-to-say patient care capacity, and better defining surge capacity will offer us a more useful framework to approach PPE supplies during the current pandemic. My department has therefore been developing optimisation strategies to provide a continuum of options at periods when PPE supplies are under stress from a demand perspective, or running in short supply from a supply perspective. Those contingency strategies and capacity measures are intended to augment conventional capacity measures and are, of course, meant to be implemented sequentially until such time as PPE availability returns to normal, in terms of both supply and patient numbers, when healthcare facilities can return to the implementation of normal practices."

The Health Secretary looked up from his notes, hoping that nobody would ask him what he'd just been talking about.

“It isn’t just about health or the economy,” said the Prime Minister a little later, once everybody’s boredom threshold had been reached and long since passed, “it’s about how we build a new Britain once all this is over. That will require new thinking on what it means to be British, and what the Britain of tomorrow should look like. I would therefore like you all to submit ideas and strategies on your vision for where we go from here, recognising that we can’t simply go back and recreate the past.”

“Why not?” asked the Culture Secretary, which was a stupid thing to ask because the Chancellor was tired of adding up large numbers on his calculator, and then having to subtract even bigger sums, mostly for a health app that might not work, and an even more eye-watering sum to better define surge capacity.

“Then perhaps the Culture Secretary might give us his thoughts?” suggested Vijay Patel.

The Culture Secretary was sitting in front of a window that didn’t have any curtains. Other members of the Cabinet strained forwards to see what kind of a room he might be occupying that didn’t need curtains. The Home Secretary put on glasses and quickly surmised that the window must have blinds. “I will, of course, consult with colleagues and forward my department’s initial ideas to the Prime Minister’s office for consideration and, in due course, I’m sure that all our ideas will be shared with Cabinet colleagues.”

“Then maybe some provisional thoughts,” said the Chancellor. “After all, without any culture going on, your department’s efforts must surely have been entirely devoted to considering what the future might look like, if indeed we have a future?”

“It’s not quite that simple, Chancellor.”

“Why not?” asked the Home Secretary, who greatly disliked the Culture Secretary, although nobody knew why.

“My department has many responsibilities, Home Secretary. In fact, I feel I should remind my honourable colleague that she simply has *Home* to worry about, while my department is the Department for Digital, Culture, Media **and** Sport. That’s four things.” The Culture Secretary, who looked like a thinner and fitter version of the Prime Minister and with neater hair, sat back rather smugly.

"Two things, by my calculation," persisted the Home Secretary, once again obliging everyone to look at her beige curtains. "Culture and sport are both in lockdown, which leaves just media and digital. Or am I missing something?"

Derek Goings, who occupied a postage stamp that nobody could see, was fast asleep, having been up all night with his mailbags, deleting two more MPs from the Queen's honours list and alerting MI5 to the possibility that the Chancellor of the Exchequer might be another traitor. Mick Gore, who occupied a blank postage stamp, recognising when a Cabinet meeting was about to end, switched off his computer, peeled off the piece of black masking tape that had been covering his computer's camera, and walked naked upstairs to get dressed.

The Health Secretary wondered, as he often did, whether the Cabinet meeting had been a success, or whether his various contributions, mostly about health, had been well received or even understood. He carefully sprayed round his office, in case his Cabinet colleagues might have been harbouring virtual germs or intelligent life forms, and was back behind his desk when there was the familiar knock on his door. The Health Secretary was by then pretending to be busy, flipping through a pile of official papers, and making small grunting noises, like a small and friendly woodland creature.

He looked up. "My God, Sir Roger! You've been in a fight!"

His Permanent Secretary's cheeks were positively glowing and his eyes were black as night.

"Not a fight, Minister."

The Health Secretary then noticed that Sir Roger's lips were painted in cerise pink, which did rather fetchingly offset his dark eyes.

"I have decided that I cannot go on living secretly with a secret," he announced. "From now on, Minister, I don't care who knows my secret!"

The Prime Minister was right, of course, as he sometimes was occasionally, although rarely about anything important such as affairs of State. The British people were tired of lockdown, he had concluded, and of having to live with people that they didn't much like, mainly their husbands, wives or children. People wanted to get back to their old lives, or make new lives for themselves with new people who they weren't currently related to by marriage. What they didn't want was an endless existence of daytime TV and pot noodles. Backing up this conclusion, the newspapers were filled with pictures of young women in tight jeans out walking in parks, or in skimpy bikinis sunbathing in parks, or with their mouths suggestively around an ice lolly, and those were just the pictures that the Prime Minister had looked at. Other countries had been a little more draconian about lockdown, requiring anybody out on the streets to have a valid reason, and a form printed from their computer to validate that reason. But Britain had not gone down that route because to have done so would have been, well, *un*-British. The British people could be trusted to stay at home with people they didn't like because it was their sworn duty as British citizens to behave in a British way, which a lot of people did – except for the other lot of people who, after several weeks of living with Benny or Sandra (or whoever else they lived with) had had enough. Those other people, in a very un-British way, were now filling parks in tight-fitting jeans, cavorting in skimpy bikinis, or suggestively eating ice lollies. Lockdown, whether anybody liked it or not, was coming apart at the seams.

The good weather didn't help, because you couldn't sunbathe in the rain and a picture of a young woman wearing a plastic raincoat didn't sell many newspapers, or so the Prime Minister supposed, leafing through the *Daily Mail* for any more pictures to support his argument.

That didn't, however, excuse anybody breaking lockdown rules, as the Prime Minister had repeatedly said on TV, radio and in newspapers – which a few people might have paid attention to, except that the sun was shining, Brighton beach was only a hundred miles away, and there was bound to be a van there selling ice lollies.

"I have some bad news, Prime Minister."

Derek Goings could have told the PM about all the traitors in his midst which, given the maelstrom that was British politics that month, might have been an important issue. But, he reasoned, identifying and dealing with malcontents was his job. He understood that politics was a dirty game, with smiling assassins around every corner, but that it was his role, among many other roles, to take care of them before they took care of him and the PM. Derek Goings was well aware of the fear and loathing he generated among the denizens of Westminster and Whitehall and, although he didn't much understand it, rather relished his reputation as a fixer who got things done, whatever reputational damage he left in other people's wake. But it meant that those malcontents would be after him as much as they would be trying to chase down the PM; for the smiling assassins, the two of them were one inseparable target. Get one, get the other for free.

"Bad news, Dee?" The sun was shining and, given the choice, the PM would much rather be jogging in St James' Park, which he did occasionally, having tipped off the media, to give the impression of being fit in mind and body. The two of them were in the PM's Downing Street office, with phones ringing in other offices, murmured conversations in the corridor outside, and a baby crying from upstairs. The PM still couldn't quite remember what it was called.

"You may recall Niall Henderson, Prime Minister?"

"Can't say that I do, should I?" The PM was looking rather wistfully out the window, perhaps wondering how he could smuggle himself to Brighton and see for himself all those selfish law-breakers in skimpy bikinis.

"He's the epidemiologist whose report warned of up to 500,000 deaths if lockdown wasn't imposed. The report that you actually read, Prime Minister." It was sometimes useful to flatter the PM, as one would a small child who has read his first sentence.

"Now that you mention it, yes, of course I remember that report. He sits on that emergency committee thing, doesn't he?"

"SAGE, Prime Minister. Yes, he does. Or, factually, no he doesn't anymore." The PM's advisor, sitting on the other side of the PM's desk, waited for the PM to finish eating a chocolate biscuit before continuing. "He was seen, if you recall, as the architect of lockdown, which makes his resignation all the more ironic."

"Ironic, Dee?"

"His mistress, sir, is married to someone else."

"Wait, wait!" said the PM in a louder voice, holding up one hand. "Is this Henderson chap married?"

"Not that I am aware of, Prime Minister."

"Then if he *isn't* married, how can he have a mistress? Surely, it's only married men who have mistresses? Not, of course, that I can speak with any authority on the matter." From upstairs came a louder howl, the PM's new baby possibly learning how to laugh.

"I will look into it, sir. However, what is pertinent is that Professor Henderson has been visited by his mistress, or girlfriend, on at least two recent occasions."

"So?"

"So, Prime Minister, he has contravened lockdown regulations."

"But *she* visited him. Surely that makes *her* guilty, not him, or am I missing something? Surely, it's her who should be resigning."

"I don't believe that she has anything to resign from, Prime Minister."

"Doesn't she, by Jove! One of those, is she?" The Prime Minister nodded wisely, or what he considered was a wise nod.

Derek Goings chose to ignore the PM's last question, as he had no idea what *one of those* might be. "The fact is, sir, is that he allowed her into his house. That makes him equally guilty. At a time when we are pleading with the British people to stay at home, avoid unnecessary contact with other people and, at all times, follow social distancing guidelines, Professor Henderson chose to flout those rules and in so doing undermine the government's strategy. After all, we can't expect the British people to do as we say if we don't do those things ourselves."

"Absolutely, Dee! Couldn't agree more! We must all set a good example to the people. It's the very least we can do to ensure that important messages are heeded. All of us, Dee, including you! So, he's resigned. From what exactly?"

"The professor is a scientist at Imperial College, sir, and a member of SAGE. He has resigned from the latter. He is, I understand, a decent and honourable person and saw that it was the right thing to do. He will be making a statement to that effect, and expressing his regret over his foolish and selfish behaviour."

The Prime Minister had eaten several more chocolate biscuits, and crumbs now covered his shirtfront. He brushed them off with a sweep of one hand, then ran his hand through his hair to properly muss it up, leaving a great many biscuit crumbs attached to his head. "I'm still not sure I really comprehend all this, Dee. As I understand it, people are allowed out for certain purposes like buying essential foodstuffs or medicines or to take daily exercise."

"Yes, Prime Minister."

"But isn't sex an essential item? Well, maybe not an *item*, unless you purchase it, of course, which I appreciate might be difficult in these challenging times. However, if for some reason it hasn't been designated an essential item or, um, personal requirement, perhaps we should add it to the list of permissible things that people can do in lockdown."

The advisor sighed, wondering – as he often did – why he bothered. "Contact with members of another household is not allowed, sir. The professor lived in one house, his mistress, or girlfriend, lived in another house."

"But sex is exercise, isn't it? That's permissible under the guidelines."

"It could be defined as exercise, sir, but, under current regulations, only between people who actually share a house."

The Prime Minister was thinking, which he did sometimes. "But what if they stayed six feet apart?"

"That might make the whole thing rather pointless, Prime Minister."

"Anyway, I don't believe the poor fellow did much wrong," said the Prime Minister, his mind on skimpy jeans and bikinis. "He was just following his instinct and, in my opinion, instinct is rarely wrong, in life as in politics. Maybe give him a gong in the Queen's honours list, Dee. That is, of course, if there are any spare vacancies on the list."

As May wore on, supermarkets realised that a great many people no longer had jobs and that their advertising strategies should reflect the new dire economic reality that was affecting so many families – supermarkets such as Tesco ('Every little helps'), Lidl ('lidl on price') and Waitrose ('Who gives a shit about money'). Hair product companies also realised that women, and some men, had problems with roots and bothersome grey hair; price comparison sites endlessly broadcast cats in parachutes or meercats in suits, while terrestrial broadcasters were patently having trouble with their schedules and showing many more repeats. Patronisingly, they also started telling viewers that 'this programme was made prior to lockdown regulations' – as if viewers couldn't work that out for themselves, particularly if they were watching a black and white Charlie Chaplin film. Subscriptions to streaming services such as Disney and Sky soared, what with those endless repeats and rubbish advertisements.

But if lockdown was falling apart, largely because young people realised that they hadn't died, and because they didn't much like their parents or care for their grandparents, who were in care homes and therefore doomed to death anyway, would it fall apart any faster if lockdown regulations were eased just a little bit? It would give people hope, went the argument: it would show people that there was light at the end of the tunnel: a light that wasn't from a truck coming the other way, but a light to walk towards in hope for a better future, and not because you'd left the bathroom light on.

But, the other argument went, if you unlock lockdown too soon, you risk a second wave of the virus. Also, any easing of restrictions risks lots of people assuming that everything was now okay, and that it was permissible to do virtually anything – including going to Bournemouth or Brighton, visiting lovers in another household and having sex less than two metres apart, or being photographed by the *Daily Mail* eating an ice lolly.

It was an issue that SAGE considered carefully, although without the sage advice of their epidemiologist from Imperial College. As always, it was chaired by Brian Whittle and, as always, was so hopelessly divided that the government could have launched a pre-emptive nuclear strike against Iceland and still been following the science. As always, therefore, it was up to government to decide which bits of science to follow. It was simply the advisors' job to advise; it was up to ministers to decide.

Against a wall of conflicting opinions, it was therefore left to the PM to follow his libertarian instincts and trust the British people, or at least that portion of the British people who didn't wear bikinis or tight jeans. He announced to the nation on Sunday 10th May, from behind a desk wedged into a doorway in Number 10, that "guided by the science, our aim will be ensuring that we avoid a second peak which overwhelms the NHS. Because protecting the health and safety of the British public is, and must always be, our number one priority. This is not the time to end the lockdown. But this is the time to make careful and deliberate measures – stay alert, to control the virus, and save lives."

The next day, Monday 11th May, the government published its strategy to ease the lockdown in three stages, with a timetable that depended on successfully controlling the spread of the virus.

Step one: Do precisely what we tell you, although you might reasonably interpret that to mean anything that you want it to mean, including doing what you want, but preferably with only a few people, if you can be bothered.

Step two: Try to pay some attention to what we suggest, because it's for your own good and you don't want to get poorly. So, if you can, try to limit socialising to people that you know, and only to complete strangers if they have promised to bring beer.

Step three: Step three is irrelevant as, without adequate policing or sanctions, everybody will have been doing whatever they want anyway.

All in all, the Prime Minister felt it had been a pretty good start to the week.

Being alert

'On May 15, the UK Office for National Statistics (ONS) released provisional figures on deaths involving Covid-19 in the care sector in England and Wales. From March 2 to May 1, 2020, Covid-19 was confirmed or suspected in the deaths of 12,526 individuals living in care homes in the two nations. Worrying as these figures are, they only capture official notifications; when taking account of excess mortality, the situation appears even worse. In an average year, the care sector in England and Wales sees roughly 20,000 fewer deaths during March and April than have been recorded in 2020.

'Once Covid-19 enters a care home, it moves quickly. By the time the first patient displays symptoms, up to half the residents might already be infected. Care homes have found it difficult to obtain adequate quantities of personal protective equipment in a reasonable time, with providers tending to prioritise the National Health Service. A survey by the Alzheimer's Society found that almost half of care homes were not confident in their supply of personal protective equipment; one facility said it had started taping bags over staff members' hands, feet, and hair.' (The Lancet)

The Foreign Secretary reverentially opened the centuries-old container and extracted the centuries-old bottle, and poured generous measures into two exquisite crystal glasses, bought especially for the enjoyment of a whisky that even the gods would fight over.

The Chancellor accepted his glass and raised it to the Foreign Secretary. "Here's to staying alert."

"Indeed," replied Rambo, "although I doubt that anybody will know what it means."

"Do you?" asked the Chancellor.

"Haven't a clue."

"Exactly, because we've replaced a clear message telling people to stay home, protect the NHS, and save lives with an exhortation to simply be alert. But alert against what? How can you be alert against a virus you can't see?"

The Foreign Secretary convivially waved the whisky bottle at the Chancellor who put a hand over his glass. Rambo poured another generous measure into his own glass, wondering how he had finished his first glass so quickly. "The Prime Minister is, alas, our leader, Vijay. Ours not to reason, and all that twaddle."

"Indeed, Timothy, and which is, perhaps, the reason why you have invited me here to drink your rather inferior Japanese whisky."

"What!"

The Chancellor indicated the label: *Sanitori. Made in Japan, last week probably. Not to be confused with real whisky, which doesn't come in a cheap box.*

"Good God!"

"I thought that, as Foreign Secretary, you were treating us to a product made by one of our great allies."

"God, no, Vijay! I really thought I was buying a very old Speyside malt." Raambo slumped back in his chair and took a gulp of his pretend whisky. Despite coming from a country that couldn't be further from Scotland if it tried, it was actually rather good, so he took another gulp and refilled his glass.

"Nevertheless," persisted the Chancellor, "you must have invited me here for a reason. Not that I don't enjoy your company, Timothy, or your choice of refreshment, usually."

"It's simply that, as ministers holding two of the great offices of State, I believe it is our duty to consider the future."

"Something which, I believe, we do every day."

"Yes and no, and only up to a point. After all, our ministerial duties are to consider the future and implement policies to deal with those futures, while not being fully in control of where the future might take us, if you get my meaning."

"No."

The Foreign Secretary again refilled his glass, because Japanese whisky couldn't be very potent and therefore could be consumed in large quantities. "I'm not sure how much more ineptitude the country can face, Vijay. We are the coronavirus capital of Europe, with more deaths per capita than virtually anywhere in the world. How could that possibly have happened?

The fact is that we locked down far too late, we allowed the virus to run rampant in care homes, and we forgot to give front line staff adequate access to PPE. The reality of that sorry mess is that it's our fault. Yours, mine and the rest of government."

"But neither of us are responsible for health policy, Timothy. Yes, we have some collective responsibility for what the government does, but that doesn't make each one of us guilty."

"But it doesn't entirely absolve us from blame either," the Foreign Secretary reminded him. "I am merely suggesting that we both have reputations to protect, and doing that requires a coordinated response from us. Look, like it or not, once the pandemic passes, we will be heading towards a general election. The Opposition will demand it and the country will support them and, given our lamentable record, we will lose that election."

"Unless, I assume, we change leaders. Is that what you're getting at?"

"Yes."

"At our last meeting when, if I recall, we actually did drink Speyside malt, we agreed that the Health Secretary was doing such a bad job that he had to stay, if only to carry the blame." The Chancellor sipped daintily at his drink, then grimaced. "God, Timothy, did you really *buy* this stuff?"

"In a most reputable and specialist shop, Vijay," the Foreign Secretary lied smoothly, which his ministerial duty required him to do on a daily basis, mostly to foreign governments who knew he was lying, while composing replies that the Foreign Secretary would also know

were lies. Diplomatic relations often required a degree of falsehood to oil the wheels of international relations, and he was rather good at it. "However, at our last meeting, we also agreed that the Prime Minister would also carry the blame for standing by a Health Secretary who was so patently useless."

"Which does, of course, mean thinking about who might possibly succeed Winston Spragg as our glorious leader. You weren't, hypothetically of course, thinking about putting your own name forward?" The Chancellor raised an eyebrow.

"With your support, yes." The Foreign Secretary realised his glass was empty and filled it up again, finally deciding that the point of their meeting was being reached, and trying to remember how much his ludicrous bottle of whisky had cost. "Well, I am the most obvious candidate, obviously, having been dealing with foreign affairs during the pandemic and, obviously, only distantly involved with it."

"Collective Cabinet responsibility means that we are all responsible for the acts and omissions of government, Timothy. We may have had our doubts about how Covid-19 was being handled, but once a collective decision was made, it also became our collective decision. None of us will be immune from blame."

"I would, of course, appoint you as deputy prime minister."

"An appointment that doesn't really mean anything," the Chancellor reminded him.

The Foreign Secretary put his feet up on the desk, momentarily admired his brogues, then put his feet back on the floor. "Then what could I offer you if, hypothetically, I was to put my name forward for the leadership and if, hypothetically, you were to support my candidacy."

"I could ask the same thing of you, Timothy."

The Foreign Secretary snorted rather derisively. "You can't seriously be thinking of running for the leadership as well, can you?"

"Why not?"

"For a start, you're Indian."

The Chancellor bristled. "I may be of Indian descent, but I am also British."

"That's not the point."

"That is precisely the point! This country needs to reinvent itself as a nation of equals, Timothy. An equality that doesn't discriminate on the basis of colour, creed or sexual orientation. That needs to happen rather quickly, whether you like it or not, and all you'll be putting forward is yet more white privilege dressed up in fine words."

"Good gracious, Vijay! I really thought you were one of us! In which case I'll put you in charge of making all that happen, how does that sound?"

The Chancellor finished his glass and stood up. "Not good enough, I'm afraid. What this country needs is someone who understands what *all* the people of this country need, whatever the colour of their skin or the size, or otherwise, of their wage packets."

"You, in other words."

The Chancellor had put on his coat and was picking up his briefcase. "I cannot support your candidacy for the leadership, however hypothetical that challenge may be, because, hypothetically of course, I may also challenge for the leadership."

There was a moment of absolute silence, while the Chancellor tried to forget about the taste of appalling whisky in his mouth, and the Foreign Secretary wondered how to kill the Chancellor without anyone finding out. "You know what this means, don't you?" said the Foreign Secretary.

The Chancellor didn't but recognised a threat when he heard one. He had also recently shared a long train journey with Derek Goings, because the PM's advisor hadn't wanted to drive because of his bad eyesight. The Chancellor had asked him how he managed to get so many people to do what he wanted and, having had several little bottles of real Scottish whisky from the drinks trolley rather than Japanese rubbish, Derek Goings had told him.

"Just remember one thing, Timothy. I know your secret."

Raambo, of course, had no secrets in his closet. He was faithful to a loving wife, a good son to loving parents, and had been fair and decent with almost everyone he had come across in life. But the Chancellor's threat had been real and barbed, while cloaked in obtuse ambiguity: did he know something that he himself didn't know? If so, had he told other people? If he killed the Chancellor, would other people then come forward to tell the world about his secret, which he didn't have? It was in this mood of worried introspection, feet up on his desk, brogues gleaming in the half-light from his desk lamp, that the phone rang, and a researcher from the BBC's *Newsnight* asked if he would be like to appear on that evening's show.

Of course, Derek Goings had forbidden ministers to appear on any radio or TV programme without his express permission and never, under any circumstances, on *Newsnight*, which was stuffed full of journalists and presenters whose political leanings would make Stalin blush.

But if the kickboxing Raambo was serious about kick-starting his leadership candidacy, he had to start somewhere, and where better than standing up to the PM's advisor and making it clear that he didn't answer to non-elected, sulphur-smelling officials in dark glasses. Of course, he said to the researcher, he'd be delighted. He then poured another very large measure of Japanese whisky into his glass and knocked it back, on top of the many large measures he had already knocked back.

"But it's simply vacuous nonsense, Prime Minister."

"It offers hope, Dee."

Derek Goings was in the PM's apartment, and deathly tired. The aftermath of Covid-19 and dealing with the PM's mail bags had taken a toll. His mind, usually faster than a computer on steroids, felt dulled. The PM was in his usual spot on the settee, with Dilyn lying warily on the floor beside him. The Prime Minister was back to red wine, although a half-eaten plate of ham salad on the coffee table in front of him suggested that his girlfriend still held some sway. In the background was the noise of a baby crying happily, or unhappily. Neither of them knew the difference.

"It offers nothing of the sort, Prime Minister, and I wish you would consult me on decisions such as this. Making decisions is my job, not yours."

"But we did discuss it, Dee."

"We merely discussed *options*, sir. I didn't know that you would be telling the British people to be alert rather than to stay at home."

"It was a rather spur-of-the-moment decision, I agree, and because it was so spur-of-the-moment there wasn't an opportunity to discuss it with you."

"I am your advisor, sir, and I do therefore expect to have the opportunity to advise before decisions are made, and not have to advise you that you've made a bad decision once it's been announced."

"The British people aren't stupid, Dee," said the Prime Minister. "They need to feel that we have made progress in wresting the virus to the ground. They need to know that, while there may still be darkness all around, a sunny upland is just around the corner." The PM tried to put a Churchillian hand in his waistcoat before realising that he wasn't wearing one. "The great British people therefore need to feel that, although this might not be the end of the end, or indeed the beginning of the middle, it is the end of the beginning."

"Very well put, Prime Minister, but being alert is still nonsense. The other governments of the UK have already rejected it."

"What! But that's impossible! I'm the Prime Minister!"

"Not, alas, when it comes to health. The other governments in Cardiff, Edinburgh and Belfast have already rejected your call to stay alert. They're sticking by their advice to stay at home."

"So, what you're telling me, Dee, is that I'm *not* the British Prime Minister?" The PM looked at his plate of ham salad, perhaps also realising that he wasn't even in charge in his own kitchen.

"Not on matters that are devolved to the other home nations." Derek Goings sensed synapses going off in his head, and all firing in the wrong order. He was tired of giving advice to someone whose only triumph was to be leading the country down a path to disaster.

"So, we stay alert, while they stay at home?"

"That pretty much sums it up, sir," replied the advisor, putting a hand to his head which had begun to throb. Normally, even driving long distances, he never got headaches, "which may become a more pressing issue because you also announced that people in England can now travel widely. In Scotland, they intend to follow a more cautious approach, and won't be relaxing their travel regulations. They continue to stipulate that people in Scotland can only travel for up to five miles."

"I'm not sure I follow, Dee."

"It means, sir, that people in England are now able to visit their second homes in Devon or Cornwall, but not to visit their shooting estates in Scotland. To enforce Scottish travel restrictions, the Scottish government may have no choice but to impose border controls."

The PM narrowed his eyes, finally realising that *stay alert* might inadvertently have consequences that he hadn't considered. "They wouldn't do that, surely?"

"The government in Edinburgh stands for Scottish independence, so they may feel that your change of message plays into that ambition. On border controls, if I was advising their First Minister, it's what I would be advising them to consider." Derek Goings closed his eyes, the dull throb behind his temples becoming a sharp and stabbing pain. He was tired, more tired than he had ever felt, and synapses seemed to be firing even more randomly.

"Dee?"

Silence

"Dee?"

More silence, except for a baby crying happily, or maybe not.

"Dee, what on earth is the matter?"

Derek Goings snapped back to life, not entirely sure what he was thinking, or whether it made any sense, perhaps brought on by having to advise somebody who was impossible to advise because he made spur-of-the-moment decisions. "Of course, sir, the issue of travel between Scotland and England is unlikely to become a constitutional crisis at this stage."

"At this stage, Dee?"

"My job, Prime Minister, is to think the unthinkable."

"*Puto enim potest.*"

"Yes, sir, the impossible as well although, in the real world, if the unthinkable can be thought it can also be made to happen. The impossible can't be made to happen because it's impossible."

"Like that old chap doing laps of his garden to raise money for something-or-other?"

"Captain Tom, Prime Minister, and he did raise a lot of money for the NHS."

"Or Westeros?"

"That's from *Game of Thrones*, Prime Minister, and doesn't exist."

"Good grief! I thought it was a historical drama. The unthinkable versus the impossible, Dee. It's a tricky one, isn't it?"

"That's why you employ me, Prime Minister. I'm the one whose job is to think the unthinkable, so you don't have to. So, let's take a hypothetical scenario, shall we? An unthinkable but not impossible scenario." Derek Goings was back to speaking slowly as one would to a small child, although he might have better luck, he thought, communicating with the baby in the next room. "Let's suppose, because of England's more relaxed approach to unlocking lockdown, that there is a new spike in infection." Silence, except for the baby and the PM pouring more wine into his glass. "Then, sir, the Scottish government might well decide on border controls with England, to prevent new infections from spreading north. It would, of course, be a political decision dressed up as pragmatic good sense."

"I possibly wouldn't have a problem with that, if it was a purely temporary measure, and unless you advised me otherwise."

"No, of course not, Prime Minister, but the problem with temporary measures is that they can have long-term consequences. Unthinkable consequences, but not impossible consequences."

"You've lost me, Dee."

"Of course, I have, Prime Minister. However, it might conceivably renew calls for some parts of England to rejoin Scotland." He allowed a few moments for this to sink in, which it patently didn't, as the PM had instead found the wine bottle and was again filling up his glass. "The R number in the north of England is already perilously close to one," continued the advisor. "In some places it might even be above one. If people see that Scotland is taking a more sensible approach to driving down the R number, they might feel that being Scottish was a safer option than being English."

"But who on earth would want to be Scottish?" asked the PM. "Apart from the Scots, I suppose," he admitted grudgingly.

"The people of Berwick-upon-Tweed have already indicated in an informal referendum that they would like to be Scottish."

"Never heard of it," said the PM, nervously taking a mouthful of wine.

"It's a town near the Scottish border which, over centuries, changed hands many times," said Derek Goings, exhibiting a patience he no longer felt. He wanted to go to sleep, to shut down his brain, to regain logical control. He also wanted to tear his hair out, while recognising that he didn't actually have any hair. "The last time it changed hands was in 1482, when Richard of Gloucester retook it for England."

"Good old Richard!" exclaimed the Prime Minister, now very inebriated, and who then realised that this happened a long time ago, back before he was prime minister.

"Suppose, sir, with a rising R number, that Berwick requests a formal referendum from the Westminster government on their constitutional future?"

"We would obviously refuse their request. Berwick-on-Something is English."

"We agreed to a Scottish independence referendum," Derek Goings reminded him.

"But Scotland is quite a big place. A town isn't exactly a big place, otherwise it would be a city, and that still doesn't make it a country, unless it's called Monaco, which Berwick isn't."

"You undeniably have logic on your side, Prime Minister. But what I am advising is that, by staying alert, you risk a rise in Covid-19 infection, and then risk breaking up the United Kingdom."

"Crikey! Why didn't you advise me of this, Dee?"

"You didn't give me the chance, remember?" The PM thought this over, poked at his ham salad, then put the plate on the floor. Dilyn wolfed down the remains, and walked off to the kitchen where they both heard the dog being sick. "My strategic worry, Prime Minister, is that *staying alert* could trigger both a domestic constitutional crisis and, unthinkably but not impossibly, a global crisis. Two words that could, maybe, lead to armed conflict."

"But Berwick is hardly strategic or global, Dee. It's just a town somewhere in the north of England." He waved a hand vaguely towards the window, realised he was gesturing south, then waved his hand over his shoulder, spilling red wine over the sofa.

"The unthinkable fact is that many countries are trying to divert domestic attention from their woeful handling of the pandemic, Prime Minister."

"But not us, of course."

"Yes, we are. Every day, at every press conference, and in every media interview, your ministers continue to try and justify to the British people that we have been doing wonderfully well."

"Haven't we?"

"No, sir, our death rate is the highest in Europe."

"Well, maybe, but it's unreliable to compare death rates between countries, or so I'm told. We have, as I hardly need point out, been following the science. By doing that, I'm sure that we are, in fact, among the very best countries in the world."

"Today, Prime Minister, we saw over 350 deaths from Covid-19. That's significantly more than Greece has suffered in total."

"Well, that's just Greeks bearing gifts, isn't it?"

"And what have Virgil and the *Aeneid* got to do with anything, Prime Minister?"

"Well, it's probably just the Greeks trying to make themselves look good ahead of the holiday season. We on the other hand are transparent, and tell the British people the unvarnished truth, even when we might also try to gloss over things a little bit." The Prime Minister lapsed into silence, as did the howling baby, which had perhaps gone to sleep, quite possibly bored from eavesdropping on its father. "You were talking global consequences, Dee?"

"I'm glad you reminded me, sir. The point is, as I've said, that some countries are using perceived external threats to divert domestic public attention. China's crackdown on Hong Kong's democratic traditions is a case in point."

"China is on the other side of the world, Dee, and even I know that." The Prime Minister laughed to indicate that he'd made a joke, although nothing surprised his advisor, who didn't laugh.

"But Russia isn't on the other wide of the world, sir. It's just on the other side of Europe, to be precise," he added, in case the PM's geography was a bit hazy. "They may also use their domestic Covid-19 crisis to ferment trouble overseas."

"You've lost me once again, Dee, although your unthinkable and impossible scenarios are most diverting. From the Latin, *derivationem*, I believe."

"Quite correct, sir. My advice would be to give Berwick the opportunity to reattach itself to Scotland, and tell Scotland that, if they agree, you will grant them another independence referendum."

"Why would I do that?

"Because of the Crimean War," replied the advisor, back to speaking slowly and clearly again. "When England declared war on Russia in 1854, Queen Victoria signed the declaration using her full title of Victoria, Queen of Great Britain, Ireland, Berwick-upon-Tweed and the British Dominions beyond the sea. Berwick, Prime Minister, occupied an anomalous position in the British Isles, having been part of Scotland many times. Berwick had to therefore be specifically included in the declaration of war. However, when peace was declared, Berwick didn't get a mention."

"So, Berwick-upon-Tweed is still at war with Russia?"

"It would seem so, although there is some suggestion that a subsequent peace treaty was signed with the Russian Imperial government. However, what with their revolution and our useless filing, nobody can now lay their hands on the treaty or, indeed, discover if one actually exists."

Despite many glasses of red wine, the Prime Minister's mind was still as sharp as ever. "Could Berwick actually beat Russia?"

"Russia has over one million servicemen and women in its military. Berwick has a population of just over twelve thousand people."

"Including women?"

"Is that important, sir?

"No, but I just want to be sure of Berwick's chances."

"However, Prime Minister, *if* Berwick was to be part of Scotland again and *if* the Russians wanted to finish the Crimean War, for purely domestic reasons, they would have to declare war on Scotland and *not* England."

"The unthinkable but not the impossible. Genius, Dee! Sheer genius! However, and with regret, I must now bring this meeting to a close."

"But there are other things to discuss, Prime Minister."

"There's a party in the Downing Street garden this evening. I rather feel it's my duty to attend."

"A party!"

"Maybe only a few dozen of Downing Street's staff."

"Prime Minister, you can't be serious! It's an illegal gathering. It's against all lockdown laws!"

"Really, Dee, don't be a party-pooper. Anyway, I've already ordered wine, so can't back out now. Besides, they are all loyal officials who can be trusted never to make it public."

"It's still illegal, sir."

"But I have ordered some excellent Merlot. 2015, Dee. A good if not great vintage. Might try to get a Party donor to help with the cost. He's been very generous at helping me pay for the redecoration of this place." The Prime Minister gestured round the room, spilling more wine on the sofa.

Derek Goings retreated to his small office downstairs and put his head in his hands. His destiny had always been to run the country, but as the dark figure in the shadows, with only the lightest touch required to steer the ship of State. Except that his brain was fizzing electricity in all the wrong places, and he had to face the uncomfortable fact that the Prime Minister was beyond not only guidance, but redemption. He put his head down on his desk and fell asleep.

The TV in his office was turned down low so that, some hours later, he barely heard the theme tune to *Newsnight*, and someone announcing that the programme would be putting questions to the Foreign Secretary. But it was enough to wake him up. The Foreign Secretary had no right to speak to anybody without him knowing about it.

The Foreign Secretary had sat for a long while, feet up on his desk, but hardly noticing his footwear. Instead he was composing clever answers to the questions that he could easily anticipate from Esme Matemore, *Newsnight's* chief presenter and who was to be his interrogator on that evening's programme.

Not that the Foreign Secretary was worried by a mere media interview; he was a veteran of many media interviews, and he knew that the key was preparedness. If you were prepared, you could evade, or at least gloss over uncomfortable facts, or ignore them completely and be relatively convincing. He had therefore prepared by drinking most of the bottle of Japanese whisky, probably distilled the week before, while anticipating the questions that Esme would probably ask, and what his answers should probably be.

He didn't much worry about the Chancellor's veiled threat, because he had no secrets, or none that he could immediately bring to mind.

The Foreign Secretary was greeted in reception at the BBC by a young man with long hair and glasses, and taken upstairs to the *Newsnight* studios. He was greeted there by another young man with long hair and glasses, but who was carrying a clipboard. He was then shown into a brightly-lit room, asked to sit down, had makeup applied, then shown into another room, which he was told was the Green Room which, of course, Raambo was familiar with, where drinks and snacks had been laid out. Raambo, a veteran of the media circuit, knew that it was never sensible to drink before searching interviews, then remembered that he'd drunk the best part of a bottle of whisky, then remembered that it had been Japanese whisky and therefore unlikely to be remotely potent, so he helped himself to a large whisky because, as a veteran of the media circuit, he was used to searching interviews, although he had by then forgotten why he was on the programme or if the researcher who had phoned him had said anything about questions.

Esme Matemore, glamorous and charming, welcomed him to the main set, asking solicitously about his family, while engineers checked for sound and lighting.

"It must be so hard being a politician at times like these," said Esme conversationally, as the clock ticked down to ten-thirty, and another young man with long hair and glasses, who was neither of the young men with glasses who the Foreign Secretary had previously encountered, dabbed at his brow with a tissue to remove any reflections, "I really don't envy your job at all, what with all the responsibilities and long hours, and everything else."

"It isn't so bad," said the Foreign Secretary.

"I'm sorry?" asked Esme, and motioned to the sound engineer to check his lapel microphone.

"I said that it isn't so bad," Raambo repeated.

"Sounds like you've got a cold," said Esme. "Hardly surprising with all that hard work. You must be absolutely run down! Would you like a glass of water?" Raambo shook his head. "The purpose of the interview is to give you the opportunity to tell our viewers all about the many wonderful policies you are implementing to keep people safe and ensure that we can, as the Prime Minister so eloquently said, wrestle this virus to the ground. Does that make sense?"

Raambo nodded.

"Excellent, Timothy! 'Can I call you Timothy? Not that I would *dream* of doing so when we're on air! And thank you *so* much again for appearing on our programme! It really is *so* wonderful of you, when I know you must have *so* much else to think about!"

Raambo nodded again.

The floor manager then shouted "one minute" and other lights came on, momentarily blinding the Foreign Secretary, who realised that what meagre notes he had brought with him were lying beside a third glass of whisky in the Green Room. He was vaguely aware of a young man with long hair and glasses, who may or may not have been one of the other young men with long hair and glasses, holding up both hands with ten fingers extended, then closing one finger at a time.

As the last strains of the *Newsnight* theme faded away, Esme turned to one of the cameras. "Tonight, we have on the programme the Foreign Secretary, a senior member of a government that has so abysmally let down the British people, with an estimated 62,000 of our citizens having died needlessly, close to the total number of civilians who died in the Second World War. And that's not counting the 181 NHS staff who have so far died, more than the total of British military casualties in the Iraq War. Or the 131 care workers who have also died so far, many from overseas, and that doesn't get close to the scandal of all the black, Asian and other minority groups who this government has failed so utterly miserably, does it Foreign Secretary? Foreign Secretary?"

With an introduction like that, Raambo had taken the prudent course of removing his microphone and tottering back to Green Room.

Naughty

At the end of May, concerns were raised about the decision to give control of the NHS Track and Trace programme to a Tory MP's wife who also sat on the executive committee of the Cheltenham Festival that allowed 260,000 people to attend, which scientists and doctors later called a 'disaster' for Britain and which accelerated the spread of Covid-19 in the UK. She was elevated to the House of Lords by her university friend and former Prime Minister, David Cameron.

"Good morning, Minister."

"Good morning to you, Sir Roger," replied the Health Secretary, trying hard to keep his voice neutral. His Permanent Secretary was dressed in a knee-length green dress, a string of pearls around his neck, makeup and, rather alarmingly, a blonde wig. "You seem to be dressed rather *differently* this morning."

"Does my attire offend you, Minister?"

"No, not at all," said the Health Secretary quickly, holding up a conciliatory hand. "I'm just not sure that male civil servants wearing women's clothes is appropriate, that's all."

Sir Roger pouted and flipped open his notebook. "Information relating to dress code is contained in the Ministry of Justice conduct policy, and clearly states that civil servants should always act in a way that is professional and, I quote, 'that deserves the confidence of all those you deal with.' Moreover, Minister, the Code also states that 'we do not have a standard dress code. As a result, this guidance is meant to provide a framework only. Ask your manager what dress code is in place in your workplace.' I have therefore made a point of asking my manager, Minister, which just happens to be me, who deemed it appropriate and professional to wear a dress at work. In seeking advice from my manager, and taking his advice based on the Civil Service Code, I have therefore fulfilled my obligations to determine if a Dior green dress can be considered as appropriate clothing."

"It is rather fetching," the health Secretary conceded. "Dolce & Gabbana, if I'm not mistaken."

"I had no idea that you were an aficionado, Minister."

"I'm not, but my wife has a dress almost identical to yours."

"Then she must be a lady of exquisite taste and a source of great happiness to you," said Sir Roger, "as it is a source of great personal happiness to me to have cast off inhibition and to emerge as the person I really am."

"Quite so," replied the Health Secretary who was also rather fetchingly dressed in a grey suit and tie. "I assume you saw the *Newsnight* fiasco last night?"

"The BBC has already received over one thousand complaints about Ms. Matemore." Sir Roger coughed and looked a little uncomfortable, although it might have just been the tightness of the dress. "Most people were complaining that Ms. Matemore didn't go far enough."

"But it wasn't exactly fair and impartial comment, was it?"

"Maybe not, Minister, and I think the Foreign Secretary acted in the most appropriate manner possible by terminating the interview. It was prudent and proportionate, and a dignified and measured response to the BBC's palpable lack of objectivity and balance."

"He did trip over a camera cable and fall over a desk."

"But in a most dignified manner, Minister," said Sir Roger, neatly folding one leg over the other and straightening his tights.

"Well, perhaps," replied the minister, not sure which bit of tripping over a cable, swearing loudly (if in a rather garbled way), then staggering across the studio to fall over a desk at which were sitting other guests for the next segment of the programme, could be termed dignified. "Anyway, what do we have on today's agenda?"

"Well, Minister, the alert levels that the Prime Minister has announced are to be run by a new and absolutely independent Joint Biosecurity Centre."

"Which is good news, I assume?"

"But of course, Minister, because anything that this department announces is taken with a pinch of salt. Giving the task of determining alert levels to a wholly-independent body, and giving it a fancy name, makes it much more credible."

It took the Health Secretary a few moments to realise that his Permanent Secretary was, in fact, less than pleased that an aspect of health policy should now be outside his control. "And what news of the app that we have been so excited about? Have things gone swimmingly in the Isle of Wight?"

Sir Roger had taken a small mirror from his handbag and was checking his makeup. 'Sorry, Minister, but I just can't decide if this blusher is really *me*." He put the mirror back in his handbag which he clicked shut. "Well, things have been *going*, if that answers your question."

"Not really, Sir Roger."

The Permanent Secretary sighed loudly, and turned his eyes to the ceiling. The Health Secretary now saw that Sir Roger was wearing false eyelashes. "As you know, Minister, the app had been developed by an American software company. It uses a centralised approach, which is in contrast to a similar contract tracing app from Google and Apple but which takes a decentralised approach."

"So far so good, Sir Roger."

"Well, the app records both the make and model of each user's phone, asks users for their postcode, and then generates a unique identification number as well as a daily identification number. It then uses Bluetooth Low Energy to record the daily identification numbers of other users nearby. Apart from liaising with other government committees with responsibility for privacy, we also consulted with GCHQ's National Cyber Security Centre. We have therefore been meticulous about setting out the groundwork for an innovative app that will be the cherry on the cake of our track and trace programme."

Such flannel could only mean that the app was not going as planned. "I thought it was to be the cake?"

"No, Minister, we have another cake now in the shape of many thousands of people, armed with nothing more than a phone and a laptop, whose job it is to contact everyone who has been in contact with someone who has tested positive for Covid-19, and advise them to self-isolate."

"So, do we therefore now need a cherry, if we have a cake?"

"Minister, I am something of a *Great British Bake Off* fan, and do rustle up a pretty good scone, even if I say so myself, so

I can absolutely assure you that cakes *do* need a cherry on the top. In any case, and as you know, Ryanair was most keen for the app to go ahead as it allowed them to market to lots of people. However, they quickly realised that the Isle of Wight doesn't have an airport. On top of that, the government then introduced a 14-day quarantine period for anyone coming into the UK, meaning that nobody was going to fly Ryanair anyway."

"But what about other sponsors?"

"The likes of McDonald's and KFC were initially enthusiastic until the Chief Medical Advisor informed them that anything that promoted an unhealthy diet, fuelled obesity and therefore adding to people's risk of dying from Covid-19, would not be acceptable. The same went for Smirnoff, Budweiser and several other drinks companies, because the app couldn't distinguish between adults and children."

"Then what about BetYourLife?"

"Oh, they were absolutely fine with it, Minister. They don't care who they make bankrupt. However, the good news is that we are continuing to develop the cherry and will, at some point this side of Christmas, proudly add it to the cake." Sir Roger swished blonde hair over one shoulder, and then examined his nails, each painted bright red.

The Health Secretary remained determined to find out what was actually going on. "So, the trial continues?" he asked.

"Not so much a trial as a competition between our original app and the Google-Apple app. Our centralised app, which worked perfectly well on Erraid, was found on the Isle of Wight to not be very good at recognising Apple iPhones. We didn't have that information before, as nobody on Erraid had an iPhone."

"All four of them."

"Being strictly accurate, Minister, all one of them, because only one person on the island had a smartphone of any sort. Dr MacDonald had a Samsung, I believe. The trial on Erraid was therefore an overwhelming success."

"But a few people probably did have iPhones on the Isle of Wight?"

"Exactly, Minister! That's when we identified the problem. However, while the Google-Apple app *is* very good at recognising iPhones, it's *not* very good at differentiating between a phone in someone's pocket one metre away and in somebody else's hand three metres away. While better at safeguarding privacy, it would also generate less information for epidemiologists to play with."

"So, what you're actually telling me is that neither of them works?"

"Again, spot on! However, sometime very soon, possibly next month, and certainly no later than the end of this year, or probably no later than sometime early next year, possibly, we should have determined which one of them works a little better than the other one."

"However," said the Health Secretary, "I do know that Germany will be launching their app in the next few days. They have also made it open source, so that we could simply take their technology for free, and therefore without cost to the taxpayer. Why can't we do that?"

"Because, Minister, we want our app to be world class, and anything world class simply *must* be developed here in the UK. In any case, our rules and procedures require any technology to be fully appraised and trialled, and I don't think that Dr MacDonald would be best pleased if she felt that we had wasted her time although, frankly, she does have rather a lot of time to waste, as she herself admits. However, she did go to a lot of trouble to help us, what with keeping her phone switched on."

It was sometimes hard for the Health Secretary to understand how Britain could have become Great Britain. "Sir Roger, if memory serves me correctly, this app was supposed to be up and running this month. We're going to be crucified about this!"

"I don't think so, Minister, because nobody really believes anything that this ministry now says. It won't therefore come as a surprise to anybody that our initial deadline has turned out to be hopelessly inaccurate."

"Are you seriously telling me that this department lacks credibility?"

"Well, Minister, it's the reason why the Joint Biosecurity Centre is being run independently." The Permanent Secretary then closed his notebook, picked up his handbag, and walked to the office door, his morning conference with the Minister over, and a mail-order catalogue for satin underwear requiring his full attention.

"One more thing, Minister, if you will. From now on, it's *Lady* Roger."

In the first week of the Test and Trace programme, out of some 8,117 people who tested positive for Covid-19 in England and had their case referred, only 5,407 (67%) of these people were reached. An MP suggested that 'you sometimes simply don't feel like answering the phone or responding to much at all' when you are unwell. Meanwhile, doctors and staff reported teething problems, while the NHS said that 'key bits' of the system were not yet operational and it could not be described, despite promises, as 'world class.'

The Foreign Secretary was also at his desk, hoping against hope that nobody in his department had watched *Newsnight* the evening before or that they had switched over before he'd fallen over a perfectly large, and therefore visible, desk. Not a bit of it, with the receptionist on the main entrance, standing in front of the Visitors' desk and telling him, "Mind your step, Foreign Secretary," which other assorted receptionists and security personnel seemed to find very funny. He made a note to ask Tony Bond why they needed so many receptionists and security personnel, when nobody was able to visit the Foreign Office and ISIS had warned against all but essential travel to Europe.

There was an email from the Prime Minister, expressing deep disquiet about the possibility of war breaking out between Russia and Berwick-upon-Tweed, "although my advisor may have been over-egging the pudding a bit." The PM was keen to find out if a final treaty had ever been signed after the Crimean War, to put Berwick's warmongering ambitions on hold, and whether, if Berwick became part of Scotland, that would change the geopolitical landscape. The PM also asked, if Russia did declare war on Berwick, with Berwick then part of Scotland, would that require the intervention of UK forces, or just those from Berwick and Scotland. The PM ended by ordering the Foreign Secretary not to raise the issue with the Russian Federation's ambassador, to avoid any diplomatic or military unpleasantness, and said that the whole thing sounded, quite frankly, a little far-fetched and that he was a little worried about his chief advisor who believes "that I am as stupid as I look, while not being remotely as stupid as he thinks I am."

The Foreign Secretary simply forwarded the PM's email to his Permanent Secretary, telling him that if no treaty could be found in the archives then to raise it with the Russian Embassy, "but only if you can be bothered because it's not something of the remotest importance."

Tony Bond then phoned the Foreign Office's registry in his department's subterranean basement, where a bored-sounding junior clerk asked when the Crimean War had taken place, who it was between, who won, and when the subsequent treaty might have been signed. He said that he'd phone Tony back.

True to his word, the Permanent Secretary did receive a return phone call several hours later from the same clerk, who still sounded bored, to say that all documents relating to the Crimean War had, it would appear, been eaten by moths.

"Moths!"

"Small winged insects, Permanent Secretary. Partial to eating stuff that they shouldn't really eat, like history. You could try the departmental archive in Kew. They might have a duplicate."

Tony Bond then phoned Kew but nobody answered.

As a last resort, he phoned his counterpart in the Russian Embassy, Dmitri Popol, his embassy's First Secretary, and explained that a treaty of no importance whatsoever between their two freedom-countries had been lost and, perhaps, he could find one? Dmitri, long used to tirades from Tony Bond on Russia's continued illegal activities on British soil, and its attempts to subvert Western democracy, listened attentively and then, in an unusual spirit of cooperation, phoned the ministry of foreign affairs in Moscow.

Within minutes, he received a phone call back to say that all files relating to the Crimean War, and all subsequent treaties that may have been signed with the Imperial government, before the Imperial government had been shot, had been eaten by moths.

"Moths!"

"Specifically, First Secretary, a species of moth known in England as the small emperor moth, or *Saturnia pavonia*, and a member of the family *Saturniidae*."

"So?"

"This is a species not common in Russia, First Secretary, and might, but only might, point conclusively to Western provocation."

As of 21st May, of those tested positive for coronavirus in the UK, 36,393 had died. The real figure, including deaths outside hospitals, was considerably higher. Of much greater importance, Derek Goings received a phone call from a journalist asking him why he'd been looking at bluebells in Durham. When the reporter said that his actions didn't look good, the PM's advisor replied "Who cares about good looks? It's a question of doing the right thing."

Dmitri Popol led a hectic life as his embassy's First Secretary, although his duties were rather part-time and consisted mostly of being lectured by the Foreign Secretary and, sometimes, his Permanent Secretary on the meaning of good diplomatic relations and why couldn't they refrain from killing people on British soil? What made his life hectic was his other job as Head of Station for the *Sluzhba vneshney razvedki Rossiyskoy Federatsii,* or the Foreign Intelligence Service of the Russian Federation, or SVR RF, which used to be the KGB, before Vladimir Putin's era of peace and love had required a strategic rebranding.

He reached into a desk drawer and extracted a cigarette and lighter, lit up, and walked to his office window which, being in a basement, looked onto the embassy's bins. He stood there smoking and thinking, then ground out his cigarette on the floor. The lighter he put back in the drawer, which he locked, not that it contained much of importance or value: merely his MP-443 Grach standard-issue pistol, a packet of wine gums, several small bottles of novichok - a relatively harmless binary chemical weapon - and a half-empty bottle of vodka. Standard procedure dictated that the novichok was only to be used if he ran out of vodka.

He quickly put on his coat and, even more quickly, drove across London.

Derek Goings phoned the Prime Minister, having run out of reasons not to phone the Prime Minister. He could have walked up the stairs, but his legs felt heavy, and there were too many stairs. He explained to the PM the circumstances of his trip north, the illness of his family, and that he couldn't have spoken to the PM before because "You were gravely sick, sir, having gone over the top and been hit by a stray bullet. I may have to resign," he finished, feeling that, for every step he took towards his destiny of domestic domination, he was also taking two steps back. He may have been the master of every circumstance but events, frustratingly, kept getting in the way.

"Rubbish, Dee, you are far too important to the wheels of government for me to accept your resignation. You are a vital spanner in the works of my administration. You were merely being attentive to the needs of your family, as should all good Englishmen. Your actions do therefore reflect well on your caring nature, and your first priority to protect the safety of your girlfriend and unborn child."

"*Wife*, sir, and my daughter is two-years-old."

"Good gracious! When did that happen?"

"Two years ago."

"Did it, by Jove! And what do you now intend to do about it, Dee?"

"I will give a press conference, sir, and explain my side of the story."

"That sounds like a most sensible course of action and, if you want any advice, please don't hesitate to ask."

"I'm sure that won't be necessary, but thank you for the kind offer."

"Jolly good! By the way, I assume you didn't drive far?"

"Durham, Prime Minister."

"And where is that?"

"Nowhere near Berwick-upon-Tweed. In fact, quite near London, sir."

The Permanent Secretary tried Kew again some time later, and on this occasion the phone was answered rather efficiently.

"Da?"

"Dmitri, is that you?

"Nein, ich habe einige worten Russki in schule gelernt, aber alles forgessen. Auf wiedersehen." It was the best that Russia's finest agent could muster, while also kicking himself for unnecessarily picking up ringing phones – an unfortunate habit from his previous job working in a Moscow call centre. He had also ascertained that security at the Foreign Office's Kew archive was virtually non-existent and that the moth infestation was also rampant in west London.

Dmitri then drove back to his command centre in the basement of his embassy and lit another cigarette. Then he poured himself a shot of vodka and drank it back quickly, making a mental note to buy another bottle before he was forced to resort to the smaller bottles.

Then he picked up his red phone, the one phone on his desk that only connected with one other phone in Moscow. "I wish to speak to the Director personally," he commanded.

On the 25th May, the PM's chief advisor stepped into Downing Street's rose garden, sat down behind a rather flimsy desk, but which was the only desk that the Irish harridan could carry, and said that, yes, people were angry about his trip to Durham, but that was only because of what the media had reported, which was mostly false, including a second trip to Durham. "I thought, and I think today, the rules including those regarding small children in extreme circumstances allowed me to exercise my judgment about the situation I found myself in," he said, in a lengthy and apologetic statement which didn't actually include the word sorry. "Any questions?"

Lauren Hindenburg: BBC virus editor: "Do you consider that you acted in any way improperly?"

Derek Goings: "No."

Lauren Hindenburg, again: "Okay, well that's all right then."

But it wasn't all right, not really. The government put out a statement, of course, drafted by Derek Goings possibly, that said that "owing to his wife being infected with suspected coronavirus and the high likelihood that he would himself become unwell, it was essential for [him] to ensure his young child could be properly cared for."

It was slightly more not right the next day when a government minister resigned over Derek Goings' lockdown trip to Durham, and the government's support of him. However, as few people, including the Prime Minister, had heard of Douglas Ross, the Parliamentary Under Secretary of State for Scotland, this didn't really matter.

What did matter was the public's reaction, the same public that Derek Goings was trying so hard to convince that the government was doing such a wonderful job on its behalf. In the aftermath of his unapologetic apology, and the government saying how much it still loved him, the Prime Minister's net approval rating, which had been a healthy 19% on the previous Friday, fell to minus 1%.

Of much less importance, in a city in Minnesota, which most people couldn't point to on a map, including many Americans, a white police officer thought it would be a good idea to kneel for several minutes on a black suspect's neck.

Secrets and lies

On 6th June, nearly thirty scientists called for a public inquiry because, despite strenuous efforts by health professionals and scientists inside and outside government, the UK had experienced one of the highest death rates from Covid-19 in the world, with the poor and certain minority ethnic groups affected especially badly.

'If, as seems probable, there is a second wave this winter, many more will die unless we find quick, practical solutions to some of the structural problems that have made implementing an effective response so difficult. These include the fragmentation, in England, of the NHS, public health and social care; the failure of those in Westminster to engage with local government and devolved nations; the channels by which scientific evidence feeds into policy; and an inability to plan for necessary goods and services, and procure them. We call on all political parties to commit to a rapid, transparent, expert inquiry to address these issues. This must avoid diverting the efforts of those responding to the crisis or apportioning blame, but should propose feasible ways to overcome the obstacles faced by those on the frontline of the response and help them to save lives.'

Derek Goings was right, as he generally was about almost everything. Russia did have a Covid-19 problem but, not being British, thought that a good strategic response would be to cause mischief. Rather like a toddler with a gun, Russia had been shooting in all directions, hoping that some of its destabilising activities would work. Russian paranoid thinking has always believed that a destabilised West would be a lesser threat, while Russian pragmatic thinking understood that cyber mischief was less of a risk than actual mischief, like poisoning people with stuff from small bottles. It was a strategy that Russia was quite good at, from meddling in the US presidential election to the Brexit debate in the UK. But the trouble with being quite good at cyber mischief was that Western intelligence agencies had also become quite good at detecting what they were up to. Official statements that Russia was entirely innocent of wrongdoing were less credible when all that fake news also carried a whiff of vodka.

Covid-19 had all started so promisingly with, on 25th March, Russia declaring a 'national paid holiday' – as if the risk of death was also an opportunity for a few days on the Black Sea. But Russia also closed non-essential shops, had closed its land border with China at the end of January, started to screen incoming passengers (which the UK hadn't seen as important) and stopped all incoming air traffic (which the UK belatedly decided might be a good idea). The mantra in Russia, as in the UK, was that everything was just fine and dandy; the country's hospitals had more than enough protective equipment and, basically, nobody should worry because Vladimir Putin is your president and, just like that rather smelly advisor to the British prime minister, is incapable of being wrong about anything.

Coronavirus wasn't listening, if indeed it had by then developed ears. By mid-May, Russia was second only to the USA in numbers of infections – close to 300,000, although official figures, as with China, were probably something of an under-estimate. For example, the Mayor of Moscow said that he believed some 250,000 Muscovites were already infected, with numbers rising rapidly. Underlining the disconnect between official figures and reality, Russia had only recorded some 2,700 deaths by then, an absurdly low figure and only partly explained by a lack of testing. After all, you can't be said to have died from Covid-19 if you haven't been tested for it. (This thinking was also tragically apparent in the UK, with the numbers for 'excess deaths' far outstripping the numbers officially recorded for Covid-19).

It was a spring that had promised great things for Russia and its ever-popular president. It had embarked on an oil price war with Saudi Arabia and was busy planning a spectacular event to mark the 75th anniversary of the end of the Second World War. It was hoped that dignitaries and world leaders would be in Moscow for it, even the US president, all standing together on the viewing platform on top of Lenin's mausoleum, and sending a clear message to the international community that the war hadn't just been won by John Wayne and a few other American servicemen. The day would end in traditional Russian fashion with feasts, toasts, more toasts, a little bit more feasting and, if anyone was still sober enough to see properly, a firework display to end all firework displays and consisting of more ordnance than was fired in the Second World War. Alas, Covid-19 made sure that little of that was likely to take place.

What did take place was a cyber campaign aimed at simultaneously downplaying the threat of a pandemic in Russia while, for its domestic audience, suggesting that the virus marked the end of the Western World and the whole concept of liberal democracy. One campaign even tried to pin the blame for Covid-19 on a US pharmaceutical company which had invented the virus to attack China. It was, however, a short-lived campaign as even the dimmest of Russians could see that killing many, many thousands of your own citizens to kill a few Chinese didn't make a lot of strategic sense. Another campaign attacked a planned US-led multinational military exercise, first, because it was clearly anti-Russian and, second, that the movement of large numbers of troops would inevitably spread Covid-19. All that was backed up with the usual incursions by Russian warplanes towards British and Irish airspace.

The swathe of fake news underlined Russia's long-held policy of international distancing, its belief in the death of internationalism, and its practice of self-isolation from the rest of the world community, partly because of its own political and territorial ambitions in Georgia, Ukraine and the Crimea.

It was, of course, the word *Crimea* that made Dmitri Popol's phone call to his Service's director so significant, and which then prompted lots of other individual phone calls, conference calls on Zoomski, as well as thousands of other highly classified communications. Russia had only annexed Crimea six years before to international condemnation, having not politely asked Ukraine if they could have it, and had ever since been stepping up its military presence in the Black Sea to project its power in the eastern Mediterranean, at a time when Europe and America were reducing their presence in the region, and putting more pressure on Bulgaria to reduce its NATO presence and encouraging a Turkish-Russian rapprochement to leverage greater influence over the Turkish Straits.

All those phone calls and other communications were duly noted by the UK government's communications intelligence service, GCHQ, from its listening stations in Ascension Island, Cyprus and Hull. GCHQ then collated all the radio traffic and sent an overnight report to the government's secret intelligence service. However, as the night duty officer was asleep, it wasn't forwarded to the Prime Minister until late the next morning, although the Prime Minister merely thought that increased traffic referred to the number of cars using the M25, and couldn't see why this should be of any concern to MI6.

Winston Cecil Montgomery Spragg wasn't from humble origins, and couldn't therefore easily portray himself as a man of the people, unless most British citizens lived in expensive country mansions with Swiss trust funds, which they didn't. Many actual people had to make do with a small flat in a tower block, a reality which he was only dimly aware of, having never been inside a tower block, although he did occasionally see them from the windows of his ministerial car. He was named after his father, also Winston, with Cecil and Montgomery coming from his grandparents. His childhood neighbours, also in expensive mansions so couldn't really be called *neighbours* in any literal sense, collectively owned much of the south of England, and large tracts of Scotland that were only fit for shooting things, which they did. The young Winston was educated at an expensive boys-only public school famed for the numbers of diplomats it had educated and, not being very bright, went on to Oxford to study politics and, still not very bright, into journalism where he was fired from at least two jobs and then, still not very bright, into politics. He decided early on in his political career that, if he couldn't present himself as someone who had personally shared any of the disadvantages of being British, he would at least make a virtue of something that the British did admire, because it was such a rare quality. Like George Washington, before him, Winston Spragg would never tell a lie. The inconvenient fact of his inherited wealth could therefore be glossed over with a thick coat of probity. This was his subtle sales card to his party and then, as advancement came, to the

British people. He understood that the electorate tolerated political incompetence because, from experience, they expected nothing less from government. After all, they expected nothing less in their own lives, from badly-cooked food to shelves that fell down. Incompetence was all around them, but rarely honesty.

The young Winston, his feet on the lower rungs of the political ladder, was delighted when he later discovered that George Washington never actually said that he couldn't tell a lie. That was an invention of a biographer who wanted to paint Washington as a role model for future generations. The fiction of him never telling a lie wasn't added until the book's fifth edition.

This anecdote-that-wasn't-true anecdote pleased Winston because it gave him a little bit of leeway. He would try not to tell lies but, if it was prudent to do so, he would tell lies, safe in the knowledge that the British knew that he didn't tell lies, particularly since they also quite liked his mussed-up hair and inability to speak in joined-up sentences. The British people, mostly inarticulate with bad hair, saw in Winston Spragg a person they could identify with.

The prime minister also had something else going for him. In a world where politicians had all sorts of closets whose doors needed to be nailed shut, Winston's life was surprisingly empty of secrets, damaging or otherwise. He only had several failed marriages, several children whose paternity he admitted, and several others that he was unsure about; he'd only had several dubious affairs with women who may have had ulterior motives for sleeping with him, and fathered other children whose paternity he strenuously denied. In short, Winston Spragg didn't have any secrets.

On the other side of the Atlantic, the American president had a rather different relationship with the truth, which he regarded as being exactly the same as a lie. Other people could be shamed for telling an untruth; but the president's untruths were always truths for the simple reason that he said them. Political expediency had therefore made the dividing line between truth and lie completely indistinguishable. Donald Trump, 'your president of law and order' as he called himself in June, made 192 false claims over a five-week period from 4th May to 7th June according to a CNN tracker. Sixty-one were about the Covid-19 crisis, mostly exaggerations about his approach to travel from China. However, the good news was that Trump's average of 5.5 false claims every day in that May-June period was below his usual average of 7.7 false claims per day, as measured from 8th July 2019 when CNN started its track and trace falsehood programme. It meant that, since 8th July 2019, Trump had made 2,576 false claims. It's not known how many actual truths he also mentioned or Tweeted.

The president's closets were so stuffed full of secrets that it would have been impossible to nail any of them shut. But the strange thing about American democracy was that a sizeable chunk of the electorate didn't care. After all, in a world where everyone has at least one secret, shouldn't the president be allowed several – and be permitted under the Constitution to spread a few lies and falsehoods?

But if Winston Spragg at least knew the difference between truth and falsehood, or was at least vaguely aware that there was a difference, the same couldn't be said of his government. It emerged during June that more than 1,000 people had died every day between 2nd April and 23rd April from Covid-19 in hospitals, care homes and in their private homes. That figure, over a twenty-two-day consecutive period, was greatly higher than the official total and was, according to a former government chief scientific advisor, 'an attempt to play down the adversity that the country was faced with.'

Britain's worst day was on 8th April when 1,445 people died. The Foreign Secretary, then deputising for the Prime Minister, said only that 881 people had died – meaning that the true figure was some 64% higher.

The Home Secretary, sitting prettily at her desk, had also been sent a copy of the MI6 report and had actually taken the time to read it properly. However, as it merely said that there had been unusually high levels of radio traffic between London and Moscow, it was impossible to deduce anything.

The Foreign Secretary, now relieved of his duty of misleading the British public on Covid-19 fatalities, was also sent a copy of the MI6 report and, like the Home Secretary, had actually bothered to read it. Like her, he didn't think that it much mattered, although there was also a second report from MI6, based on satellite heat-signature information, to suggest that the flagship of Russia's Northern Fleet, the Kirov-class nuclear battlecruiser *Pyotr Velikiy,* was preparing to put to sea, alongside other escort vessels. The MI6 report said that this did not constitute unusual activity, as ships were designed to put to sea from time to time. It also noted that, in March, at the start of the Covid-19 crisis, seven Russian warships had sailed close to British territorial waters in another needless provocation, and had to be shadowed by nine British ships, including four Type 23 frigates.

The Foreign Secretary didn't much worry about this as he had something else to worry about, not including his rather inept departure from the *Newsnight* studio. He hadn't, of course, worked on secondment for a human rights NGO, and nor had he been an advisor to the World Bank in the Middle East, neither of which he could have done as he was working as a sales assistant in Primark at the time. What was worrying him was something else entirely. He hadn't been captain of his university's kickboxing team. He had merely been its vice-captain, in a club of only three members, and a falsehood of such magnitude on his CV that could cost him the premiership.

But how could the Chancellor have found out?

If the American president saw truth and falsehood as being exactly the same, just spelled differently, the Prime Minister's advisor did know the difference, but was happy to use either as political expediency dictated. He arrived, as always precisely on time for his morning meeting with the Prime Minister, to find him at his desk, with his computer switched off, having read a tedious and irrelevant report from MI6 on traffic levels in and around London and decided that there were much better things to occupy his time. Instead, on his desk were spread B&Q colour charts. He was so occupied with those that he didn't immediately hear his chief advisor come in.

"Good morning, Prime Minister," said Derek Goings, noting the Prime Minister's unusual concentration and the colour charts.

"Ah, Dee," he replied, "and a good morning to you as well. Any more trips to Durham planned?"

"No, Prime Minister. All's well that ends well."

"Excellent! It's just that I saw on the news that some people think your trip may have been a little bit unnecessary. Can't think why, of course."

"It's of no consequence, sir. I have of course told the unvarnished truth about my trip to Durham."

"Of course, you have, Dee. Still, we mustn't be too careful, can we? We can't set rules for them, and have different rules for us, eh?"

"Absolutely not, Prime Minister."

Derek Goings could have mentioned a YouGov poll that said that 70% of the public thought that his actions would make it harder for the government to get across any future lockdown messaging, a finding that crossed regions, ages and political persuasions. The poll also showed that the public thought that his Durham escapades would make it more difficult for the government when the next change in messaging was made. However, he had decided that the Prime Minister did not need to know this small and irrelevant piece of information.

There followed a lengthy silence as the Prime Minister shifted colour charts about, his brow a furrow of concentration.

"I assume, sir, that you have been following the Black Lives Matter protests?" asked the advisor, now that Durham seemed to have been dealt with, and in an effort to move the Prime Minister's attention back to what he was actually paid to be attentive to.

"Yes, of course I have. If I open the window, Dee, I can *hear* them out on the Mall. What with them shouting from outside, and a crying baby shouting from inside, it quite spoiled my breakfast, such as it was," said the PM, whose not-so-chubby-anymore girlfriend was still insisting on health over volume.

"I'm sorry to hear that, sir. How is Wilfred?"

"Who?"

"Your baby son, Prime Minister."

"Oh yes, that Wilfred. In jolly good form, Dee, jolly good form, probably."

"I'm very glad to hear it, sir. However, the Black Lives Matter demonstrators must be listened to."

"I have listened to them, Dee. I can't do anything else *except* listen to them!"

Derek Goings took a deep breath. "I really meant in policy terms, Prime Minister. Listening and doing are two separate things. Racial equality is now an important issue, and one that the government can't avoid."

"Well, announce another enquiry, that usually works."

"Since the Stephen Lawrence murder, Prime Minister, there have been several enquiries, but without much being done. Instead of a new enquiry, why not just implement the findings from *those* enquiries, at enormous saving to the taxpayer, of course. This isn't going to go away by announcing yet another enquiry."

"Won't it?" The PM looked rather disappointed.

"The demonstrators want action, not words. They want to see this government take action on both the symbols of racism and the reality of it. Don't forget, they have pulled down a statue in Bristol and defaced Winston Churchill's statue in London."

"My statue, Dee! My statue!" The PM thumped a fist on the desk. "Well, not exactly *my* statue, that would be presumptuous, but the person after whom I was named. A prime minister, Dee, who stood up to Nazism and gave us the freedoms we now enjoy today."

"Not if you happen to be from a minority background, sir. I need hardly remind you," said the advisor, knowing full well that the PM needed to be reminded about everything, "that black people are several times more likely to be stopped and searched than white people, that police force is used more often against black people, and that there are enormous disparities in the justice system. That's not to mention educational attainment, and the disproportionate numbers of health workers from black and ethnic backgrounds who are dying from coronavirus."

"Well, yes, but apart from that, we've created a perfectly equal society. A nation of *aequales inter pares*! A society of equals, Dee! A nation, furthermore, that is the envy of the civilised world!"

"Not from where a great many British citizens are standing."

The Prime Minister frowned and ran a hand through his hair. "I am, of course, fully aware of this black problem. The Chancellor and Home Secretary, don't forget, are both black."

"They are of Asian descent, Prime Minister, and would hardly define themselves as black."

"Well, maybe not black. Brown, I suppose. But not white, Dee, that's the important thing to remember," said the PM, also remembering that the Home Secretary was also from the wrong sex, and trying to think why he had appointed her to the job. "However, I have been giving the issue a great deal of thought."

"You have?" Derek Goings couldn't help but sound surprised.

The Prime Minister gestured to the colour charts that littered his desk. "I have decided to repaint my plane!"

The advisor opened and closed his mouth, not being able to think of anything to say and unable to discern, not for the first time, what course of thought the prime minister was embarked upon.

"My official plane, Dee, is very boring. It's grey."

"It's an RAF plane and used for the purpose of air-to-air refuelling. It's painted camouflage grey for a reason, Prime Minister, to avoid it being shot down."

"It's still boring, particularly since we're not actually at war with anyone, are we?" The advisor shook his head. "I therefore have the perfect solution. Suppose, we paint one wing of the plane black, to show that we understand that some people in this country aren't white?" Derek Goings simply stared at him, open-mouthed. "I thought that would impress you, Dee! The power of lateral thinking in creating a new symbol for racial harmony! But my idea goes much further than that. Suppose that we paint the other wing pink in solidarity with queer people."

"I think you mean the LGBT community, Prime Minister."

"Well, maybe I do. Anyway, let me show you the fruits of my deliberations," said the PM, opened a desk drawer and took out a badly-made Airfix plastic model of a World War Two bomber. "Bought this for little what's-his-name, but then realised he's probably a bit young to be accidentally sniffing glue." The plane did indeed have one black wing and one pink wing, but with splodges of other colours down its fuselage. "We are a rainbow nation, Dee! A country of northerners and southerners, with a few Scots and others thrown in. We are a nation of white people, and some other people as well. We are the nation of Shakespeare, Bronte, John Lennon, and Einstein!"

"Einstein was German, Prime Minister."

"What! Well I never, poor fellow."

Derek Goings looked from the PM to his plastic plane. "You're not really being serious, are you? You have kind of removed its camouflage, which is the whole purpose of it being painted grey."

"On the contrary, Derek, I have given it new purpose! A new role as an ambassador of our rainbow nation! Well, what do you think? The Prime Minister sat back in his chair, ran a paint-splattered hand through his hair, giving his fringe black and pink highlights.

Instead of answering, Derek Goings retreated back to his office and, not for the first time, put his head despairingly in his hands. He had been wanting to discuss ideas for a new Britain after Covid-19. Perhaps to pledge new funding for cancer research, and make cancer a thing of the past within ten years. Or divert the international development fund into funding things that were actually useful, like helping give the world's poorest access to clean water. Things that JFK would have spoken about, or Roosevelt, to articulate a changed Britain and a changed world in which everyone could share. A bold vision to help the country recover, and give itself new pride and a new role in the world. Then he extracted a sealed and padded envelope from his desk and walked out of Downing Street to put it in a nearby post-box.

In early June, backdated data showed the real number of deaths in Britain had gone beyond the 50,000 mark, making the

UK Europe's worst-hit nation. The Prime Minister told MPs: 'I take full responsibility for everything this government has been doing in tackling coronavirus and I am very proud of our record.'

Elizabeth Ludlow was one of the few people in the country genetically unable to tell a lie, and would therefore have been useless as a UK government employee. She was, however, on top of her day job as an artisan crafter with an arts and crafts shop in Berwick-upon-Tweed, a clandestine employee of the Russian government which, under President Putin, did sometimes tell the truth, or what it purported to be the truth, and which sometimes was the truth. She had been trained over several years by Directorate S of the SVR, the fun-loving successor to the KGB, which included weapons handling, martial arts, surveillance and counter-surveillance, sending and receiving coded messages, learning perfect English and idioms commonly used in the north-east of England, and how to paint water-colour dog pictures.

This last skill was vital to her deep-cover role as Russia's sleeper agent in the north of England, although it wasn't a job that entailed doing very much. Actually, she had to admit, it had entailed nothing at all, since she first arrived in England ten years before as a tourist. Then she was given a new identity, complete with false passport, driving licence, bank account and a diploma in dog-painting from an established arts college. She had soon settled into her new life in Berwick, splitting her time between working in the craft shop, which had taken one look at her French poodle paintings and welcomed her in, and listening to Moscow Radio. She didn't much miss her old life in Siberia, largely because it was colder than England, and her new country didn't have bears. She was also happy in her own company although she positively hated dogs and having to paint them. The laptop her agency had given her had one small and insignificant piece of software installed; her link to the real reason for being in England. Over the past ten years, this small and insignificant bit of software had done nothing more than wish her happy birthday or happy Christmas.

Elizabeth was at her kitchen table, sketching out a picture of a West Highland terrier with an ice-pick in its back when, to her surprise, her laptop bleeped. She checked the calendar on the wall to make sure it wasn't her birthday or, somehow, had become Christmas without her noticing. Then, becoming excited, she shut the curtains and opened her laptop. Closing the curtains was unnecessary as she lived in a third-floor flat overlooking the sea, but it was standard SVR operating procedure.

On her screen was a long string of numbers. 4/8/13 8/16/2 89/22/10 and so on for page after page. She took down her copy of *Fifty Shades of Mucky* and began to decrypt the message. The first number signified the page number, the second number the line on the page, and the third number the letter on that line. So long as both she and her controller in Moscow were working from the same novel, it was foolproof. Problems only arose if the wrong novel was used, and that happened rarely, although sometimes with unexpected results.

She worked assiduously for quite some time, eventually decrypting the secret message from her handlers.

Hello from Moscow. Hope you are well. It's unusually warm here for the time of year. However enough unnecessary chitchat. We would like you to make a reconnaissance of the Berwick area for us for reasons that need not concern you and which are completely routine, and ascertain whether or not the town has any sea defences and if there are any military bases in the area. Warm best wishes and kind regards. Moscow Centre.

Elizabeth felt that the message could have been shortened a little, given the length of time taken to decrypt it, although she had been distracted towards the end of the message when reading that the book's hero had gone to the shops to purchase a cucumber and two carrots. She'd read on to find out what he could possibly have been planning for his girlfriend, only to discover several pages later that he was, rather disappointingly, making a carrot and cucumber salad. Decryption complete, she put on her coat, ventured outside and drove her unobtrusive Maserati slowly out of the town. (Her dog pictures were very popular). The sea defences part of the message could be easily answered as she could see from her kitchen that there were no sea defences. The military bases part of the message she was less certain about, although she had yet to encounter a soldier or sailor in the town.

She had just reached the AI heading north when she was pulled over by a police car. She stopped in a lay-by and wound down her window.

A decadent capitalist in a blue uniform and cap leaned in. "Could I ask what you're doing, Madam? You're still only allowed from your home for essential purposes."

"I am looking for military bases," she replied, unable to resist the genetic flaw of honesty that the SVR had, surprisingly, not picked up on.

"There are none," the police officer told her, seemingly unsuspicious by her reply. ISIS had, after all, banned travel to Europe. "Best go home would be my advice," which she did take and spent only a few minutes composing her reply to Moscow Centre.

None, was her message.

Her terse reply took the cypher clerk in the SVR's basement communications centre some time to decrypt, largely because he too was fascinated by the book's hero buying a cucumber and two carrots and wanting to find out what he could possibly want with them. However, unlike his agent in the north of England, he read on to the end of the chapter, and was greatly surprised by what you could get up to with half a cucumber and one carrot.

His report to the Director of Operations was marked Top Secret.

The GCHQ report that night, despatched to MI6 and onward to ministers and the chiefs of staff, reported satellite imagery from high above Severomorsk, a cultural and vibrant city on the Barents Sea, and home to Russia's Northern Fleet and, adding to its charm, a city that also boasted a bakery, sausage factory, soft drinks bottling plant and swimming pool. GCHQ reported that the nuclear heat signature from the *Pyotr Velikiy* had dimmed considerably and that the battlecruiser and its escort vessels would probably be remaining in port, at least for the time being, which, the report advised, wasn't necessarily surprising as ships not at sea can often be found in port.

Later in June, the government announced that nearly £1 million would be spent on repainting the Prime Minister's RAF Voyager aeroplane in Union flag colours, and said that it would be done to ensure 'value for money for UK taxpayers.' The Culture Secretary defended the decision, saying the government should be promoting the country's creative industries and the work on the plane is 'part of that.'

Pubs and pepper spray

Britain's excess death toll at the peak of the Covid-19 pandemic was the highest among 11 countries analysed by The Guardian. *The UK had the biggest spike among countries including Sweden, France, Germany and Spain. At its peak the UK death toll was more than double that of an average week, at 109%, compared with Spain's peak in week 14 where the death toll was double the average at 100%. By week 20 of 2020 the UK death toll - inclusive of both Covid-related and non-Covid deaths - was 21% higher than the average of recent years meaning, for every five deaths that occur in the UK in a normal year, six people had died.*

Different countries developed different strategies to deal with coronavirus which were dictated by individual circumstance. New Zealand, for example, with low rates of infection and, by extension, very low mortality levels, could realistically set a target for the elimination of the virus, which the World Health Organisation defines as four weeks without a single case, the equivalent of two incubation periods. Elimination requires effective border surveillance to ensure that no new infections are imported.

Border surveillance in New Zealand found two new cases on 13th and 15th June, both from people returning to the country from India on repatriation flights. They brought the total number of active cases in the country to nine. Shortly before, New Zealand reported its first coronavirus cases in more than three weeks after two women who travelled to the country from the UK were found to have Covid-19.

Countries like England could only look realistically to elimination if a vaccine was found. The virus was, simply, too prevalent within the population. The other UK nations were able to choose different paths based on their different levels of infection. Scotland, for example, with a lower incidence of the disease, more localised test and trace programme and stricter mitigation regulations was looking for elimination. For England to follow an elimination strategy would require an absolutely watertight lockdown for a lengthy period, with enormous social and devastating economic cost. It wasn't therefore feasible.

However, it was hoped that a contain and suppress strategy until a vaccine was found would allow the country to ease lockdown restrictions and that, if the virus did surge again, it wouldn't overwhelm the NHS.

While not ideal, it was a strategy preferable to that of Belarus whose president said in March that worries about the disease were a 'psychosis' and variously suggested drinking vodka, going to saunas and driving tractors as ways to fight the virus. It is not known how many of his countrymen followed that advice, how many died because of it, or whether President Trump considered Tweeting about it.

In Russia, contain and suppress was also the prevailing strategy, although figures on mortality were somewhat opaque. For example, in Dagestan, in the south of the country, hundreds of deaths were recorded as 'community-acquired pneumonia' – although their symptoms were identical to Covid-19. Indeed, the work of a new hospital that opened in Dagestan to great fanfare, was curtailed when 50% of medical personnel fell ill with the virus.

Over at least a seven-day period in May, over 10,000 people per day were being infected although, by June, that figure had dipped to some 7,000 infections. All in all, it was a health crisis that President Putin could do without, particularly since he was seeking a change in the Constitution to enable him to stay in power for another two terms.

All of which fed into the Russian government's sense of paranoia, and a feeling that it was, once again, under attack from a foreign enemy that, in this instance, it couldn't see. However, it only needed a small shift in official thinking to divert that paranoia onto an enemy that it could see. The Crimea was at the hub of it.

The Foreign Secretary was not at his best, beset by worries about the Chancellor's possible ambitions for the top job, and equally worried that his damaging secret could become public.

How could he have been so stupid! Being vice-captain was nearly as good as captain, he tried to tell himself, and nobody was going to dig through university records to determine that his club had only three members, would they? Yes, they would, he decided, because the Chancellor must have done so, and would now have to be dealt with, temporarily or permanently.

Tony Bond was, as always, at his best, notepad at the ready, enigmatic but eager-to-please smile in place, his tie perfectly knotted and shirt perfectly creased. "You seem out of sorts, Minister," was his opening comment, noting the Foreign Secretary's rather crinkled shirt and, as the politician had his feet up on the desk, his shabby old brogues.

"Not feeling too well, Tony," he replied, "but nothing to worry about," he added, as his permanent secretary surreptitiously moved his chair backwards. "Is there anything on the agenda for today?"

"Everything is, as is now the new normal, rather quiet, Minister. Right now, governments aren't terribly occupied by foreign relations, and aren't doing much of them."

"China?"

"No sabre rattling from China, I'm afraid. Not yet."

"America?"

Tony Bond consulted his notepad. "President Trump did say that police hadn't used tear gas on Black Lives Matter protestors outside the White House when he wanted to have his picture taken outside a church."

"And did they?"

"No, Minister, they used pepper spray."

Raambo tried to think of any other trouble spots around the globe and took his feet off the desk. His shabby shoes perfectly matched his mood. He rubbed sleep from his eyes and blinked rapidly several times, briefly considering – as he had done several times – how to remove the Chancellor from his mind, temporarily or permanently.

"There is one small thing, Minister," said his Permanent Secretary, extracting a piece of paper. "I received this message from the Russian ambassador this morning."

Raambo took the piece of paper, read it, and handed it back. The message merely asked the British government to clarify if its position had changed as regards Russia's perfectly-legitimate and lawful annexation of the Crimea in 2014, and which had been ratified by the freedom-loving peoples of the Crimea in a perfectly-legitimate and lawful referendum of all those people living in the Crimea who could speak Russian. "I'm not sure I understand, Tony. What's the Crimea got to do with anything?"

"Well, sir, I'm not entirely sure."

"Not *entirely*, Tony?"

"Well, sir, you'll recall that the Prime Minister did ask if we still had a copy of the Crimean War peace treaty. Well, we don't, because our copies have been eaten by moths. So, I asked the Russians if they had one."

"And?"

"Theirs have also been eaten by moths."

Raambo put his shabby feet back on the desk and looked sourly at his shoes. "And is this in any way important?"

"Absolutely not, Minister!" The Permanent Secretary smiled reassuringly over the desk. "However, *technically*, it may be that a state of war still exists between Russia and Berwick-upon-Tweed."

If Russia was considering using the Crimean War as a pretext for something-or-other in the north of England, the Prime Minister should perhaps have been considering the same. On 3rd June, the UK recorded more Covid-19 deaths than the 27 countries of the European Union put together, according to Our World in Data. Four days later, on 7th June, a study warned that by the end of June the death toll from Covid-19 infections and other excess deaths would likely 'approach 59,000 across the entire English population, of which about 34,000 (57%) will have been care home residents.'

The Health Secretary was also feeling a little frazzled, having read a triumphant memo from the Culture Secretary saying that he could now announce, with great excitement, that his department had been working tirelessly on a new design for the Prime Minister's plane, and having been bombarded with questions from his children over breakfast. They were, understandably, keen to get back to school or, more precisely, they were keen to get out of the house and away from being home-schooled by their mother, who was now giving them intense lessons in ironing, hoovering and dusting, but very little in the way of subjects on the school curriculum. Their mother, they complained, now spent the day watching TV, sporadically checking on their housework rotas, and making only occasional trips to the supermarket to buy more toilet rolls and pasta.

"When can we escape?" one asked over his bowl of cornflakes. "I miss school *so* much."

"Soon," replied Kevin.

"When is soon?"

"Soon is when it's safe to do so."

"Which might be never," said his son, now snivelling.

Of course, while the issue of a return to school had been uppermost in government thinking, demonstrably so because its thinking had changed several times, the British people were more concerned about when the pubs were going to reopen. This, and other decisions of national importance, were issues for the Health Secretary to have firm opinions on, based purely on the science.

"Good morning, Minister."

"Good morning, Lady Roger." The Permanent Secretary was chic in a shimmering blue dress with matching handbag, diamante earrings and bouffant pink hair. "I believe you wish to discuss the next phase of easing restrictions."

"Yes, Minister, but let me first say that I think it's *so* wonderful how well we have handled everything!" Lady Roger patted his hair. "We have been a team, you and I, and a team that continues to shine as a beacon of hope and fortitude to the rest of the world." The Health Secretary knew that this kind of waffle signalled bad news. "We can therefore safely ignore the latest National Audit Office report that says that it's not possible to estimate how many of the 25,000 people discharged from hospitals into care homes at the peak of the outbreak were infected with coronavirus."

"Can we ignore it?"

"Of course, Minister! The sun is shining, the pubs are about to open, and I absolutely dispute the contention from a former government advisor that the coronavirus outbreak had been doubling in size every three or four days before lockdown and, if lockdown had been introduced just a week earlier, the UK death toll could have been reduced to just 10,000 people."

"Can we ignore that as well?"

"Absolutely, Minister! It's from that Henderson chap who had to resign because he was visited by his girlfriend, or mistress, for, I understand, purposes of a carnal nature." Lady Roger had lowered his voice to say this, or maybe *her* voice, and had framed his (or her) mouth in a disapproving oval. "The British people don't like adulterers, sir, and take anything they say with a pinch of salt."

"Even if it's true?"

"Particularly if it's true, Minister! The British people aren't stupid, you know."

The Health Secretary couldn't quite fathom what Lady Roger was getting at, so chose not to reply to that point. "Very well, is there anything that we can't ignore?"

"Yes, Minister. You'll be aware, I assume, that the Transport Secretary has announced that face coverings will be mandatory on public transport in England from the fifteenth of this month."

"I was aware of that, yes."

"Then we must also announce something, sir, because it's simply *intolerable* that the transport ministry should be announcing health things. After all, we don't go about willy-nilly announcing rules and regulations on buses, do we?" Lady Roger stamped his/her foot. "I therefore suggest, as a matter of urgency, that we announce that medical and other staff should have to wear surgical masks at all times. I also recommend that visitors to hospitals and outpatients attending appointments should be refused entry if they're not wearing a face covering."

"Is that really necessary?"

"Necessary? Vital! I'm not happy one little bit that the transport minister has had the effrontery to announce a health something without us also announcing something."

"I thought that the science didn't support the wearing of face coverings?"

"Apparently, it does now, sir. Inconvenient, I know. Also, the World Health Organisation seems to have changed its mind as well. They now support the whole idea of face coverings."

"So, by making a new announcement on face coverings, which is completely different to other announcements we've made on face coverings, we are simply following the science."

"Precisely, Minister!"

The Health Secretary put his elbows on the desk and momentarily put his face in his hands. At that moment he could happily have walked out of his office and gone to the nearest pub, and had to remind himself that they were still closed.

On 9th June, the government had the lowest approval rating in the world over its handling of the Covid-19 pandemic, according to a YouGov poll. Just 41 per cent of Britons said the government was handling the crisis well, with 56 per cent saying it was handling it badly to give a net score of -15, down from -6 the previous week, and even lower than Americans rated Donald Trump.

The Director of the SVR was, outwardly, a rather avuncular man who epitomised the new face of modern Russia. He was cultured and well-read, understood the ways of the West, and had actually visited bits of it. He was, however, someone who presided over an agency that liked to kill people in rather imaginative ways or, as in Salisbury, also kill and injure the wrong people with even more imagination. Not that the UK or any other Western country seemed to mind. After a little huffing and puffing, there were never any consequences. He had known Vladimir Putin when they were both young officers in the KGB's spy academy, chasing each other naked down corridors with wet towels, a fact that probably now explained his lofty position.

In the new Russia, governed by a government that was the best government in the history of governments, nothing was allowed to go wrong. When it did, it was always the fault of someone else, and that was the opportunity and danger he now had to balance. Yes, annexing the Crimea had been a little hasty, but it was a done deal. The Crimea was now part of Russia, and everyone was delighted, particularly Russian-speaking citizens of the Crimea. The West had, of course, failed to lift a finger, contenting itself with faint mutterings of outrage. But was there now another more secret agenda? Why had London asked Moscow if a Crimean War treaty still existed? Was it their way of reminding Russia that it was still at war with an insignificant town that he'd never heard of? Was it a veiled threat? A threat from a government that had failed to tackle Covid-19 and might now seek to divert public attention to something more military? He looked again at the Top Secret report on his desk:

Berwick-upon-Tweed is a town in the county of Northumberland. It is the northernmost town in England, at the mouth of the River Tweed on the east coast, and four kilometres south of the Scottish border. The area was for more than 400 years central to historic border wars between the Kingdoms of England and Scotland, and several times possession of Berwick changed hands between the two kingdoms. The last time it changed hands was when Richard of Gloucester retook it for England in 1482. To this day many Berwickers feel a close affinity to Scotland. Berwick remains a traditional market town and also has some notable architectural features, in particular its medieval town walls, its Georgian Town Hall, its Elizabethan ramparts, and Britain's earliest barracks buildings.

The Director marvelled at the speed and efficiency of his agency's researchers. However, if the researcher had bothered to scroll down Wikipedia a little bit, he would have seen:

...some proclamations referred to 'England, Scotland and the town of Berwick-upon-Tweed.' One such was the declaration of the Crimean War against Russia in 1853, which Queen Victoria supposedly signed as 'Victoria, Queen of Great Britain, Ireland, Berwick-upon-Tweed and all British Dominions.' When the Treaty of Paris was signed to conclude the war, Berwick-upon-Tweed was left out. This meant that, supposedly, one of Britain's smallest towns was officially at war with one of the world's largest powers.

The BBC programme *Nationwide* investigated this story in the 1970s, and found that while Berwick was not mentioned in the Treaty of Paris, it was not mentioned in the declaration of war either. The question remained as to whether Berwick had ever been at war with Russia in the first place. The true situation is that since the Wales and Berwick Act 1746 had already made it clear that all references to England included Berwick, the town had no special status at either the start or end of the war.

But the Director didn't read that because the researcher who wrote the Top Secret report hadn't read that far because he'd been keen to get away from his desk, go to the nearest market, and buy a cucumber and two carrots. His report abruptly finished with the highly-classified and up-to-date intelligence from an asset of the Service in the area that the whole Berwick coastline was undefended.

The Director picked up his red phone, the only phone on his desk that only connected with one other red phone on another desk, and thought back fondly to the sound of wet towel on naked bottom.

Vouchers and vaccines

Public Health England releases its report into the disproportionately high number of people from ethnic minorities dying from COVID-19. The report finds that age, sex, health, geographical circumstances and ethnicity are all risk factors, with those of Bangladeshi origin experiencing a particularly high number of fatalities. Thirty medical organisations representing black, Asian and minority ethnic doctors and nurses wrote to the Health Secretary to express their concern.

In a sign that everything was absolutely fine and completely back to normal, despite dozens of people still dying every day, parts of the Health Protection (Coronavirus, Restrictions) (England) (Amendment No. 4) Regulations 2020 (SI 588) came into effect on 13th June in England and Northern Ireland, allowing households with one adult to become linked with one other household of any size, allowing them to be treated as one for the purpose of permitted gatherings. This also allowed the members of one household to stay overnight at the home of the other, which the government referred to as a 'support bubble.'

Unsurprisingly, few people paid much attention to this because most people had been doing just that for some time, with many support bubbles bringing beer or sausages for the barbeque. What was of much greater concern were the remaining provisions of the Health Protection (Coronavirus, Restrictions) (England) (Amendment No. 4) Regulations 2020 (SI 588) which came into effect on 15th June, and allowed the general re-opening of English retail shops and public-facing businesses, apart from those on a list of specific exclusions such as restaurants, bars, pubs, nightclubs, most cinemas, theatres, museums, hairdressers, indoor sports and leisure facilities. It now meant you could shop all day, wearing a face mask if you could be bothered, and then spend time in your social bubble, or however many of them who had brought beer or sausages you could fit into your home.

On the same day, and adding to human euphoria, endangered species also celebrated the opening of outdoor animal-related attractions such as farms, zoos and safari parks. Places of worship also opened for private prayer, although not for communal worship. Four days later, the UK's Covid-19 Alert Level was lowered from Level 4 (severe risk, high transmission) to Level 3 (substantial risk, general circulation), following the agreement of all four Chief Medical Officers. The Health Secretary described the change as 'a big moment for the country.'

The Prime Minister, still jubilant over his private jet's paint job, had put away his colour charts and was sitting at his desk, with his computer actually switched on.

"Well, Dee, we wrestled it to the ground, just as we said we would!" The PM seemed buoyant, despite having only a cup of black coffee in front of him, or which looked like a cup of black coffee. "On top of all that, we can now travel to France! Isn't that absolutely splendid!"

"France has indeed lifted its border restrictions, sir. Is that of particular importance?"

"Wine, Dee! People can now travel to vineyards and purchase claret and burgundy!"

"They could also just go to the supermarket, Prime Minister."

Derek Goings was not feeling in a buoyant mood. Other countries were also wrestling the virus to the ground, with only small rises in infections, even smaller numbers of deaths, and an easing of restrictions that erred on the side of caution. The Prime Minister, as always, was filtering out inconvenient scientific opinion. The PM's advisor had also made a decision, a decision that could cost him his job, future, and marriage, which worried him because his wife was warm, witty, intelligent and, now back to full health, in possession of a functioning vagina.

"Supermarkets are a pale imitation of the thrill of adventure, Dee! The thrill of discovering a new vineyard. It's not just the taste of wine, it's the taste of freedom!" Derek Goings now realised, and perhaps should have realised sooner, that the Prime Minister was inebriated which, being Prime Minister, he was entitled to be, even though it was only ten o'clock in the morning.

"I'm sure that most British people will still prefer the supermarket, Prime Minister. However, perhaps I could remind you that, because of travel restrictions in Scotland, English people can now travel to France, but Scottish people still can't travel to England."

"Can't they? Good gracious! There again, why would they want to? We've only got that muck that they make in Kent." The Prime Minister took a swig of his coffee and burped rather loudly. "However, I have been giving this whole Berwick thing a bit of thought. Even asked the Foreign Secretary about it, and he had to ask the Russian embassy about it." The Prime Minister ran a hand through his hair, just in case it had returned to normal neatness. "Then Claire had the bright idea of having a look at Wikipedia, which I don't suppose is something you've ever come across before. It's on the internet, just in case you want to have a look."

"Caroline, sir."

"No, Wikipedia, Dee. Most informative! It says that Berwick *is* part of England after all, and has been for a very long time. So, no need to worry because we're no longer at war with Russia, if indeed we ever were," added the PM, not entirely sure of this last point.

This came as something of a surprise to the advisor who, unlike intelligence agencies, knew that Wikipedia couldn't be entirely relied upon. He did, however, make a mental note to double-check Berwick's status as regards Russia, but filed his mental note in a cabinet marked Not Particularly Important, as he was sure that the Foreign Office and Russian embassy would quietly and efficiently have sorted out any historical misunderstandings.

"I have, however, made a decision," said the Prime Minister, finishing his coffee – without offering his advisor any – and then retreating to the kitchen for a refill. Derek Goings heard the kettle boil and a bottle being unscrewed. The PM settled back in his chair and looked at his computer, wondering why CandyCrush was so hard to master.

"You said you'd made a decision," the advisor reminded him, never liking it when the Prime Minister made decisions.

"Yes, I have," replied the PM, leaning back in his chair, and placing the coffee mug on the swell of his belly where it made a round stain, "because, Dee, I am a huge sports fan and believe that all sporting stars, whatever ridiculous sport they mistakenly play, should be listened to."

This was news to Derek Goings. "I thought you only watched rugby, Prime Minister?"

"Rugby *and* lacrosse."

"I see," said the advisor, who didn't see, mentally or physically, although his eyesight had miraculously improved since his trip to Durham.

"Specifically, Dee, women's lacrosse because I find it so exciting and so graceful. I can watch it for hours, endlessly admiring the majestic skills and athleticism of the players." The Prime Minister lapsed in silence, perhaps thinking about sporting skill and athleticism or, maybe, short skirts and the glimpse of ladies' knickers. "I watch it whenever my duties allow on YouTube, which you also may never have heard of."

"You said you had made a decision, Prime Minister."

"Well, yes I have. You see, Dee, there's an English lacrosse star called Danielle Rashbrook, who is particularly skilled and graceful although, of course, that has nothing to do with anything." The Prime Minister took a large gulp of his coffee, which didn't seem to be very hot, although it did make his eyes water. "She was talking on YouTube about our school meals voucher programme and how it was disgraceful that we weren't doing it through the summer holidays."

"You only announced a few days ago that it wouldn't be extended over the summer, Prime Minister."

"My decision, Dee, is that we *should* now extend it. We owe it to struggling mothers and fathers to give their children a decent steak once in a while."

"While also travelling to France to buy claret, Prime Minister?"

"Precisely, Dee! I have therefore decided to take Danielle's advice and do something that many people in this country will be grateful for. To give people yet another good reason, on top of many other good reasons, to continue to put their faith in me and my government. Frankly, it's such a good idea that I'm surprised that you didn't advise me sooner on this course of action."

But Derek Goings, the man in the shadows, with every fact at his fingertip – except about Berwick, maybe – was starting to play a different game, which had nothing whatsoever to do with lacrosse. "But you couldn't do one thing, Dee, could you?" asked the Prime Minister in his most plaintive voice. "Get me Danielle's phone number? Purely to thank her personally for her contribution, of course."

Soon afterwards, the Health Secretary did indeed thank the sports star for her contribution, but in a media interview afterwards mistakenly referred to her as 'Marcus Rashford' – a footballer, apparently, who few people had heard of.

The Chancellor was more usefully occupied, reading a report from the Organisation for Economic Co-operation and Development that said that the economic impact of Covid-19 would be 'dire' everywhere, with Britain's economy likely to slump by 11.5% in 2020, and outstripping falls in other developed economies such as Germany, France, Spain or Italy. It also said that, if there was a second peak in the pandemic, the UK economy could contract by 14%.

He often wished that he could have responsibility for a different department. Being Culture Secretary would have suited him just fine, with very little to do lately except make announcements on a new colour scheme for the PM's plane. It was a role he was well-qualified for, being genuinely cultured. He enjoyed the theatre, he read novels that didn't have pictures of bunny rabbits or kittens in them, and his palate knew the difference between Scottish and Japanese whisky.

Instead, he was Chancellor of an exchequer that had nothing in it, with a wife whose wedding finger contained more gold than the country's gold reserves, and a national debt mountain that, in the real world, should have obliged everyone in the UK to rely on foodbanks, except children in receipt of free school meal vouchers.

But the one job, apart from Culture, that he wanted most of all was the one now occupied by the Rt Hon Winston Spragg, First Lord of the Treasury and Prime Minister, who would be voted out of office soon enough by anyone who was still alive, except that there was one other man standing between him and his destiny.

His phone rang and, when he answered it, he could almost hear a well-shod foot tapping on the floor.

It wasn't all bad news. On the 16th June, the low-dose steroid dexamethasone, that had been part of clinical trials for existing drugs that could be used to treat patients with Covid-19, was heralded as a major breakthrough after it was found to cut the number of deaths. Experts estimated that up to 5,000 lives could have been saved in the UK had the treatment been used from the outset. The Prime Minister described the news as 'a remarkable British scientific achievement.' It was also announced that AstraZeneca and Oxford University had reached a deal to begin manufacturing a potential vaccine, although without clinical approval, with a plan to stockpile the vaccine ready for its approval. Just over a week later, scientists at Imperial College London began human trials of a Covid-19 vaccine after tests on animals indicated an effective immune response.

The man with the other red telephone on his desk took a phone call and listened attentively. Then he went to his window overlooking Red Square and pondered options. Surely the British government wasn't considering some form of military adventure to divert public opinion from its appalling Covid-19 record? There again, he had to admit, it was a strategy that Russia endlessly deployed to blame the West for everything, including a few things that the West could legitimately be blamed for. But, if the British were thinking along similar lines, what might their military ambitions be? Was the Crimea a valid pretext for dragging up ancient conflicts? Did Britain really care about the Crimea? The Charge of the Light Brigade was a footnote of history; Florence Nightingale was dead and buried.

If his country was still at war with Britain, or a very small bit of it, should he order an amphibious assault? After all, the Berwick seafront was scandalously undefended. A pre-emptive strike followed by a protracted peace process offered all sorts of positive possibilities, not least to demonstrate Russia's military superiority and divert the Russian people's attention from his own rather shoddy Covid-19 response.

But in his heart of hearts, he didn't believe that the British would risk a military option. For a start, it wasn't in their nature, with all that stiff-upper-lip nonsense about fair play. In any case, the British didn't really have any armed forces anymore, or none that couldn't be swatted away by a nuclear battlecruiser. But he still had a nagging doubt about the British Prime Minister because, in his view, someone so verbally inarticulate must also have an inarticulate mind: a mind full of swirling and conflicting thoughts that could land absolutely anywhere.

Under his leadership, Russia had become great again by being prepared to wage real or proxy wars whenever and wherever it wanted – in Ukraine or Salisbury, or anywhere in between, or in places nowhere near Ukraine or Salisbury. But having another country possibly threatening Russia with what it had been happily doing for years was new territory. Out on Red Square, troops were practicing for one of Moscow's many military parades. He watched, proud of his armed forces, as two tanks collided with one another, and two tank commanders in big coats emerged from them and started brawling. He would have to think carefully before making his next move, a move calibrated to ensure that there could be no political or military misunderstandings.

He had no idea who had just phoned him. He couldn't speak English and didn't know what a chicken korma or onion pakora were.

The Foreign Secretary, what with nothing going on in the world, decided to phone his permanent secretary and ask what he'd told the Russian embassy in response to their rather passive-aggressive message earlier. It was a loose end that needed to be tied up, before his evening meeting with the Chancellor, and the

Foreign Secretary was good with loose ends having already been out to buy a real bottle of Scotch whisky. "Quite simply, Minister," said Tony Bond, "I merely reiterated the position of Her Majesty's government on the matter."

"Which is?"

"That we regarded the annexation of the Crimea to have been a hostile act in contravention of international law, of UN protocols governing land or border disputes between nations, and that our position on that illegal and hostile act hadn't changed."

"So, the matter is now closed?"

"Yes, Minister."

The Foreign Secretary put the phone down and smiled grimly. The Chancellor would be arriving shortly, once everyone in his outer office had left. It was time for the final showdown, which might or might not involve bloodshed.

The Prime Minister claimed that no country had a working coronavirus tracing app - only to be told that 12 million people had already downloaded Germany's version. He also dismissed criticism over the failed NHS software, which was initially billed as crucial for controlling the disease before being abandoned. Ministers had to admit that it failed to work on almost all iPhones, and that they were now focused on a hybrid model built by Apple and Google. The Minister for Innovation at the Department of Health and Social Care said the contact tracing app was 'not a priority' and might not be ready until the winter.

Ken Stamper was quite new to his job as Leader of the Opposition and had rather hoped for a quieter introduction. His first priority had been to start on a total reformation of his Party because his predecessor, a bearded maverick whose Left-wing politics made Kim Jong-un seem positively decadent, had rendered the Labour party unelectable. Ken's very long agenda involved forging a new political consensus that didn't involve the abolition of capitalism, the nationalisation of all industry, the abolition of all military forces, the abolition of the police, and the extension of free school meal vouchers to every adult and child in the country because money would also have been abolished. His reform agenda required both charm and steely resolve: to win back the Party's grassroots from his predecessor's activists, and slowly purge the Party's higher echelons of those who believed that radical socialism would best be achieved by executing entrepreneurs, artists, journalists and Jews. But the trouble with bold socialist visions is that they inspire blind fervour among the very dim or utterly deluded, and his Party was stuffed full of them. Getting the Labour Party back to being a pale imitation of itself would be a long, hard struggle, and Ken was up to that task, except that Covid-19 had made it impossible.

Instead, Ken's agenda was now one of soft words and olive branches. His Party wouldn't oppose everything because the country expected its politicians to demonstrate unity of purpose. In a time of crisis, it wanted a government of all the people, even the dim and deluded: a coalition that would, of course, entirely unravel once the crisis passed. Ken's strategy was equally simple: to wait. Once the British people were given a chance to vote, they would also remember that many of their loved ones were no longer around to vote, and would therefore vote on their behalf: electing a new government that had one huge advantage. It wasn't the old government.

Pondering this wait-and-see strategy, Ken opened a padded envelope that had just been delivered to his House of Commons office. Inside was a mobile phone and a message in bold, black capital letters: *Just answer it.* There was no indication who it was from, although the message had been written on 10 Downing Street headed paper, which the sender had tried to disguise by badly crossing the address out. No sooner had he read the message when the phone rang.

"Hello?

"This is Jackdaw."

"Is that you, Derek?"

"This is Jackdaw. I have never heard of anyone called Derek."

"Look, Derek, I know it's you." Ken Stamper could smell sulphur radiating from the phone and into his ear and, presumably, his nose. "What is it that you want?"

Derek Goings sighed and then removed the sock from the mouthpiece, a muffling strategy that hadn't worked as well as he'd anticipated. "Very well, I admit that I might be the person to whom you seem to be referring."

"In which case, could I ask you again what you want?"

"The government for which I work is useless. It is no longer a winning government. I only wish to serve and guide winning governments."

"Derek, you know I couldn't possibly employ you. For God's sake, you're the Prime Minister's chief advisor!"

"And you will shortly be the next prime minister," Derek reminded him. "I would merely be continuing in my current role."

"Maybe, but I would be a Labour prime minister!"

"Your politics are of no concern to me, Mr Stamper."

"Look, Derek, this is ridiculous! In any case, I already have a chief advisor."

"That Cummings fellow! He's useless, and you know it."

"I'm sorry, but what you're suggesting is unethical, probably illegal and, quite frankly, more than a little mad."

"No, it isn't," said Derek with soft precision.

"Why not?"

"Because I know your secret."

The Foreign Secretary had been right to worry about Hong Kong. At the end of June, the Chinese imposed a new security law in Hong Kong that the Foreign Secretary termed 'a clear and serious breach' of the handover agreement between the UK and China. Several hundred pro-democracy activists were then arrested.

The man with a red phone on his desk and a view of Red Square also had another red phone on his desk, which was connected to only one other red phone, and not to someone speaking in a fuzzy English accent. He picked up this other red phone which was answered immediately by someone who, reassuringly, spoke Russian. He gave his orders and then stood at his window, with its view of Russian military history, and where rival military units were now exchanging small-arms fire, and wondered what the future might hold.

The end of the beginning

With lockdown easing, and the two-metre rule being relaxed, and pubs to open, the World Health Organisation warned that millions of people across the world could die if there was a second wave of coronavirus. An assistant director-general for strategic initiatives at the WHO said the pandemic had so far spread as health officials had anticipated, and compared the virus with the Spanish Flu outbreak of 1918-19 which had ravaged countries around the world, including Britain, where there were more than 220,000 deaths and the US, where 675,000 died.

The WHO also noted that, towards the end of June, thirty countries in Europe had seen an increase in cumulative weekly cases for the first time in months and that, if unchecked, in eleven of those countries, it would again push health systems to the brink. The WHO urged governments that the pandemic is speeding up and 'the worst is yet to come.'

In the UK, the sun was shining, the virus was beaten, and the Joint Biosecurity Centre concluded that transmission of the virus was no longer 'high or rising exponentially,' although the government's chief scientific adviser and the chief medical officer for England stressed the Prime Minister's plan for unlocking lockdown was not 'risk-free.'

The country's upbeat mood didn't stop the killjoy presidents of the Royal Colleges of Surgeons, Nursing, Physicians, and GPs signing a letter published in the *British Medical Journal* which called for an urgent review to determine whether the UK was properly prepared for the 'real risk' of a second wave of coronavirus, warning that urgent action would be needed to prevent further loss of life.

However, most people didn't bother with all that depressing nonsense. They were now quite happily living in their various support bubbles, which collectively contained everyone they had ever known, family, and complete strangers who had brought beer, and chose only to hear the Health Secretary's announcement that the easing of restrictions was a 'big moment' that showed the ‘government's plan is working.’ Nobody thought to ask what the government’s plan actually had been, or whether it still had a plan.

Evening, and the Health Secretary was in an exceptionally good mood although, as someone who rarely smiled and who looked permanently worried, it was hard to tell. He’d been able to announce that the government’s plan for coronavirus was working and that the Prime Minister would be reducing social distancing from two metres to one metre, or to whatever anyone thought appropriate, necessary or could be bothered with - a complete vindication of the government’s handling of the crisis.

His wife was in the driveway loading things into their car boot when his ministerial limousine dropped him off. His children were jumping around and looking excited.

“I thought we’d go to the beach tomorrow,” she informed him, “now that we don’t have to worry about anything.”

“Social distancing hasn’t been abandoned,” he reminded her.

“Well, I’m taking the kids to Bournemouth, Kevin, and you’re more than welcome to come too. It’s going to be hot tomorrow, and the kids need a bit of sun after being cooped up inside.”

“Social distancing still hasn’t been abandoned,” he repeated, wondering if maybe the Prime Minister had announced its complete abandonment during his journey from central London which, knowing the Prime Minister, was quite possible.

“It’s Bournemouth, Kevin, so hardly Saint Tropez. Anyway, who the fuck ever goes to Bournemouth beach?”

When he checked in the boot, it was full of toilet rolls and packets of pasta.

Evening, and there came a soft knock on the Foreign Secretary’s door. It was time to face down his principal rival.

A leading scientist from the University of Edinburgh and advisor to the Scottish First Minister said at the end of June that Scotland should consider quarantining travellers from England, with rates of infection in some parts of England above those in

Scotland. If that were to happen, said critics, it would be seen by some people as a first step towards border controls. There has not yet been any reaction from Berwick-upon-Tweed's town council.

In July, Scotland's First Minister said that any move to place restrictions on visitors from England to Scotland would be based on risk, not politics. She said that quarantine for visitors from elsewhere in the UK could not be ruled out.

Evening, and Ken Stamper was staring out of his office window into Parliament Square. He had a decision to make although, in his heart of hearts, he had already made it.

Evening, and the Chancellor knocked softy on the Foreign Secretary's office door. It was also time to face down his principal rival.

At the end of June, the UK was warned by a member of the government's Scientific Advisory Group for Emergencies (SAGE) that it remained 'on a knife edge.' The warning came following large gatherings around the UK during a recent heatwave, including illegal street parties in London, Manchester and Cardiff, and crowding on beaches, including Bournemouth. England's 23,000 pubs opened on the first Saturday in July.

Evening, and Derek Goings was also staring out of his window. In the next room was his wife, who still had warmth, wit, intelligence and a functioning vagina. He too had a decision to make. Now that he was completely bald, and with everyone who mattered frightened of him, should he keep taking the sulphur tablets? Everyone, that is, except Sir Roger Smallwood who had phoned earlier to say that he didn't care who knew his secret any more. This had meant nothing to the PM's advisor.

He also had another decision to make, although this decision depended on someone else's decision. However, having considered every fact from every angle, he had already decided what that other person would decide, and had provisionally made his own decision.

Evening, and a GCHQ report to MI6 and then forwarded to government ministers and the chiefs of staff, said that the *Pyotr Velikiy* was again displaying a nuclear heat signature. However, as its heat signature was now some twenty nautical miles west of Severomorsk, it could reasonably be deduced that the battlecruiser and its escort vessels had put to sea.

A nationwide round of applause took place in early July to mark the 72nd anniversary of the NHS, an idea inspired by the success of the weekly Clap for Carers, which saw households across the country show their appreciation for NHS and other key workers. The PM was joined on the steps of Downing Street by Annemarie Plas, who founded the Clap for Carers initiative. In a Tweet, the Prime Minister said: 'In these past few months, indeed the past 72 years, you have represented the very best of this country. Our gratitude to you will be eternal.' Earlier that day, to show the PM's personal thanks, medics were invited to Downing Street, including Luis and Jenny.

Evening, precisely 1,635 miles from Severomorsk, if you happened to be a very fit crow with a good sense of direction, and the Prime Minister was alone in his Downing Street support bubble. His girlfriend was staying with friends or family for the night, without specifying which, and had taken their child and several bottles of Merlot with her. He was in an unusually reflective mood, thinking back on his own brush with death, and having only learned of the recent death of Dame Vera Lynn, presumably from coronavirus because that's what all old people die of nowadays. A living link to the Second World War had been lost; no longer would we meet again or see bluebirds flying over the white cliffs of Dover: a reminder of Britain's finest hour was gone. He was, of course, thankful for his own return to health and had earlier, remembering his two valiant nurses and how he had failed to name his son Jenny or Luis, phoned St Thomas' Hospital to thank them personally, only to be told that the hospital had no record of them.

In July, families who lost loved ones to coronavirus announced legal action against the government over claims they would not have died had ministers locked down the country sooner. Around 1,000 grieving relatives said the government 'gambled' with people's lives by failing to act quickly enough. Later in July, according to Sir Patrick Vallance, the Chief Scientific Advisor to the Government, SAGE advised the government to enter lockdown on March 16.

The Prime Minister was writing an article for *The Times*, a task that his chief advisor would normally have done. However, he hadn't been able to reach Derek Goings on his office, mobile or home phones and had decided that, as prime minister, he was perfectly capable of scribbling down a few sentences. He had already written quite a lot, about how his government had followed the science at every step and then thrown up protective shields everywhere.

He conceded that people had died, even Dame Vera, but thousands had been saved because of his government's forward planning and prompt action. His prose was interspersed with appropriate Latin phrases and, throughout, a great many Churchillian quotes, which meant that he didn't need to think up much that was original, or even articulate. He had just written: *The virus has received back again that measure of fire and steel which it has so often meted out to us.*

He drank from his glass of Merlot, wondering how many bottles his wife had left behind, and pondered how to finish the article. Then he remembered, or thought he did, the rest of Churchill's speech, and thought how the next day's media would react. Rather well, he concluded, and that his chief advisor would be so proud of him! The Prime Minister sat back at his computer and wrote: *This is not the end. It is not even the beginning of the end. But it is, perhaps, the beginning of the end.*

As of January 6th 2022, over 173,000 people in the UK have died from Covid-19.

About the author

Charlie Laidlaw teaches creative writing, and lives in East Lothian. He is a graduate of the University of Edinburgh and was previously a national newspaper journalist and defence intelligence analyst. He has lived in London and Edinburgh, and is married with two children. His other novels are *Everyday Magic*, *The Things We Learn When We're Dead, The Space Between Time* and *Love Potions and Other Calamities*.

W: www.charlielaidlawauthor.com
T: @claidlawauthor
F: @charlielaidlawauthor

Printed in Great Britain
by Amazon

15054015R00131